WARRIOR
OF THE WILD

TRICIA LEVENSELLER

SQUARE
FISH

NEW YORK

SQUARE
FISH

An imprint of Macmillan Publishing Group, LLC
120 Broadway, New York, NY 10271
fiercereads.com

Square Fish and the Square Fish logo are trademarks of Macmillan and
are used by Feiwel and Friends under license from Macmillan.

Our books may be purchased in bulk for promotional, educational, or business use. Please
contact your local bookseller or the Macmillan Corporate and Premium Sales Department at
(800) 221-7945 ext. 5442 or by email at MacmillanSpecialMarkets@macmillan.com.

Library of Congress Control Number: 2018945026
ISBN 978-1-250-23365-3 (paperback)   ISBN 978-1-250-18995-0 (ebook)

Originally published in the United States by Feiwel and Friends
First Square Fish edition, 2020
Book designed by Liz Dresner
Square Fish logo designed by Filomena Tuosto

10 9 8 7 6 5 4 3 2 1

WARRIOR OF THE WILD

For Johnny,
because you introduced me to Overwatch,
where we get to be warriors! Thanks, bro.

"BRING YOUR PRETTY FACE TO MY AX."
—GIMLI
The Lord of the Rings: The Two Towers

PART 1

THE
TRIAL

CHAPTER

1

An ax swings for my head.

The dull training weapon may not be enough to decapitate me, but I know all too well the sharp sting of metal on skin.

I duck.

A whoosh of air sails over my head, and while I'm still crouched, I thrust my ax straight out so the blunt tips of the double heads whack right into Torrin's armor-clad stomach.

He lets out a sad breath of air. "Dead again."

Ignoring the instinct to correct his form, I opt for a quick "Sorry," as he rubs at the spot where I struck him.

He grins at me. "If I had a problem, I would find a different sparring partner."

That smile of his sets my stomach to fluttering. It gets more and more charming every day.

But shame spreads through me when Torrin's eyes raise to my hair. He hasn't said anything about it, and I'm in no hurry to offer an explanation for its shorter length. Thankfully, Master Burkin strides over to us, saving me.

"Well done, Rasmira," he says. Then to Torrin, "You're too slow on the recovery. Unless getting eviscerated was your intention?"

A look of annoyance flashes over Torrin's face, but it disappears as quickly as it comes. "Maybe it was, Master Burkin."

"And maybe you'll fail your trial tomorrow. This is the last day for me to shove any more training into your thick skull. Let's pair Rasmira up with another boy so you can watch."

Being put on display is the last thing I want. It separates me even more from the rest of the trainees. I already receive more attention, receive the highest marks. It's as if my instructor, my father, and everyone else are *trying* to make life harder for me.

Burkin searches through the other pairs practicing in the training house. "How about . . ."

Not Havard. Not Havard. Not Havard.

"Havard!" Burkin calls on the second-highest rank in our training group. "Come pair with Rasmira so Torrin can observe how to properly recover from his own swing."

"I know *how* to recover," Torrin says defensively. "Rasmira is just fast."

"The ziken are fast, too," Burkin says, "and they will not have blunt claws for weapons. Now watch."

I've spoken to my father about Burkin belittling the other students in order to raise me up. Complained profusely.

Nothing has changed.

So I'm forced to face off with Havard. He's the biggest boy I've ever seen, with a scowl across his lips to heighten the effect.

No one ever did like being second best.

Then again, perhaps no one ever hated being first more than I.

I swing for Havard's head, just as Master Burkin wants. Havard ducks and thrusts out with his ax just as I did before. With the same momentum of my initial swing, I curve my blades around, effectively blocking the jab toward my stomach.

"Perfect," Burkin says. "Now step it up, Torrin. Else tomorrow will be the last day any of us sees you alive."

And with that, Burkin stomps off to find other students to nag.

"Doesn't he realize how hard it is to take this seriously when it's the last day of training?" Torrin asks.

I'm about to respond, when a blur streaks toward me out of the corner of my eye.

I throw my ax up just in time.

It would seem that Havard isn't done with me yet.

"Something is different about you," Havard says, looking me up and down. The motion makes me feel dirty.

But then his eyes fix on my hair.

He laughs once. "You've cut your hair. Were you trying to make yourself uglier? Or does Torrin prefer it this way?"

I shove at our joined axes, sending Havard back a step. He has a knack for finding just the right ways to bring me down low. My eyes sting, but I have long since learned to control tears.

My father cut my hair last night. It used to flow down to my waist in blond waves. I loved my hair, despite the fact that it's more white than golden, like my mother's and sisters'. But now it barely reaches my shoulders, just like the rest of the men wear their hair.

I know that if my father could somehow force me to grow a beard, he'd do that, too.

My knuckles whiten where they grip my ax.

Havard notices. "You're going to strike me?"

"I'm considering it."

He snorts. "How would it look if the village leader's daughter started a fight the day before her trial?"

"Like she got pissed off by the village idiot."

His eyes sharpen. "You want to be very careful of what you say to me, Rat."

Rat—his charming nickname for me. Havard has been using it since I was eight. He said I scurried like one every time I tried to find my feet after he'd knock me down in training.

And when I would come home covered in bruises from my shins to my cheeks, Father began training me at home, too. For the last ten years, I have learned very little other than how to handle an ax.

But that is why I'm the best.

Because I know he's not expecting it, I fling my fist at Havard. His eyes were trained on my ax, not my free hand. The blow catches him on the chin, and I'm pleased by the way my knuckles smart. It must mean I hit him hard.

Havard cannot keep challenging me. I have to put him in his place. For one day, I will be his ruler, and if I cannot keep one bully in line, I'll never be able to look after a whole village.

When he sends a returning fist my way, I move to block it with my ax.

But he uncurls his fingers, wraps them around the shaft, and traps my ax in place. After dropping his own weapon, he sends his now-free hand toward my face. I feel my skin split across my cheekbone as my face wrenches backward.

Burkin notices.

"Havard! No fists! You will apologize to Rasmira."

Havard is furious at being caught when I wasn't. Rage fuels him now—he's past the point of listening. Past the point of being sensible, which is right where I want him.

He picks his weapon back up and flies at me, ax, legs, and arms swinging intermittently. I block each attack one after the next, just waiting, waiting, waiting.

There.

After a sweeping move meant to cleave me in two from head to toe, Havard's ax nicks into the dirt floor.

I've already sidestepped it, and now I sweep his legs out from under him, landing him on his ass for the whole room to see.

"Quicker on the recovery!" Burkin barks out. "By the goddess, do none of you listen?"

Some of the trainees laugh, but I barely hear it. My entire focus is latched onto Havard lying on the ground.

I kick his weapon far from his reach, then lower my ax to Havard's neck so the two blades rest on either side, pinning him to the floor.

"Dead," I say. And then lower, so only he can hear, "Challenge me again, and the next time we face off, it won't be with training weapons."

Havard answers with a disturbing smile. "You won't live long enough for us to face off again."

7

I kick him, send my leg straight down into his stomach. "And you need never rise from this floor. Apologize if you wish me to free you."

Once he catches his breath, Havard tries to use his hands to thrust my ax away from himself. I kick him again. This time my heel comes down on his nose.

Burkin does nothing. Will never do anything, because I am my father's daughter. Displeasing me would displease Father.

A little voice scratches at the back of my mind, warning me that incensing Havard is no way to earn his respect and loyalty. I'm abusing my own power.

But a much more prominent voice practically shouts, *Make him bend.*

Finally, through a blood-soaked face, Havard says, "Apologies."

I let him up, and training resumes.

TORRIN WALKS ME HOME, as he's done every day for the last month. Though now it feels as though he's always been by my side, we only became friends about six weeks ago. Before that, he was part of Havard's group, just another face in the crowd of my tormentors.

I remember vividly the day everything changed. Havard thought to gang up on me with the help of his best friends, Kol, Siegert, and Torrin. But instead of siding with Havard, Torrin helped me fight them off. Afterward, Torrin begged my forgiveness for playing the part he had the last several years. He said that as our trial had grown closer, he'd given some serious thought to what it means to be a warrior. "It never sat right with me—the way Havard treats you," he said, "but rather than face what I believed to be wrong, I did the easy thing. I don't want to be that kind of man. I know it's too late to take back what I've done, but I'd like to start changing now. I hope you can forgive me for the past."

I didn't think I was the forgiving type. I didn't think I believed people could change. But as I watched Torrin start living his life separate from Havard, I started to become closer to him. For the first time, I had a friend. Someone who didn't hate me for what I couldn't control, for being my father's daughter.

Now Torrin gently touches my cheek where Havard struck me. "We need to get this looked at right away."

I'm torn. I want to shrug him off because I don't need him fussing over me. He would never treat a male warrior this way. And yet, I don't want him to stop touching me.

"Irrenia will do it when she gets home," I say.

"Even with the cut, you're still lovely. How do you manage that?"

Lovely.

I have received praise for being brave and strong, for having impressive aim, for holding my ax properly.

But no one has ever praised my looks.

A blossoming warmth spreads inside my chest, traveling upward. It envelops the pulsing sting in my cheek.

I have no idea how I'm supposed to respond to something like that. How do women handle such praise? Saying *thank you* doesn't seem right. Especially when I don't agree.

Thankfully, Torrin saves me from having to respond. "I overheard some of the trainees talking about sneaking out tonight to witness the Payment. Do you want to go? Not with them, obviously. With me. Separately." He takes his hand back, and we continue walking toward my home. He moves slightly closer to me so that our arms brush as we walk. It's such a subtle change, but I notice, as if he'd bounded into me headlong.

At this point, I'm convinced I would do anything as long as it means spending more time with him.

"Sure." I try to sound as though I couldn't care either way. I hope he doesn't realize just how good it feels for me to be around him. While I'm almost certain he feels the same way I do, it's impossible to tell for sure. But why else would he look for reasons to touch me? Why would he try to spend as much time as possible with me outside of training?

But if he does like me, then why hasn't he kissed me yet? Maybe he is just as nervous as I am. Maybe it's his first experience with courtship, just as it is mine. I've never seen him with another girl.

We pass through the streets of Seravin. Homes made from rock slabs line either side of the street. The gray-black stones have been painted over with deep azures and muted greens—the colors of the sky and sparse grass that breaks through the rocks. To the right, a cart is being heaped with chunks of meat to be presented for the Divine Payment. Two nocerotis, large beasts with sleek hides and two horns jutting out of the tops of their heads, are attached to the front, ready to pull once smacked on their hindquarters. Children, too young to begin training for a specific trade, play a game of pebbles in front of their homes.

And all the while Torrin's fingers are inching closer toward mine.

"I hope this year's Payment doesn't require us to skip meals again," he says as he watches hunters layer more and more valder into the cart. Each one is the length of two handspans and has enough meat to fill a small family. "There were several times during training last year that I thought I would pass out."

My chest tightens at those words. Peruxolo, the low god, demands payment each year. He collects different resources from every village. Ours is responsible for providing him with the best game. Our hunters are the most skilled of all the nearby villages. Even still, there is not always enough meat to go around.

Sometimes the Payment is so great that some in the village must go without food for days at a time. Parents and older siblings, like Torrin, skip meals so the younger ones can fill their bellies. Because of who my father is, my sisters and I have never had to go hungry. Other families are not so lucky.

Hunger is a better fate than facing Peruxolo's wrath, but I still feel sick to think of people starving.

"You will not go hungry during this Payment, Torrin," I say as I take his hand in mine. "I will make sure you and your brothers are fed each mealtime. My family always has more than enough food."

Torrin turns toward me, a peculiar expression upon his face. Confusion? Guilt? No, perhaps just surprise?

"You would do that for my family?"

"Of course I would." His intent eyes make my insides squirm. I try to lighten the air. "Because I don't want to be seen with you if you don't keep up your impressive physique."

He laughs, and the action makes me smile in return.

We've reached my home now, and Torrin releases my hand. I try to keep from frowning until I realize his face is approaching mine.

This is it, I think as my heart begins racing. *He's going to kiss me.*

And he does.

On the cheek.

I don't break eye contact as he pulls away. Maybe if I just look at him longingly, he'll see what I want and he won't be afraid to give it to me.

He looks back at me, his eyes deepening again. I think he might be reading my mind.

"I'll pick you up tonight outside your window so we can witness the Payment. I can't wait." He rubs his thumb against my lips before departing.

But it's still not a real kiss.

I **NEARLY FALL OUT** of bed when knuckles rap against my bedroom window. Of course, I've been expecting Torrin, but I'm not used to sneaking out at night. I may be excited, but perhaps a bit anxious as well.

I've never left the boundaries of the village before.

When I rise and go to the window, Torrin has his face squished against the glass and is making a funny face.

My lips tilt in a smile as I open the window.

"Ready?" he whispers.

"Yes." I grab my ax—a sharp blade meant to do damage, not a training weapon—from beside the window and sling it through the strap on my back. Then I lift myself through the window one leg at a time.

Torrin doesn't waste any time at all lacing his fingers through mine. My home is among those at the edge of the village boundaries, so it isn't long before we are in the wild. We take the rough terrain at a steady jog.

Everything in the wild is dangerous, including the ground, which is composed of broken-up rocks teetering against one another. It's difficult to find even footing. Any step could result in a twisted ankle, and rockslides are frequent. Though a more traversable road wends through the wild, we can't risk taking it, else we might be seen by the adults tasked with delivering the meat to the god.

We have to give the inna trees a wide berth. Their branches grow to a couple feet in length and naturally sharpen into deadly points that can pierce through our armor if we aren't careful.

As we walk, a lonely valder blurs across our path. As soon as I blink, it's already moved on. The valder are our main source of meat, but they run so fast, they're easy to miss. Our hunters are trained to be quick with their throwing hatchets—the only weapons that can be thrown fast enough and hard enough to catch them. I'm shocked to find one so close to the village. It's as if it knows it's not in danger now that all the meat has already been collected for the Payment.

As we veer around another tree, a distant cackle carries to us on the wind.

That'll be the ziken.

They're the reason we need to train the best warriors. With their paralyzing venom and ability to regenerate lost limbs, the ziken are formidable foes. The beasts love nothing more than the taste of human flesh, and they know exactly where to get it. That's why we always have warriors scouting the perimeter of the village.

As soon as Torrin and I pass our trial tomorrow, we will join the ranks of warriors and be charged with the village's safety. Our lives will be consumed with killing the beasts.

I wonder if any will come out to play tonight.

TORRIN AND I STAND in the shadows of the trees, waiting for the god to appear.

In the clearing ahead of us, seven wagons wait in a line, heaped with various goods: precious stones and gems, fine clothing sewn with metallic hems, preserved fruits and pickled vegetables, flasks of fresh water from the Sparkling Well, herbs and medicines, fresh and dried meat—and in the final wagon . . .

I cannot bear to look at that last wagon.

"What do you suppose the god looks like?" I whisper.

"They say he never shows his face," Torrin whispers back.

"Maybe he doesn't have a face."

"Maybe his nose is embarrassingly large, and he doesn't want anyone to know."

My lips twitch, but I cannot manage a smile with the threat of danger surrounding us.

The light of the full moon makes it easy to spot my father standing next to our wagon. The nocerotis are harnessed to the front. They are restless, sensing the tension of all the men waiting. My father reaches out a hand, patting the rough hide of one of the beasts.

I wonder if the god isn't watching them, relishing their discomfort. In making them wait.

"You don't think he knows we're hiding out here?" I ask.

"Your father?"

I shake my head. "The god."

Torrin doesn't say anything for a moment. "Havard's boasted of sneaking out before to witness the Payment, and he's still alive."

Unfortunately.

Still . . .

"Maybe we should turn back," I say.

"Rasmira—" Before he can say anything else, the heads of all the nocerotis snap to attention, focusing in the same direction. The fidgeting of the leaders stills, and many of their faces go pale.

My father is the most skilled warrior I have ever seen. How terrible could the god be that even he would be afraid?

Tree branches on the opposite side of the clearing rustle, and it takes me a moment to notice the hooded figure in black furs and armor.

Because he isn't on the ground.

He's floating in the air.

A cape drapes across his shoulders and hangs just above his boots. He's impossibly tall, yet slimmer than I imagined, even with the furs giving him extra bulk. Over his right shoulder, I spot the head of an ax.

The only uncovered parts of Peruxolo's body are his hands, which are . . . surprisingly normal. He has, at least, the hands of a human, but what lies beneath that hood?

Every leader in the clearing drops to their knees. The god does not approach them, though his voice is not difficult to hear.

"The gems are few tonight," he says, a deep and cruel rumble that I feel in my bones. A man stands from his kneeling position, presumably the village leader responsible for providing the gems.

"My god—" He is cut off by a raised hand.

"Come forward," Peruxolo purrs, and just by the tone of it, I know something awful is about to happen.

The leader hesitates, and I can see him swallow from this distance.

Peruxolo cocks his head, and that is all it takes for the leader to obey.

"That's enough," Peruxolo says after a moment. And the man opposite bows his head to the ground.

I know already that he will not rise again.

With a single flick of Peruxolo's wrist, the bowing leader topples over, blood pooling around him, choking gurgles coming from his lips.

We've been told stories since we were children of the god who can kill without touching his ax, but to see it . . .

Torrin trembles slightly beside me as the leader goes still and silent.

"I trust that someone will let the Restin village know I expect double payment on their gems by next month."

The guards who accompanied their leader from Restin start to move toward the body.

"No," Peruxolo drawls out lazily. "You will leave him for the ziken to feed on."

It's a shameful thing. Our people are buried under rock so thick that no animal can desecrate their bodies.

Almost without thinking, I grab Torrin's hand. His fingers curve around mine, and I look down at the sight of our joined hands. A rope bracelet peeks out from beneath his sleeve, lengths of his little sister's hair woven with the reeds—the child his mother lost at birth last winter.

Despite the danger, my racing heart calms somewhat at the sight.

"If I don't receive double by next month," Peruxolo says, "I'll pay a visit to the village."

Everyone in the clearing cringes at those words.

"Back up," he continues. The leaders and guards do so, stepping away from the wagons. Only then does Peruxolo descend. He curves through the air in an arc before bending at the knees to catch himself on the ground. He rises, head held high, hood still firmly in place.

Peruxolo climbs into the last wagon in line.

He leans down to examine the drugged girl lying across the floor. He places a thumb and forefinger on either side of her chin, turning it from side to side as if she were a doll.

"She's pretty. She will make a fine sacrifice. At least I can count on the Mallimer village to do their part each year."

The Mallimer village leader nods. Actually nods. As though he's done some great service.

My father turns away from the scene. Does he imagine how it would feel if one of his own daughters were taken? I know how much our people suffer, because I see the shrunken bodies and hollow cheeks that follow the Payment each year. But now I'm reminded how some villages have a heavier Payment than we do.

"Hitch the wagons together," Peruxolo orders.

My father and the others remove the nocerotis from each wagon, yoking them all together in front of the first wagon. They connect the wagons in one long train. Peruxolo sits at the head of the reins and slaps them down on the hides of the wide beasts in front. So very slowly, all those goods, the wealth of seven different villages, roll away.

My whole life, I have heard whisperings about the god Peruxolo. He moves objects without touching them. Kills men who displease him with a look. Floats above us in the air. Sometimes the ground shakes when he walks. He has even been known to kill entire villages. Only twenty years ago, the Byomvar village was eradicated in the short span of a week when they failed to meet the requirements of their Payment for the second year in a row. They all grew sick until their bodies collapsed.

Peruxolo appeared hundreds of years ago in our lands and made it his home, demanding tribute every year in exchange for not slaughtering us all where we stand. His power is unlimited, he himself is immortal, and we have no choice but to abide by his wishes.

We're taught to pray for Peruxolo's mercy each night, but I do not. My prayers are only for Rexasena, the high-goddess. She is an unseen deity who lives in the heavens. But I feel her all around me. In my sisters' laughter. In the sun's warm rays. In the peace I feel inside. She encourages goodness and kindness in this life so we may experience bliss in the life to come. But Peruxolo? He is a bane on the mortal realm, making us suffer unnecessarily for his own gain.

"Let's go," Torrin whispers. "Your father's leaving. We should try to beat him home. We don't want him to notice you're missing."

I nod and let Torrin lead me back the way we came. Despite the dangerous terrain, my thoughts circle around that girl in the last wagon. I wish I could help her. But to do so would be to doom the entire Mallimer village to a worse fate. We have no choice but to let her go.

I shiver from the thought of the death that awaits that girl.

"What's wrong?" Torrin asks as we dodge another tree branch. "Did you see the gunda?"

I nudge him with my shoulder. "The gunda isn't real."

"How would you know? You've never been out in the wild before."

"It's an imagined monster meant to scare children away from the dangerous wild."

"Don't shrug it off until you see one."

"You do realize the flaw in that logic?"

He grins, and I look away so as not to be caught staring at his mouth.

"Come, now," Torrin says. "You'd love to stride back into the village carrying the gunda's head. Imagine the look on Havard's face!"

I know he's trying to make me feel better, and I let him, because I *want* to feel better.

"Imagine how spent we'd be then before tomorrow's trial," I say.

"Worried you'll fail?" he teases.

Though we're both eighteen, we will not be considered adults by the village until we pass our trial. It is a dangerous challenge filled with ziken, the same creatures that roam these very woods. And the consequence for failing is no small thing. Tradition dictates that those who fail face banishment and the mattugr. It is the absolute worst disgrace to be bestowed by my people. If any individual isn't excelling in their profession, they're smart enough to switch to something more befitting their abilities before the year of their trial.

"If I were to fail," I say, "who would trounce you so thoroughly during training drills?"

"An excellent point. We'd best stick together tomorrow, then."

I don't think I'll ever tire of hearing the word *we* leave his lips.

After tomorrow, things are going to change. When I beat my trial, I can finally move out of my father's house. I can see Torrin whenever I like. No more sneaking around because Torrin is afraid of my father.

And I'll finally be free of my mother.

A sharp yank snaps my head backward. I think I've caught my hair on something, until I'm suddenly spun around, and a powerful pain shoots clear to the back of my skull, starting at my right eye.

I barely manage to catch my balance as my hands fly over my eye. Then I hear quiet laughter.

It would seem that Torrin and I were not, in fact, the only ones to sneak out tonight.

"Something in your eye?" Havard taunts as he shakes out the fist that struck me. That sends his accomplices, Kol and Siegert, into a fit of laughter.

I wipe at my watering eyes so I can properly see the threat, but my right eye appears to already be swelling shut. I can't believe I didn't hear Havard coming. I was too distracted thinking about Torrin.

"Go back to the village, Havard," I say. "I beat you at every fight you instigate. How could you think this would be any different? Are you so fond of pain that you now seek me out for it?"

An unkind thing to say, for sure, but sneaking up behind me to strike was low of him.

Havard rips his ax from off his back and advances toward me. "Let's have it out here, then! See how you do against a real weapon."

The shout sends bats sailing upward from the trees, their chirping and clicking following them into the night, and I hope no ziken were near enough to hear Havard's outburst.

I pull my ax from my back, preparing to defend myself against Havard and his friends. Torrin does the same beside me. We spread our legs apart, one foot forward, in a readying stance. Kol and Siegert mirror their leader, advancing in a straight line.

"Rasmira."

Everyone freezes at the new voice.

Havard's shout didn't alert the ziken.

It brought my father.

CHAPTER

2

My father, Torlhon Bendrauggo, is flanked by three other warriors from our village. He surveys the scene quickly: Havard, Kol, and Siegert charging toward us with their axes as Torrin and I are about to defend ourselves.

"You're injured," Father says, as though I maybe hadn't noticed the flaring pain in my head. "Which of these boys hit you?"

"Master Bendrauggo," Havard starts as he hides his bloodied knuckles behind his back, "we—"

"To the village. Your excuses can wait until we're out of the wild."

No one dares to argue. Five axes are returned to their owners' backs, and we're shuffled along with my father and the guards dispersed among us—as though we'd try fighting one another with them here.

It is a long trek back to the village boundaries. We take the road this time, which is much easier. We need not worry about brushing against stinging agger vines, skimming poisonous yoonbrush needles, or getting a foot stuck in a snaketrap plant.

When at last the road dumps us into the village, Father rounds on the boys behind me.

"Since you four seem to think you're already men, you can take watches tonight. Show us your prowess at protecting the village."

Havard won't look my father directly in the eye as he asks, "For how long?"

"Until you're needed for your trial."

There is the punishment. No rest before the most important day of our lives.

"What about Rasmira?" Torrin asks.

"That is none of your concern. Now stay here. If I hear word from any of your parents that you returned in the night, it's banishment and the mattugr for all of you."

We are all silent at that.

In the old language, *mattugr* means "might." But it has no implications of strength. No, the mattugr is a challenge. If one has been issued the mattugr, it is because one has lost all honor, and the only way to redeem oneself is to attempt the challenge given. Attempt, because the quest is always something that is meant to end in death.

A mattugr has never been issued from my village during my lifetime. But I have heard stories of challenges given in the past.

Walk for a thousand days without pausing to sleep or eat.

Jump from the tallest peak and land on your feet.

Sleep for a night at the base of a pool of water.

Other challenges are less obvious in their implications of death, but they are no less deadly.

Kill the gunda and bring back its carcass.

Take a tooth from the mouth of a living mountain cat.

Face the ziken without a weapon.

That my father would threaten us with the mattugr—

He is *furious*.

"Rasmira, follow me." Father turns on his heel and leads me deeper into the village. All is quiet, for all are asleep save the warriors left roaming the outskirts, watching for danger.

Father marches right through our front door without bothering to check that I follow still. I'm half-tempted to make a run for it. Mother's likely still up.

But I follow through, and the metal door doesn't make a peep on its hinges as it closes behind me. Very little is built out of wood, for it soon becomes brittle and fragile once the ground no longer nourishes it. The wagons carrying the god's spoils will crumble in a few days.

Our home is the largest in the village, with a massive receiving room. It's bedecked with the finest decorations to show our standing: furniture handsomely crafted out of marble and cushioned with bird feathers, mounted horns from various beasts my father has killed, jewels cut and crafted into the most beautiful designs.

My mother and sisters come running into the room at the sound of the front door closing.

"You're safe," Mother says. "Bless the goddess!" She tries to throw herself at my father, but he stays her with an upraised hand.

"Did you know Rasmira had left the house?" Father demands.

Mother finally takes notice of me standing behind Father. She debates for a moment. I can tell she wants to lie, to say she did know. But to be caught in a lie is a grave sin.

"I hadn't! I thought her in her room." That's probably not entirely true. I doubt she thought of me at all.

Father looks pointedly at the three girls standing beside her. "Tormosa, Alara, and Ashari are not in their rooms."

They are second, third, and fourth oldest, respectively. Salvanya is the oldest and already married and living in her own home. Irrenia is number five, but it would appear she isn't home yet.

"You know how Rasmira is. She keeps to herself! How was I to know?"

"Rasmira is important," Father begins. I close my eyes, dreading this turn. I know that when I look at my mother, she'll be livid. "She will be a warrior and will protect this village. She will lead our people after I am gone. Already she is the best of the apprentice warriors. Who else will carry my legacy but her?"

The last line was too far. Mother shrinks back. She never wanted to have children. I know because she's said so more than once. She'd hoped to give Father a male heir and be done with it. But then girl after girl after girl was born. Six of us. My birth was the most difficult, and now she can't have any more children. A blessing for her, but something my father is always throwing at her, as though it's somehow her fault.

"I left of my own will, Father," I say. "I'm to blame. Not Mother."

He ignores me. "Do you have any idea how important tomorrow is for her? She will participate in the most difficult test we've ever devised, and afterward, she will finally become a ma—woman. A woman."

"Father—" I try again.

"Go to your room, Rasmira. Get rested."

"But you're making the others stay up to guard the boundaries! What is my punishment?"

"Your eye is swollen shut. That's punishment enough. The boys were fighting you in the woods. Their punishment is more severe."

"Torrin wasn't, though. He was on my side."

"And is he the one who convinced you to sneak out of your bed tonight?"

My silence is answer enough.

"Go to bed. Now. The rest of you girls go to your rooms as well. Where is Irrenia? She should see to Rasmira."

"Still out," Mother rushes to say, glad to have an answer to something.

"All right. You can wait up for her and direct her to Rasmira's room when she gets in. I'm to bed."

Father pats me once on the shoulder before shuffling off. A sign of affection that Mother watches with a sharp eye.

"I'm sorry," I whisper to her.

"Torlhon said you're to go to bed," she bites out. "So be off. Tomorrow we can finally be done with you."

She sits herself in one of the cushioned chairs, staring fixedly at the door. My sisters go to their rooms, and I do the same, unwilling to be left alone with Mother.

My room is the last at the end of a long, empty hallway. Embers from the fire set the room aglow. Elda, the housekeeper, lit it before I climbed into bed—shortly before I climbed out of it and snuck out the window.

I don't go to the bed now. If the boys are punished with a night without sleep, then I will be, too. I sit on the floor, reach under the bed, and pull out a small box.

26

Good thing Elda doesn't bother with cleaning under the bed.

I open the lid and stare at the shiny contents.

My mother and sisters (save Irrenia) all chose jeweling as their professions. All the miners bring the best finds to Mother with the hopes of earning her favor. She's also the most beautiful woman in the village—a fact she never lets me forget—and sometimes miners will seek her out when they don't have jewels to sell. They shower her with compliments. No one has a larger section in the high goddess's Book of Merits than my mother, I'm sure.

At the top of my jewelry box is a sapphire necklace, the centerpiece the size of the pad of my thumb. Salvanya, my eldest sister, gave it to me as a gift for my last birthday. Beneath it is a bracelet rimmed with rubies. That's from Tormosa. Alara and Ashari made me matching ruby earrings.

I've never worn anything in this box outside the confines of this room. If my father saw me dressing in such finery, he'd be ashamed. Warriors do not wear jewelry. Even Torrin gets reproach for the sentimental bracelet he wears, which is why he tries to keep it hidden under his armor at all times.

And if my mother saw me, she'd laugh and probably make some comment about how gems could never hide how ugly and unfeminine I am.

I wade through more items: a turquoise choker, a topaz anklet, an emerald-dressed headpiece.

At the very bottom are two plain items, but they're my favorite. I pull them out, even dare to put them on.

Black earrings. My ears were pierced by the time I turned six, but before that, I longed to wear beautiful earrings like my older sisters. Mother knew this, so she made me earrings out of special plain black rocks. She called them lodestones. Some natural reaction between the two ends draws them together, holding up the pieces with my ear suspended between.

I remember what she told me, how I was one end of the earring while she was the other, held together by a powerful force.

That was before I declared myself a warrior. Before my mother hated me. I wouldn't dare wear them in front of her now. She might demand them back.

But I dream of wearing them in front of her, of her seeing them and remembering the words she once spoke.

I know it's foolish thinking—nothing could sway her now. She wears her hatred like an armor fused to her skin, never to come off. It is the only thing that protects her from my father's constant rejection.

She doesn't realize I would give up his praise in an instant if it meant I could have a real mother. One like Torrin's, who grieves every day for the child she never even knew.

A door slams, and I hurry to throw everything back in the box, pulling the stones from my ears and chucking them inside, closing the lid, and shoving it under the bed.

My door opens not even a second after the box slides out of sight.

"What did I miss?" Irrenia asks. She is only one year my senior and the sister I cherish the most.

"I snuck out of the house. Father blamed Mother for it."

She opens her mouth, likely about to demand more details, but then she sees my face. "There's a cut on your cheek, and what happened to your eye? Mother didn't—"

"No. It wasn't Mother." She is not foolish enough to actually strike me. Not when I am warrior trained.

Irrenia enters the room fully, gets behind me, and steers me down the hall. "Tell me everything."

I do so as she plunks me into a chair in her room and digs in one of her drawers for some sort of salve. She rubs it onto my swollen eye, and it begins to twitch from the stinging sensation caused by the salve.

"Ow," I say.

"Oh hush. It'll feel better in a moment."

I close my other eye and take in the rich scent of Irrenia's room. She does not work at the jewelers with everyone else. Irrenia trained to become a healer. She passed her trial just last year, but she's already the best with medicine in the village. Her room is filled with her own concoctions, and it smells of soothing herbs. Lately she's been experimenting with ziken venom, trying to find a way to make the warriors immune to their paralyzing bite.

Irrenia has the kindest spirit of anyone I know, which is why she is always home so late. She can't bear to turn away those who are sick or injured. She continues to work each day until she has no more patients or until she drops from exhaustion.

Though I still cannot open my injured eye, the stinging sensation abates, replaced by a soothing numbness.

She rubs more salve onto the wound, and I finish telling her everything that happened tonight, leaving out no details.

"Sneaking out was stupid," she says when I'm finished. "There are a hundred different ways you could have been injured or killed. I'm just relieved a punch to the face is the worst of your injuries. What if you'd run into the ziken in the wild? We wouldn't have even recognized your remains in the morning! And what would happen to Father then?"

"Oh yes, poor Father. Whatever would he do without an heir to carry on his legacy?"

"He loves you, Rasmira. It would break him to see you go."

Because of his own investment in me. It has nothing to do with me as a person.

"At least Mother would be happy then," I say.

She flicks my swollen eye with a finger.

I let out a sound that probably wakes Ashari over in the next room. "What the hell, Irrenia!" I cup a hand gently over my eye.

"I don't want to hear you talking like that. Everyone has problems. Don't make Mother's and Father's your own. You are not at fault for anything." She puts a finger under my chin to raise my eyes to hers. "I love you. It sounds like that boy of yours is quite fond of you. Your instructors adore you. But even if they didn't, it doesn't matter. You are worthy of love. Not everyone knows how to love the right way. But you remember how that feels and vow never to do it to others."

"You're awfully wise, you know that?" I say. "And you're the kindest person I know." I tell her that last part every day. If there is anyone who deserves a place of honor in Rexasena's Paradise, it is Irrenia. And I remind the goddess every day through my compliments.

"Enough about me," Irrenia says. "Let's discuss how we're going to get this boy to kiss you."

CHAPTER

3

Despite all of Irrenia's wild ideas ("Find a way to get trapped in a dark, tight spot with him," "Pretend to trip in his direction so he has to catch you with your lips inches from his," and "Tell him you've got something stuck in your eye, and you need him to take a look"), I've decided that I will not wait any longer for Torrin to make the first move.

I'm going to kiss him.

As soon as we've both passed our trial—it's the perfect moment.

I fall asleep on the floor of my room with that thought in my mind. The next morning, I take some satisfaction in my aching back and neck. Torrin had to stay up all night. I'd tried to do the same, but at least I can say I'm being punished for my part.

I do not need long to prepare myself in the morning. I wash

myself down with a rag and soapy water, put on a fresh set of warm hides, buckle my boots, and then survey my armor lying out on the far table. Our metalsmiths pound iron into flat sheets and shape them to our bodies. Mine fit perfectly, and I take pride in the simple act of donning them each morning. I like to start at the bottom and work my way up. First come the greaves, which consist of two separate sheets for each lower leg and slide into thin openings in my leathers. I curve one over the top of each shin; the other two slide over my calves. The thigh guards are a bit trickier due to the size, but they slide on the same way. I pull my breastplate over my head and tighten the straps, remembering the embarrassment on Father's face when the smithy had to round it out more for my breasts. My forearm and upper arm guards go on next.

Last and most importantly, I slide my ax through the sheath on my back.

I check and double-check everything. Ensure that all is secure, tight, and comfortable.

At a knock on my door, my heart skips a beat. I know it can't be Irrenia. She said the previous night that she was to go see patients until the time of my trial.

It's Father.

He strides into my room and looks me over from head to toe, hands hidden behind his back.

When he finishes his assessment, he nods to himself. "Your eye is better. Irrenia did fine work. And I'm proud of you, Rasmira. You will do splendidly today. Let us forget last night's escapade ever happened."

I bet Torrin wishes he'd extend the same sentiment to him.

"It is customary for family members to bestow a gift after you complete your trial, but I wish to give you mine now."

He shows me what he'd been hiding behind his back.

There's no other word for it. The ax is *beautiful*. I take it in my hands to inspect it. The iron has been polished until it shines. It is a bit heavier than my first ax, the shaft as long as one of my legs. But the weight is perfectly balanced. The double ax heads are wickedly sharp, ready to cut through flesh as effortlessly as a fish skims through water. Etched into the blades are a series of swirling knots, alluring and intricate. Some of the designs morph into dragon-like figures; others take the shape of birds.

Black leather coats the handle, giving me a perfect grip.

"It's exquisite," I say. "Thank you."

"You haven't even seen the best part. The bladesmith has added a new feature." Father extends his hand, reaching for a notch I hadn't noticed along the handle. He presses it down.

A metal spike springs from the tip of the shaft, right in between the blades.

I gasp in excitement. "This is wonderful."

"Only the best for my daughter."

I set the ax down to grip my father in a hug. He pats my shoulder once before holding me back at arm's length. Warriors do not embrace. Men do not like long hugs.

For the hundredth time, I wonder why I can't be a warrior *and* a woman.

But I don't let Father see my disappointment. I lift my old ax from my back and replace it with the new one.

"It looks good on you," Father says. "Now come. We're due at the amphitheater."

We jog past many townsfolk on their way to the trial: miners with soot-stained hands, broad-shouldered builders, hunters with throwing hatchets hanging off belts at their waists, jewelers wearing their best pieces as advertisements, healers heavy-laden with slings of bandages, ointments, and other remedies.

Today no one has to work. Today is a day of trial, and all the apprentices who have turned eighteen throughout the year will get to partake in the individual trials of their trades. The whole village shows up for the warrior test—even those who don't have children participating. Simply put, ours is the most exciting to watch.

I'm sure my mother would prefer to stay home, but she wouldn't dare disappoint Father by not showing up to give her support.

An arena is located on the most eastern edge of the village. An amphitheater was carved out of rock hundreds of years ago; in the center rests a maze built of rock and metal.

Most of the village has already gathered. Old men with metal staffs hobble up the stairs. Children cling to their mothers, anxious over the close proximity of the wild resting beyond the inna trees. Warriors who have already passed their trials stand guard at the tree line and around the maze, ready to step in should any of the beasts inside get loose.

I should probably be nervous, but I'm not. I have fought the ziken before during training exercises. And it's hard to be scared with the heavy weight of an ax against my back.

Father separates from me once we reach the ground level of the maze to talk with Master Burkin about the trial. As I watch him go, I see movement out of the corner of my eye. Irrenia is waving wildly to get my attention from up in the amphitheater seats. I return the gesture, happy that she's here. Mother and the rest of my sisters are there as well, seated beside her. Salvanya and her husband, Ugatos, stand and offer brief waves. Tormosa, Ashari, and

Alara stand as well to show their support, and the latter puts her fingers to her lips to give off a loud whistle. Only Mother is seated and purposefully looking away from me.

Someone nudges my shoulder.

"Are you nervous?" Torrin asks.

"Torrin, I'm so sorry. How are you feeling?" His eyes are rimmed with sleepless red, and his body sags with exhaustion.

"Never better," he says, completely undaunted. "Think nothing of yesterday. I'd do it again to spend more time with you."

My face warms at the words. I answer his initial question. "I'm not nervous. Are you?"

"Of course. Everyone's watching. Your *father's* watching."

I know he says this because my father is the most important man in the village, but part of me hopes it is also because he plans to court me after the trial and he wants to make a good impression. Especially after last night.

I remember my resolve to kiss him after the trial, and my heart does a flip in my chest. It must be a private moment. I don't think I'm brave enough to kiss him in front of the others. And if he rejects me, then I don't want anyone to witness that, either.

"You're staring at me," Torrin says.

"You're the only thing here worth looking at." I'm surprised by the brazen words after they've left my mouth.

But Torrin doesn't tease me for them.

"That's not true," he says, locking eyes with me.

For the first time today, a bit of nervous energy stirs in my belly. I laugh off his comment.

"Warriors, quiet yourselves!" Master Burkin calls, silencing our chatter. "There are various entrances to the maze, so I will be spreading you out. Follow me. Be ready when the doors open, but don't enter until you hear the horn blow.

"The rules of the trial are simple. The hourglass will turn. By the end of the hour, you all must have killed at least one ziken and you must avoid being bitten. Anyone who fails to meet *both* requirements will face banishment and the mattugr."

A spike of fear ripples down the assembled warriors.

Burkin turns. As one group, we follow. A foot blocks my path, but I jump over it before I can trip.

"The maze is a dangerous place for a rat," Havard says. "There's more than ziken to worry about in there."

I narrow my eyes at Havard. It would be just like him to spoil this for me, to try to get me banished and left to die outside the village.

"Tell me, Havard, will you be able to see the ziken charging at you past your broken nose?"

It's swollen to twice its usual size and bent horribly to the side. I hadn't realized I'd kicked him so hard during training yesterday, and it must have been too dark last night for me to notice.

Havard scowls at me. "You'll get what's coming to you."

He walks off. Torrin steps in front of me before I can get any ideas to follow.

"You four, enter here," Master Burkin says. He starts divvying us up, putting three to four people at each entrance as we circle around the arena.

"Rasmira, Torrin, Siegert, and Kol, you stand at this door. Best of luck, Rasmira, though I know you don't need it."

"Thank you," I say flatly, irritated that he hasn't given anyone else the same good wishes.

A look of frustration crosses Torrin's face at the words. Before I can say anything to try to make up for what I cannot control, the look disappears.

"It's a lot different viewing the maze from this angle, isn't it?" Torrin asks as he pulls his ax off his back.

The rest of us do the same. Siegert and Kol glance at me with cruel smiles on their lips, as if they know something I do not.

"The walls seem higher," I say, avoiding their stares.

The metal door starts to lift, pulleys screeching as it heaves upward. While we wait for the horn to sound, I take another chance to survey the crowd. My father has joined the rest of my family. Their eyes are all on me. Now I really feel waves of tension. *Mother is watching me.* I can't mess up. Even if it's impossible, I have to try to make her proud. I cannot be hated by her my whole life. Once I pass my trial and become a woman, I have the option to live in my own home. She'll have Father at the house without me. She'll get the attention she craves from him. Goddess knows I receive too much of it.

Everything will be the way it should have been from the beginning.

The deep blare of the horn sounds above the chatter of hundreds of voices. My stomach plunges to my toes, and Torrin and I are off.

The ground is uneven. I lift my feet high above the rocks as I run to avoid tripping. Some grass cracks through in places, breaking up the ground further. Siegert and Kol race against us. At the first fork in the maze, they veer right while Torrin and I head left.

I relax a little once they're gone. It's easier to focus when it's only me and Torrin. Now if I could just forget the fact that my mother is watching me from the seating above the arena . . .

Low shrieks sound throughout the maze. Someone has run into the ziken already.

"Come on," I say, excitement pulsing through my veins. Torrin quickens his pace to keep up with me. We turn right, left, left, right, plunging as deep into the maze as possible, listening to the hungry calls of the ziken.

We take one more turn before a flash of black streaks across my vision.

"Finally," I breathe.

The ziken halts and turns as soon as it hears us coming.

When standing on all fours, most ziken are between two and three feet tall. Instead of fur, they have a shiny black exoskeleton, as thick as any armor forged by man. Their eyes bulge outward, like an insect's, and I can see my reflection multiplied a hundred times in the faceted eyes of the beast before me. Its legs end in sharp claws, and its mouth unhinges to let out an unsettling cackle. Bulbous red-orange eyes fix on me, and then it flies toward us at a gallop, tail whisking behind it.

"I've got this one!" I shout to Torrin.

I sprint headlong toward the ziken, holding my ax so it is parallel with the ground. The creature never wavers in its direct path to me. I hear my blood in my ears, see my breath pool out of me in the cool morning air.

I dare a glance up into the stands, unable to help searching for the look on my mother's face. Will she seem anxious or eager? Will she be watching me at all?

But what I find is worse than all the options I'd considered.

Indifference.

If I win my trial, I will be a woman, finally able to leave her household and live on my own. She never has to see me again.

And if I die or lose, I will also be gone from her sight forever. Either way, she wins.

I return my gaze to the creature just in time. A jolt runs up my arms when we make contact, my ax connecting with the creature's neck. I'm bigger, stronger, and the ziken skids backward, its neck trapped in the space between the ax blades. A sharp crack ricochets around me as the tips of my blades connect with a stone wall of the maze.

My finger slides across the switch, and the spike drives from the tip of my ax, piercing the creature's neck. With the ziken's next cackle, brown blood bubbles from its throat.

I brace a foot against its body and pull my ax free, a liquid slurp coming from the wound as I do so. I flip the switch again, allowing the spike to slide neatly back into place. The ziken falls to the floor, blood oozing from the wound. But almost instantly, the skin starts to heal over. Before it can recover, I lift my ax above my head and bring it down on the creature, successfully severing the head from the body—the only wound the beast can't recover from.

Blood drips from my ax as I look up into the seating once more. My father stands and clashes the rod of his ax against the ground in approval. Everyone in the crowd stomps their feet. My eyes seek my mother's face. She still watches me, and I swear I see the almost-imperceptible movement of a nod. If it was a nod, was it one of approval? Was it her face turning downcast in disappointment? A physical sign of her resigning to her fate?

I am a skilled warrior. She knows I will not fail. She will have to walk this world knowing I'm in it, too, somewhere, keeping her husband from her as Father trains me, dotes on me.

"Well done," Torrin says, pulling my attention back down to

him, "but the next one's mine." The eagerness is apparent in his voice.

"Of course. I bet I can kill more than you by the end, though." We're running again, searching right and left for more signs of the creatures.

"Are you willing to wager on that?"

"Of course."

"All right, what do you want if you win?" he asks.

I know what I want, but I'm still not brave enough to ask for it. No, I will surprise him with a kiss after the trial. "If I win, you have to clean and polish my ax after the trial—and every day for the next month after we start taking rotations guarding the village boundaries."

"That is easily doable."

"What do you want if you win?" I ask.

"That's—"

A ball of smooth black skin attaches itself to Torrin's back. For a moment, I'm unable to move, horrified by what's in front of me. He can't be banished. I need him.

A second later, I'm launching myself forward. Grabbing the ziken with my bare hands, I tear it from Torrin's back and throw it in the opposite direction. The beast is heavy; it doesn't sail more than a few feet. But by then, Torrin has turned around, fire in his eyes, ax straight. He takes a swing at it, severing off an arm and biting into the neck. With a second swing, he detaches the head.

"Torrin," I say, barely above a whisper, staring at the little drops of blood falling from his neck. He probably can't hear me over the sounds of the audience's loud exclamations.

"It's okay. Those are claw marks. It didn't bite me."

I don't dare believe him without checking. I inch down the armor at his back to get a better look at the exposed skin of his neck. Yes, claw marks. And he hasn't started shaking from the venom spread through their bite.

I sigh in relief.

"Did you honestly not believe me? Or were you simply desperate to see beneath my shirt?"

I glare at him. "Don't you scare me like that again."

"It's all right. I won't. Come, now. We've done the hard part. All that's left to do is survive without sustaining a bite. Let's go on."

We're running again. Despite the previous scare, we're still eager to reach more of the deadly beasts.

"What were you going to say?" I ask. "What do you want if you kill more of them than I do?"

"That's easy. I want you to put in a good word for me with your father."

"Oh." It makes sense, I suppose, but it bothers me that he wants to use me like that.

"Get that frown off your face, Rasmira. I want you to put in a good word for me so he'll give me permission to court you."

I nearly drop my ax.

"Don't look so surprised."

"I'm disappointed that I have to let you win now."

He smiles at me, and it makes the future seem so bright. I don't even care if I have to deal with my mother's hate. My teacher's false praise. My father's single-minded adoration. As long as I can protect this village, spend time with my sisters, *and* have Torrin, I don't need anything else.

We round another corner and stop dead in our tracks.

Five ziken beasts block our path, almost as if they were waiting for us.

They cackle at the sight of us, and the sounds send a shiver down my back.

"The one in the middle is enormous," Torrin says.

My grip on my ax tightens. "Then I'll kill it and leave you to deal with the hatchlings."

Torrin snorts. The others can hardly be called newborns. They are only marginally smaller.

"The sensible thing," Torrin says, "would be for one of us to take on three, and the other to take on two, including the big one."

"I don't think they're going to give us much say in the matter."

As if in agreement, all five of them race for Torrin, clinging to the left side of the path where he stands, instead of spreading to the right side where I am.

I try not to be offended. He is taller, bulkier. And while I am certainly no fragile or dainty thing, I must not look as threatening.

How very misguided of them.

"Rasmira, get over here," Torrin says. It's not fear in his voice. Mostly anticipation, but he doesn't like his odds five on one.

"Perhaps I should just run. I need only be faster than you."

Torrin gives me a gesture, and by the gasps in the audience, I can tell at least a few people saw it.

I laugh and leap to his side just as the horde reaches us.

They pounce, hind legs sending them flying through the air, jaws unhinging, teeth flashing in the light of the sun.

I hold my ax out in front of me, turn it sideways, and use the length of the rod to connect with three separate ziken, careful not to let teeth get anywhere near where my hands are spaced apart. I skid back across the rocky soil at the impact. One of the beasts takes the rod in the mouth, another at the neck, and the third—the monstrous one—hits at the knees and continues sailing over my head.

Brown blood smears the rod from the ziken who took it in the mouth, but that particular beast finds its feet and licks its lips, as though even more crazed by the taste of its own blood. A tooth flicks to the floor as it roves its mouth with its tongue. A canine. Good.

I bring my ax down on its head, the sharp blade sinking in deeply, right between the beast's eyes. Before I can pull it back out, the monstrous ziken charges me again, this time from behind.

I spin my body around, bringing both ax and impaled ziken with me. The two beasts collide, and my ax finally dislodges from the first one's head as both beasts are sent flying off to the left.

The final ziken, the one that took the rod to the neck, is still wheezing on the ground. I step up beside it, raise my ax high in the air, and bring it down across its neck. The head rolls off to the side, brown liquid spreading across the rocky ground.

Another loud whistle rises up from the stands.

I look up at Torrin. He's swinging his ax back and forth, keeping his two ziken at bay.

"They're both still alive?" I ask. "Come, now, Torrin, I've already killed one, and I got stuck with three of the beasts, as well as the large one that made you piss yourself."

"Then give yourself a pat on the back!" he shouts back to me.

I laugh and turn, ready to meet the two beasts that have found their footing once again.

My hands tighten around my ax, loving the feel of the leather-laced handle. I feel powerful when I hold it, unstoppable, even. My blood sings in my veins from the thrill of battle, and I eagerly await the next onslaught.

The ziken that took my ax between its eyes has already healed itself. Its armored skin has reconnected so perfectly, one wouldn't be able to tell it was ever injured.

And the large one—its eyes flash orange with the direct sunlight shining on them. Thick droplets of saliva hit the ground as it licks its lips.

"Come take a bite of this," I say as I swing my ax at it.

It dodges to the side before taking a swing at me. One clawed foot connects with my breastplate. Sparks rain to the ground at the contact, and the ziken cackles menacingly at the sight. It's startled by the hot sparks, and I use the beast's confusion to send another swing its way.

My ax embeds into its shoulder, and I yank it back out as the other ziken decides to pounce again. In the same motion, I swing my body around, connecting with the smaller ziken's side.

I remove its head with the next swing.

That leaves the big brute. It eyes me warily, takes in the dead ziken we've already dispatched—

And runs off down the way Torrin and I just came from.

"Get back here!" I yell as I bound for it.

Torrin catches me by the arm and halts me. "Leave it, Rasmira. Let's see if we can reach the middle of the maze before the time runs out!"

I wipe my bloodied ax blades on the leather covering his greaves.

He leaps backward. "Disgusting."

I grin. "Race you there!"

It doesn't take long to reach. The middle of the maze is a vast opening. It seems that everyone else has already arrived, and they're all battling their own ziken—some taking on two or three at a time.

Torrin takes no time at all to launch himself into the fray as if he didn't sustain an injury. I hop in after him. The hourglass must be done soon, and I don't want to waste a minute of this experience. It's an opportunity to show everyone what I can do.

The ziken are everywhere. It's a wonder we ran across any in the maze. But they are no match for us. We have been trained for the last ten years to do one thing: kill them. They don't stand a chance.

Axes swing. Heads roll. Brown blood flies everywhere. It's disgusting and thrilling and freeing. I don't care that I've got blood in my hair, that Havard will probably pass his trial and continue to cause trouble in my life. I don't care if my mother still doesn't approve. In just a few more seconds, I will be a woman. I will be free from my father's household. Torrin will court me.

Everything will be different.

I step onto a loose head and nearly lose my balance. I huff out a laugh before continuing onward, swiping at the nearest beast to me.

Torrin sidles up next to me, holding a ziken head with one hand below its mouth and the other at the apex of the head. "Rasmira," he says in a childish voice, moving the ziken's mouth so it looks like it's speaking. "Torrin has killed eight beasts. How many have you killed?" His puppeteering act draws a laugh from me.

"Just because we have to kill them, it doesn't mean—" I start.

A loud howl rises above everything else. The entire crowd leans out of their seats, straining to get a better look.

Over on the far edge of the maze's center, Havard battles with his own ziken.

Did he get bitten? I wonder with equal parts eagerness and pity.

No. It is merely a battle cry. Undoubtedly an intentional one so everyone can see him swipe the head off the largest ziken in the maze, the brute I faced earlier. It must have found its own way to the center. The crowd's quiet anticipation allows us all to hear the ziken's head bounce onto the stone floor.

A sharp pain takes hold in my left forearm. I suck in a breath and look down only to find nothing there. I look around me. There are no ziken nearby. Yet, as I squint at my arm, I can see—

No.

How can it be?

My first instinct is to look up into the stands to check if anyone saw. But everyone is still awing and clapping over Havard's kill.

Everyone except my mother, who watches me as if I'm the only person out here.

I start to panic. I don't understand. What happened? Where did the teeth marks on my skin come from? The leather is torn there, right in the gap between the two sheets of armor. How—

I finally catch sight of the head still grasped in Torrin's hand. Only now it has red coating its teeth.

My blood.

Stupidly, I think Torrin must have accidentally hit me with it. But once I find the courage to drag my eyes up to his face, my world shatters.

He's shaking with laughter. Cold. Fierce. Laughter.

When he catches his breath, he says to me, "Your life is over, Rat."

CHAPTER

4

The horn blows, signaling the end of the trial. Pulleys yank up sections of the maze, and older warriors enter to deal with the rest of the ziken. Cheers ring through the amphitheater as families congratulate the victors. My father and sisters part the crowds, racing down to me.

Foolishly, I hide my left arm behind my back, as if that will stop the venom coursing through my veins.

Torrin walks over to Havard and claps him on the back. He whispers something to him, and the two laugh and turn in my direction.

There are words I should say. Things I should do. Emotions I should feel. My body wants to fight. My mind wants to run. I'm frozen like that. Just staring at Torrin with Havard, trying to understand what it means. Trying to understand what is going to happen to me.

Then the venom hits.

I collapse.

My muscles flare with pain, pinching and tightening, roiling. My arms and legs spasm as the venom works its way through my bloodstream. Uncomfortable screeching fills my ears as the armor at my back rubs against the rocky ground. My head darts every which way as my neck twitches.

A flash of blue sky.

Rocky soil in my mouth.

Torrin's brown eyes.

"Rasmira's been bitten!" he shouts for all to hear.

The cheers and stomps go quiet as I become a spectacle for all to see.

A sickening sensation spreads through me. Something that has nothing to do with the venom.

Humiliation.

I've been such a fool.

Torrin is an excellent actor. My aggressors have always openly hated me. It never once occurred to me that someone could hate me under a facade of friendship.

As I lie here, helpless to control my own body, a series of unseen moments flashes before my eyes: Torrin and Havard planning this move from the beginning, Torrin inwardly blanching every time he had to touch me, Havard's secret smiles every time he saw me under Torrin's spell, Torrin and Havard laughing over my gullibility.

The truth is so clear now.

Torrin put up with me for six whole weeks, pretending to be my friend, pretending to want to be more than my friend, all so that on this day I would let him get close enough to me to sabotage my test.

And to think, I thought I would finally have my first kiss today.

Bile heats the back of my throat. I vomit all over myself, start to choke on it as I'm still facing toward the sky, unable to roll on my side because the venom still controls my limbs.

Until someone is there, turning me.

"Get back!" Irrenia yells. "What's wrong with all of you?"

She helps me to my side, places my head in her lap so I can't injure myself as we wait the venom out.

Where is my father?

"It's all right," Irrenia says, stroking my hair. "It'll be over in just a few seconds."

She sees to the wounds of our warriors all the time. Of course she knows the effects of a ziken bite. But why is she lying to me? My shaking might stop soon.

But everything will not be all right.

FINALLY, MY BODY CALMS. My muscles are enflamed. I feel sluggish, tired, but I stand anyway, try to regain what dignity I have left as I wipe my face on the hides covering my forearm.

Then my eyes land on Torrin.

I want to curl into myself, hide my face from the world, from the shame, from the knowledge of what he did to me. From what will happen to me.

But then rage strikes like a bolt of lightning, infusing my limbs, making me forget all else.

Before I realize I've even moved, he's flat on his back. I must have kicked him in the stomach.

"You bastard. You disgusting, pathetic, lying worm—" I hurt every inch of him I can get my hands on. It's a good thing I dropped my ax when the venom took over, otherwise he might no longer have a head. As it is, I've knocked the wind out of him, so he's unable to defend himself from my blows. His so-called friends just laugh at the display, but I don't spare them a glance. I'm determined to have at Torrin until his own mother won't be able to recognize him.

A strong set of arms yanks me back. "Rasmira!" my father shouts.

I try to pull against him. Torrin needs to suffer. He needs to be the one twitching on the ground while everyone watches.

"You will calm yourself, now!"

"He set me up," I yell back. "I didn't get bitten. It was him. All of them. They—"

He slaps me.

The shock is enough to distract me from my need to disfigure Torrin. My father has never struck me. He's never needed to. I have always been his perfect child. His favorite. But as I look into his eyes now, I can see nothing but disappointment. Anger. Even hate. As though he is the one about to be sentenced to death in the wild.

I collect myself, breathing in and out slowly. This time, with no mania, I try to explain again, loudly for all to hear. "I was not bitten by one of the creatures. He clamped one of the severed head's teeth onto my arm. They're *trying* to get me banished. I swear it, Father."

A group of the village elders stand behind my father. Edelmar, the oldest and wisest of them all, speaks up. "Can anyone confirm Rasmira's story? Did anyone see?"

I look around, but I now realize the reason for Havard's battle cry. He drew everyone's attention to him, and Torrin was so close to me, he could have easily ruined me without anyone noticing.

My eyes land on my mother.

She saw.

I'd looked up and seen her watching me. I remember. She saw the whole thing. She can save my life.

"Mother?" I plead.

Uncertainty crosses her face for a moment. She has an important choice to make. One that could change her life and mine.

Finally, she says, "I cannot lie. The goddess forbids it. I won't do it, not even for my own daughter. I saw nothing."

Whatever hope I might have been clinging to vanishes. *I* vanish, blowing away on the next gentle breeze. My world has ended, and I can't feel anything anymore. I am only a collection of thoughts.

The odds that nobody saw what truly happened are so slim, but no one would dare refute my mother. Not the village beauty. The wife of their leader. Not when they could use their knowledge of the truth to gain favor with her.

"Very well, then," Father says. His voice is calculated, free of emotion. "Rasmira Bendrauggo, daughter of Torlhon, you are to be banished. You have until morning to prepare yourself for the wild. By that time, the council will decide your mattugr."

IT REQUIRES ALL MY concentration just to put one foot in front of the other. Hundreds of eyes burn into my back. I can feel them even if I can't see them judging me. When at last I step into my home, I allow my shoulders to slump, my head to fall.

I head for my bedroom. I need to pack.

I need to think.

I need to breathe.

My thoughts jumble together as I try to remember all the supplies I will need for the wild. Hides, food, candles, flint and pyrite, soap, water flask, blanket, whetstone, oil.

I crouch down to my knees to look under the bed for a leather pack to store it all. Instead my eyes land on the jewelry box.

Mother's earrings are inside.

Before I even know what's happening, the box is in my hands and I'm hurling it across the room. A scream fills my ears. My scream.

The box shatters as it hits the wall, and the light from my window flashes across the gemstones as they rain to the ground. I rip the ax from my back and let it clatter to the floor. I slam a fist into my feather-stuffed pillow. My eyes and nose burn.

I come apart where no one can see and no one can hear.

SOMETIME LATER, I lie in bed, staring at the rock ceiling. I've already finished filling my pack with provisions. There is nothing to do now but wait.

It seems as though my memory must be faulty. Some nightmare that I've confused with reality. But as I listen to the sounds of the village's celebration, I remember that I'm not invited. I am not an adult like the rest of the warriors of my age group. I'm an outcast.

I hear the door to the house slam shut. A rush of footsteps. Then my door bursts open, Irrenia spilling in, her arms barely containing an assortment of objects.

"Sorry it's taken me so long to come," she says. "I had to grab a few things." She sets everything on the floor and starts sifting through it. "Fever reducer," she says, holding up a few leaves in a glass jar. "Pain reliever." She raises a bottle of rosy pink liquid. "Muscle relaxant. This one wards off infection, and—"

"Irrenia."

"Drink this one with water. It'll make sure you get all the nutrients you need. Plants will likely be scarce out there."

I stand and walk over to her, trying to still her frantic hands. "Irrenia."

"No! You need to remember this. It's important."

"How can I possibly fit this all in my pack?"

"Take two packs."

"I may be strong, but I also need to be able to walk."

Her head snaps up. "This is no time to joke! You're going to— going to—" She bursts into tears.

I have little desire to comfort her when I am the one being sent to my death, but I remember the right motions. I wrap my arms around her dainty figure. She's beautiful like Mother. Out of all of us, I think she looks the most like her. How did she become Mother's opposite in everything else?

She lets me hold her only for a few seconds before pushing me away. "Don't do that. I should be comforting *you*. I'm horrible. I—I—I just stood there."

"What do you mean?"

"All I had to do was say I saw that boy do it. It didn't matter that I didn't see anything. I still should have done it. For you."

My heart seems to grow within my chest. "I don't expect you to lie for me. You cannot jeopardize your soul, Irrenia."

"I should have done it anyway. I would do anything for you. I just hesitated. I thought of myself first. I'm despicable. I—"

"That's enough. You are the furthest thing from despicable. You are one of the only people in this village who truly cares for me. You are kind and good. Nothing in this world has made me happier than having you for a sister."

Tears start to fall from her eyes again. "But it's not fair. They set you up."

"I know."

She grabs one more thing off the ground. "All right, it might have been silly for me to bring so much, but you at least have to take this with you. It was your present for after the trial. And now—" She clears her throat. "Now that your trial is over, I can give it to you."

She forces a smile and hands me a canister. I take it, open it, and sniff at the contents.

"Ugh. It's brown. Is it dung?"

"No. It's much more useful than dung. I've been experimenting."

"With dung?"

"No! With ziken blood."

Now she has my attention. "You didn't!"

Her tears disappear. The healer in her comes forth. "I did. If you're injured out in the wild, smear this cream on the wound. It will heal most cuts and scrapes instantly. It won't mend broken bones, and it won't re-form lost limbs. I can't figure out how they manage to grow those back. I'm still working on it, and I have much to figure out, but—"

I embrace her before she can finish. "It's wonderful. I'm sure it will help."

Maybe I'll last two days out on my own instead of one now.

Hurt spreads through my heart as I hold my sister. My hours with her are numbered, and I don't know how I'll possibly let her go.

UNSURPRISINGLY, I CAN'T SLEEP. I'm half-tempted to leave while everyone dreams; that way I don't have to face them all in the morning. But if I don't stick around to hear what my quest is to be, I'll have no hope of returning home, no chance of redeeming myself so I can enter the goddess's Paradise.

There's also no chance I could leave without waking Irrenia, who refused to sleep in her own bed despite my protests. She said she was going to stay by my side for as long as she could.

Bugs chirp loudly outside my window, counting down the seconds until I have to leave the safety of the village.

I try to close my eyes, but when I do, I see my father's face. That look of disappointment. Of embarrassment. Of anger. All of it for me.

Could I have misread his face? Surely he was only surprised? My father couldn't have really turned against me so quickly, could he? Not after all the years of training. We've grown so close in all that time.

I remember the day when things finally changed between Father and me. It was ten years ago, and it was the same day I realized my mother would never love me again.

My whole life I'd been mocked for my bulkier form. Even

when I was so young, I knew I was different with my short torso, wide shoulders, muscled figure. I knew that I didn't look like my sisters, and all the village kids my age would tease me for it. My father barely looked at me back then. I was daughter number six. His sixth disappointment. He never had time for me.

I was sick of it. Sick of being told I wasn't pretty like my sisters, sick of being told I took more after my father, sick of my father not paying attention to me.

At the end of the year, all the eight-year-olds were lined up and told to declare their professions. Father had every child come up to the village square one at a time and state what they would do for the rest of their lives. Then they went to stand with the masters of that trade.

When it was my turn, when my father finally looked at me for the briefest moment and then looked heavenward, as though he were embarrassed to even acknowledge my existence, I said, "I will join the warriors."

I remember being surprised by the words. I'd thought for sure I would join the jewelers like my four eldest sisters and mother. It's what I'd been planning.

But then my father looked at me. Really looked at me.

"Rasmira, don't waste our time. What is your real choice?"

I stared him down, held myself as high as I could. "Give me your ax."

While much scoffing and laughing came from the villagers, my father listened. He took that ax from off his back, an ax that Irrenia and Ashari couldn't hope to heft an inch off the ground, and handed it to me.

I took it. I lifted it high. And then I threw it. The ax embedded firmly into the nearest tree with a satisfying *twang*.

I couldn't remember anything feeling so right. While I enjoyed jeweling immensely, I realized that I wanted this more. Especially with the way my father was now looking at me.

I said it again. "I will join the warriors."

Father escorted me himself over to Master Burkin. As we walked, he said, "You're to listen to Master Burkin in all things. If you can prove yourself, if you become the best, I will make you the next ruler of this village."

All my father's attention suddenly became mine. He watched over me, trained me, talked with me, loved me in his own way. Mother lost her husband to me. Because I was like him, he loved me more. And once she realized things would never be the same for her, she began to treat me the way Father did her.

I was ignored, ridiculed, held to different standards. I was always a disappointment to her.

I took comfort in my prowess with the ax, but that only drove me further and further away from her.

I did nothing to deserve my mother's hate. How could I help the way Father reacted? I used to try to ignore him as he did Mother, hoping he would understand and start being kind to her again. But that only resulted in me being neglected by both of my parents, and I couldn't stand that.

Apparently, I drove my mother so far away that she would rather lose her immortal soul than finish out her mortal life with me in it.

But not Father. I'm his pride and joy. He won't send me into the wild with an impossible task. He can't. He needs me to carry on his legacy. He needs me to be the next ruler. He won't allow the council to assign me too harsh a task. It'll be something difficult but doable. Something I can accomplish and, once done, return with glory.

Only that thought is what finally lets me drift off . . .

I'M HYPERAWARE OF MY surroundings as I walk to the village square, my pack and ax strapped to my shoulders. Irrenia walks beside me, but she doesn't say anything. What do you say to someone who's about to go to their death?

I shake away the dark thought. Not death. Father will help me. He loves me. He'll make the council see reason.

The air feels unnaturally cool this morning, raising bumps along my skin underneath my furs. I notice the coarse grass swaying in the wind, rocks skittering out of my path as I walk, the buzzing of insects in the early morning.

Irrenia places her hand on my arm and gives it a squeeze, offering me strength, as people start to stare.

"It doesn't matter what they think. The goddess knows what really happened. You will not lose your place in her Paradise. Because your place is right next to mine. I cannot live happily if you are not there."

"Thank you, Irrenia."

"You will try, won't you?"

"Try what?"

"To complete your quest. Whatever it is. Promise me you'll try. You have to come home to me."

She's on the verge of tears again, so I say, "Yes, I promise. I'll try."

But even as I say the words, I wonder if I'm lying.

"RASMIRA BENDRAUGGO, daughter of Torlhon, come forth."

That's the second time my father has addressed me this way. As though he is not Torlhon. As though I am not anyone or anything to him. It must be an act. It has to be. I kindle the hope inside me. He's putting on a show, trying not to express favoritism before he gives me my mattugr.

It would seem that everyone has come out to watch my banishment. Kol, Siegert, Havard, and Torrin push their way to the front of the crowd. They share a bag of myrkva seeds between them, cracking the shells with their teeth and spitting them to the ground, as though I were some sort of summer play about to start.

How is it so quiet? Even children don't speak as everyone stands in a semicircle in front of me. There is nothing but the *crack, crack, crack* of those damn seeds.

I step forward, turning bright eyes to my father.

"Rasmira—" There's a hitch in his speech, his voice breaking for the briefest of moments to show his emotion.

I make the mistake of glancing to his left, where my mother stands. She tries to hide the smile on her face, but I see it clearly. She couldn't be more thrilled by the whole situation.

"Rasmira," he tries again, "you are my daughter. I taught you myself. You've had the best training under Master Burkin. You may be a woman, but you are held to the same standard as everyone else your age. You have had many female ancestors who have passed their trials. There's absolutely no reason why you shouldn't have.

"You made a statement by entering that maze. You told everyone that you had the confidence to succeed. That you deserved to be a warrior.

"You lied. And as *my* daughter, you're being appointed a special quest."

My back straightens. This is it. He's going to spare me. I'm going to be given a special quest, one actually capable of being accomplished.

"For centuries," Father says, "we have lived as the hunting tribe. We are responsible for supplying the meat for Peruxolo as our yearly tribute. Our children starve as a result. Our hunters exhaust themselves. Our habitat spreads thin."

He's lost me. Am I supposed to get more food for the village? I can learn to hunt. If I can take out a ziken, how hard could it be to catch a valder?

"And so," he continues, "for your mattugr, you are tasked with killing the god Peruxolo."

THEY WANT ME TO *WHAT?*

I repeat the words three times in my head before they take root.

"Should you complete your mission, you will be granted the highest honor available to a mortal. You'll be welcomed . . ."

I stop listening. Nothing else matters. He couldn't say anything to lighten the revelation.

The most powerful being in our land, and I'm supposed to kill him.

My father must truly loathe me to demand such a mission of me. He's *ensured* that I will never come back home. Surely an immortal cannot be killed.

". . . time for you to leave now," he says. "You've had plenty of time to say your good-byes. Go now or face eternal exile from Rexasena's Paradise."

I don't dare look at my mother. I don't want to see the joy that lights up her eyes. I don't want to see the faces of those I trained with ever again. It's bad enough that each step I take is echoed with the cracking of a nutshell. So I look to the one group of people I still can count on. Salvanya, Tormosa, Alara, Ashari, and Irrenia. My five sisters huddle together. Tears on their faces. Love in their eyes.

That is the last image I see before turning my back on my home.

The last image I see before I leave my life and brace myself for death.

PART 2

THE
WILD

CHAPTER

5

Birds squawk loudly from the inna treetops. I focus on their drab brown-and-gray wings. I imagine that I can fly and take myself away from this horrible place.

The last time I walked this way, I was with Torrin.

I've kept to the road. It doesn't seem as though I've been walking long, but I've already reached the clearing where our village paid tribute to Peruxolo just two nights ago.

Peruxolo. The god I'm supposed to kill.

A bitter laugh bubbles up from my chest. A god cannot be killed. I'm not meant to return home. I'm meant to die. My father sent me here to die.

This is it. The farthest anyone travels away from the village. Beyond this point, the wild is lethal.

But I have to keep moving. If I'm not moving, I'll be forced to think. And thinking isn't an option right now.

To the north and west lie more villages. To the south is Seravin. And to the east—

That's where Peruxolo went with the wagon train. I can see the faint outlines of a less traveled road, one traversed only once a year when the god takes away all our food.

I follow it.

The farther I go, the more wildlife there is to be found. Thorny vines the color of blood wrap around the bases of the trees. Indigo berries hang off the vines. Though I've never seen nor heard of them, I assume they're poisonous. Surely nothing so bright in color could be edible. Crying saplings peek through gaps in the taller trees. The white bark peels back on its own in strips, which is how the trees earned their name.

My steps grow louder as I step on dried leaves atop the rocky ground. A snaketrap gapes open in the middle of the road, two handspans in length. The plants are camouflaged to match the color of the rocky ground, easily missed if one isn't looking for them. I step over this one. In another hundred yards, I find a closed one, a wriggling tail flapping out of the side. The plant constricts, and the snake stills.

Yellow eyes peer at me from dens in the trees. Since nothing ventures onto the road, I assume I'm too large of prey for the predators attached to those eyes.

Far, far up ahead, I see the outline of a mountain through thick clouds. Unless the road changes direction, it appears to head right for it. I wonder if that is where Peruxolo makes his home.

I sip from my canteen and chew on a dried strip of valder meat. Before I know it, night falls. Still, I walk. It isn't safe to stop and sleep. I should have built a shelter. But I didn't. Because I'm not thinking, I'm moving.

My head twitches at every little noise. The sounds of the wild change at night. High-pitched trills echo through the starry expanse. Branches crack and rocks roll across the ground. Bugs buzz all around me. It's hard to tell just how close any other noises might be. I'm unsure if it's safer or more dangerous to light a torch.

So I do nothing but walk.

I carry my ax in my hands, ready to use it at the first hint of danger. My mind is wide awake but scratchy from the pain of two nearly sleepless nights.

It's harder to keep the dangerous thoughts away now.

I see their faces—Havard's, Torrin's, Siegert's, Kol's. I can imagine them snug in their beds, content and proud of themselves.

And I entertain the notion of sneaking back into the village, knocking them unconscious one by one and dragging them from their beds to tie them to trees in the wild, leaving them for the ziken.

Perhaps it would be worth getting caught and exiled from Paradise forever.

When my legs finally tire, I find the largest tree lining the road and sit with my back pressed firmly against it, my ax balanced across my knees.

Tonight the moon is mostly full. Silhouettes fly across the sky, some small, some the length of my arm. I watch them chase one another through the open air. Listen to the chattering. Now that I am still, cold seeps in through my hides. I pull the spares from my pack and don those, too.

Then I wait to see if I will survive the night.

I MUST HAVE DOZED at some point, because consciousness suddenly jolts through me. My eyes are still closed, but heat pelts into my face from the sun.

No, not the sun.

The sun doesn't smell of blood and rot.

I hold perfectly still except for my hands, which search my lap for my ax. Bless the goddess, it's still here.

I crack open one eye.

An unhinged ziken mouth is inches from my face, tasting my breath. A tongue lolls out and touches my chin. A cackle, so loud it hurts my ears, unleashes from its mouth.

Fear floods through all my limbs.

I realize then that even if I don't have any answers, even if I don't know where to go or what to do, I now know one thing.

I don't want to die.

My instincts kick in, and quick as I can, I raise my ax and press the shaft between those gaping jaws.

Red-orange eyes flash, and the muscles beneath the beast's natural armor bunch. It presses against my ax, trying to reach my neck in earnest now that it knows I'm awake, alive.

I'm alive, and I'm going to stay that way.

My muscles strain, weaker than usual because I just woke up. Slowly, the beast gains inch by inch on me. One prick from either of those canines and I'll be helpless while the beast takes its time consuming my flesh.

Promise me you'll try. You have to come home to me. Those were Irrenia's last words to me.

I intend to keep them.

I let out a battle cry and shove the creature away long enough to find my feet. It charges, but I leap aside, and it crashes face-first into the tree. I bring my ax down on its neck with all my might, severing the head with one blow.

It picked the wrong girl. I killed a dozen of its brethren yesterday. I took on three ziken at once at the trial. One beast is nothing, so long as I'm not asleep.

I breathe deeply, trying to shake off the fear in my chest, the pounding in my head from the lack of sleep.

How long was I out? The wild is lit with a predawn glow. Likely four hours at the most.

My pack of supplies is still strapped to my back. I shrug it off my shoulders to grab some breakfast: a small loaf of bread. Holding my meal between my teeth, I return the pack to my shoulders and sling my ax onto my back. I leave the ziken carcass for scavengers to feed on. Ziken meat is bitter, completely inedible for humans. Useless.

I take back to the road, this time at a quicker pace. My body courses with extra energy from the ziken encounter. My head pounds, and everything crowds in at once. I'm too tired to put up a shield against it all.

I feel everything.

The betrayal. The lies. The hurt.

Everything pours into me.

I start running, as if that will somehow let me escape it.

I THOUGHT I LOVED TORRIN. I thought for the first time in my life, someone wouldn't hate me for what I couldn't control. I don't ask for the praise I'm given—*was* given. I didn't get a big head or flaunt my talents. I didn't ask for any of it. But my fellow trainees were still angry enough to get me banished. To send me to my *death*. Their malice ran so deep they had Torrin spend weeks pretending to be someone else. Pretending to like me.

I should have known. Mother told a *lie*; she put her eternal soul in jeopardy to see me gone. If my own mother could hate me so much, how could I ever have deluded myself into thinking that a boy could care for me?

My legs ache, but I run faster, trying to outdistance the tears.

They come anyway, my first in years. I don't fight them like I usually would; why would I when there is no one to see them?

Father would make the biggest complaint. I can hear his voice perfectly. *Warriors don't cry.*

He could have helped me. Could have saved me, but he didn't. Instead, he gave me the most difficult mattugr ever conceived. He, too, sent me to die.

How can a person hurt so much? The ache throbs up and down my body, soaking me in it. Pushing deeper and deeper.

A lone ziken rushes across my path. My hand flies to my back before I realize it's not coming at me. It crosses the road and takes off through the opposite copse of trees.

I turn sharply to follow it, anger suddenly fueling my weary limbs.

Because—despite how everything played out—

I could have done it.

I would have beaten my trial had no one sabotaged it.

I can prove it. I'll kill every ziken out in the wild if I have to. Maybe I'll throw a head into the village boundaries every day until I die to prove it.

The ziken leaps over a fallen log, tramples over a small fern, churns up rocks in its haste.

Where is it going?

It zips between two trees and finally comes to a stop.

There must be at least a dozen of the beasts in the small clearing. They're focused on some heap on the ground. I can't get a good look at it because the ziken crowd it, all trying to sink their teeth into it, but it's large.

My hand grips the cool metal just beneath my ax blades as I pull it from my back.

A horizontal swing takes off the head of the nearest ziken. It lands on the rocks below, but none of the other creatures take any notice. They're too excited by the meat before them.

So I wreak havoc.

I put the faces of those whom I despise most across them. This one's Torrin. That one's Havard. Father, Mother, the council. Mother again. And again. And again. Her face is everywhere. That satisfied smirk, showing the pleasure she feels knowing she will never have to look upon my face again.

My chest heaves from the want of air. More of it. Faster. My thoughts are spinning.

Now that I've dispatched over half their numbers, a few of the ziken finally look up from the body before them. Oh goddess, I think it's human. I'm certain it's dead, but the muscles still twitch from all the fresh venom trapped within.

My foot steps on something that is distinctly not a rock, and I risk a glance down. It's another battle-ax.

With my free hand, I lift the weapon from the ground. It feels heavier in my less dominant hand, but still right. An ax always feels good within my grasp.

Two ziken leap at me, red blood dripping from their maws. I bring both axes down, embedding the blades into their skulls. I pull the right ax out and use it to decapitate the other beast. Then I bring both axes down on the other one's head.

More ziken follow. I spin and twist, duck, thrust. My boots make a squeaking noise as they skim across a blood-soaked stone.

I cross my arms and launch outward with my double axes, severing two heads simultaneously with the movement.

That's all of them.

I drop the metal from my hands, the weight of the axes suddenly too much to bear. Sinking to my knees, I take in the flailing body before me.

It's a boy.

He looks my age, maybe a little older.

He lies on his stomach, the back of his shirt ripped open to expose skin covered in bites. Blood drips steadily down his sides to the ground. Were he still alive, he would be in unbearable pain, especially with the way his body contracts where all those wounds are. Ziken venom truly is a nightmare.

His hair is a deep brown with lighter streaks glinting in the sunlight as his head twitches. His eyes are closed, and the cheek I can see is covered in scratches, likely from flailing against the rocks beneath him.

His eyelids slam open, and I leap backward with an "Ah!"

I try to reassure myself it's just the venom controlling the body, when he lets out a groan.

Blue eyes flick to me, and that's when I finally move.

I vault to the ground, place the stranger's head on my lap so it can't sustain any further damage, and wait with him for the venom to cease its course.

His arms flail uncontrollably. A fist flies at my thigh, but I don't move. It's not his fault.

I don't know what I'm doing. A group of boys is what landed me out in the wild in the first place. They can't be trusted. I blame Irrenia for my urge to help him. It's what she would do. I can only imagine her disappointment in me if I left him to die in the wild when I could have helped.

It must be at least another five minutes before his muscles calm. I brush a spot of dirt near his eye away.

"Are you all right?" I ask.

A pause. "No."

Obviously. Stupid question.

"Hold on," I say. As gently as I can, I lower his head to the ground. In the next moment, I dig into my pack for Irrenia's salve. When the canister is in my hand, I say, "I'm going to rub this on your back."

I pop off the lid and dip my fingers into the brown liquid.

"What is it? It reeks," he says.

"It should help."

"Should?"

"I haven't actually used it before."

He thinks a moment. "Do it."

I start with the biggest of the bites, one near the center of his back, where a good chunk of flesh is missing.

As soon as my fingers touch the wound, he lets out a growl.

"Sorry!" But I don't let up. I rub the ointment in faster. How much does it need? The stranger tries to throw me off, but I hold him down with my knees against his lower back, where the bites are fewer, and begin to rub more of Irrenia's gift into the next wound.

Only a few seconds pass before he relaxes underneath me. I watch in wonder as his skin begins to reknit together, even re-form in places. It pains me to see that half the ointment is already gone, but I can't bring myself to stop helping someone in need. It's what Irrenia would do.

"What is your name?" he asks.

"You first," I say as I continue rubbing the foul-smelling cure into his skin.

"Soren."

"I'm Rasmira."

"Thank you for saving me."

"You should be thanking my sister. She's the one who made this miraculous ointment."

He lets out a labored breath as my fingers brush against another wound. "But she's not the one who fought off a dozen beasts that tried to devour me."

I raise a brow.

"I saw most of your fight before I passed out," Soren explains. "You're incredible with an ax."

The praise makes me uncomfortable, so instead of thanking him, I say, "You must be terrible with one."

A short laugh escapes his lips. "Not usually, but when it's one against twelve . . ."

"What are you even doing out here?"

"I live out here. The wild has been my home for a year."

"A year!" I exclaim. So that means . . . "You were exiled after last year's trial."

For some reason, he grins at me. "And you must be this year's failure."

I wince and withdraw my hand now that Soren's back is mostly healed. I place my focus on returning the lid to the canister. Three-fourths of the salve is now gone. I didn't regret helping him until his last comment, however.

"Sorry," he says quickly. "Too soon. I'm an idiot."

"Almost a dead idiot." I rise and wipe my hands off on my pants.

Soren tries to get his hands underneath himself to push onto his feet. He rises maybe an inch before falling back down.

"Do you think you could help me stand?" he asks.

"Roll onto your back."

He grimaces.

"Your skin has healed over," I say.

"What? How? I thought you gave me something to numb the pain."

I tell him about Irrenia's experiments with ziken blood. When I finish, he dares to roll onto his back.

"She sounds amazing," he says.

I swallow a lump in my throat. "She is." I hold down my hand to him, and he takes it. Once on his feet, I let go, but he sways to one side. I throw Soren's arm over my shoulder to ground him.

"Side effect of your magical cream?" he asks.

"I don't think so. You lost some blood. It's made you light-headed, and you're likely exhausted from your ordeal."

"And you're not?"

Truth be told, I feel ready to sleep for a hundred years, but having someone else to take care of is giving me the strength to go on. I answer with a shrug.

"This way," Soren says. "I have shelter."

We walk side by side. I hadn't realized when he was on the ground, but he's barely an inch taller than I am. Something tells me it's never been a problem, however. Any other girl would think him handsome with his bright blue eyes, strong jaw, and long black lashes. But not me. I will never think of a boy that way ever again.

"So, Rasmira," he says. "Do you have a boy waiting for you back home?"

I drop him.

All the air leaves him as he crashes to the ground. I hadn't meant to let go of him, but the question was so startling, so *painful*, and Torrin's face worked its way to the front of my mind.

"Ow," Soren moans.

I reach down to help him back up, shaking brown eyes from my thoughts. "Sorry. That was an accident."

He clings to me with more strength this time, as though he doesn't trust me to hold on to him. "What, did you trip?"

"Something like that." It's such a bland response to get around telling a lie. He probably sees right through, and I expect him to call me out on it.

"You didn't answer my question," Soren says instead.

This time, my tone turns harsh. "No, I didn't."

He may be injured, but at least he's not stupid. Soren takes that for the dismissal it is, and only points if I start going in the wrong direction.

"Should have kept better track of the days," he says as we veer around a large boulder a few minutes later.

"Why's that?"

"The Payment can't have been long ago if you're here. Peruxolo would have traveled through with a cart heaped with meat. The ziken are following his trail. That must be why there are so many out and about. I shouldn't have come anywhere near here."

And I've been following the same trail. No wonder one of them found me early this morning.

"A whole year," I say, thinking of Soren's earlier comment. "So it's possible to survive in the wild. How have you not gone mad being out on your own for so long?"

"I haven't been alone. We've arrived."

We duck some thick branches and stop in front of—

Another tree.

Only this one has a house built into its branches. It's small, perhaps the size of my bedroom back home, and it's made out of—

"Is that wood?"

Soren's eyelids flutter. Must be taking him some effort to keep them open. "Our best discovery out in the wild. There are trees out here that stay strong long after they're cut."

His eyes close, and suddenly he's all deadweight.

My back slams against the base of the large tree supporting Soren's home. I try to lower him as gently as I can the rest of the way to the ground.

He plops against the rocks, and his eyes suddenly shoot back open.

"Are you all right?" I ask.

"So . . . tired," he says.

I take in the tree. The branches near the base look sturdy, and they're spaced evenly apart to make for easy handholds. But there's no way I'm getting Soren up there on my own.

"Hello?" I venture, raising my voice. Soren said he didn't live alone. "Anybody up there?"

Silence.

"Soren's in bad shape, so if you're up there, I could use some help."

There's a loud thump in response, like someone dropped something. In the next second, a piece of the flooring raises—a door.

A head sticks out, takes in Soren on the ground and me standing next to him. It's another boy. He immediately starts climbing down the tree. He looks the same age as Soren. His hair is much lighter, a brown so bright it is almost blond. He's also taller than his friend, with leaner muscles. An ax rises over his right shoulder. Another warrior.

Once he hits the ground, brown eyes lighter than mine size me up from head to toe. When he finishes his assessment—presumably coming to the conclusion I'm not an immediate threat—he leans down to check on Soren.

"What happened?" he asks.

"Ziken horde," I explain.

The new boy lifts up the tattered remains of Soren's shirt. Looking for bites, I realize.

"Not injured, Iric," Soren groans out. "She . . . healed me."

The boy, who must be Iric, gives me yet another once-over. I can't imagine what exactly he must think, but his eyes land on my ax. "Can you help me get him up there?" He jerks his head toward the tree house.

"I think so."

"I'll be right back."

Iric scurries up the tree. In another moment, he drops down a rope with a loop around the end. "Can you put that under his shoulders?"

Understanding what he intends, I manage to get the rope over Soren's head and under his arms.

"What's going on?" Soren asks.

"This might hurt a bit, but we're going to get you up where it's safe," I answer.

I hoist myself onto the nearest branch. I loved climbing trees when I was little, and it would seem my body hasn't forgotten the motions. I get myself up through the hatch in the floor and briefly take in the shared living space.

Two small feather-stuffed mattresses, a fireplace, a wooden table and chair, and a pile of what I suspect is dirty clothing by the smell of it.

I get behind Iric and grab a section of the rope. A pulley dangles from the ceiling. They must hoist things through the hatch regularly. Likely firewood to cook their meals in the fireplace. I hope the pulley is strong enough to manage a body.

"On three," Iric says.

The two of us start heaving. Even with the pulley, we have to strain our muscles to get Soren up and over the trapdoor. Iric unhooks him from the pulley and drags him over to one of the mattresses.

"How many ziken got ahold of him?" Iric asks as he stares down at Soren.

"A dozen," I answer. "I found him twitching on the ground. Thought he was already dead."

"You killed a dozen of them?" he asks, a note of suspicion in his tone.

"It was easier because they were distracted by the raw flesh." I nod at Soren.

"He doesn't have any bite marks, but he's covered in dried blood."

Though I'm loathe to have another person know about Irrenia's miracle cure, I explain about the salve. I hope these boys wouldn't steal from me after I helped them.

"You have my deepest thanks . . ." Iric leaves the ending open for my name.

"Rasmira," I offer.

Though I'm in no way fishing for compliments, I'm surprised he doesn't send one up to the goddess for me. It is the polite thing to do. But then another thought hits me. These two boys have lived in the wild for a year. This house is so permanent. Have they even *tried* to complete their mattugrs? Maybe they don't believe in the goddess. These two aren't from my village. They're both warriors, so I would have met them if they were. Do not all villages know of the goddess?

The distinct sound of a slap pulls me from my thoughts. I look down to see Iric standing over Soren, the latter boy's left cheek now red. "Wake up!"

Soren's whole body jolts. His eyes shoot open.

"What the hell were you doing?" Iric asks.

"I was . . . hunting," Soren manages.

"You nearly got yourself killed. You nearly left me *alone*, you arrogant ass!"

"I'm . . . sorry."

"Not yet you're not. But you will be once you're healthy enough to receive the beating that's coming your way."

Soren smiles. Smiles! And then his eyes drift closed once more.

"Is he safe if I leave him with you?" I ask.

"He's fine," Iric grits out. "Did he hit his head at all?"

"Not that I saw."

"Good." He takes a deep breath and lets it out. "We don't have a lot of space, but you're welcome to find a free spot on the floor to sleep on. You look ready to drop."

Nothing could wake me up more.

"Thank you, but I need to be on my way."

"Are you going somewhere? You're not in exile like we are?"

"I was banished and given my mattugr. I intend to complete it."

Iric smiles, and I'm not entirely convinced it's a kind one. "You're going to complete your mattugr, are you?"

"Complete it and go home or die trying. Either way, I will be with the goddess in the next life."

His lips press together, as though to keep from laughing.

"What?" I snap.

"You just saved Soren. I shouldn't."

"Say it anyway."

"All right. Rasmira, was it? There's no delicate way to put this, so let me be up front. You're never returning home. No one completes their mattugr. They're *designed* to be unbeatable. We are the ones no one wants, the ones everyone is ashamed of. The sooner you accept that, the better off you will be. You will never see your family or friends ever again.

"And your so-called goddess? What kind of gracious deity demands that her subjects die horribly in order to be received into her Paradise? Dying horribly is stupid. I suggest you make yourself a shelter, get yourself into a routine, and accept that this is your new life.

"Welcome to the wild."

CHAPTER
6

Bastard.

I'm glad to be free of that stuffy tree house full of idiot males.

Somehow I manage to find the road again. I walk down it for several minutes before crossing to the other side and plunging into the foliage. Everything Iric told me was false and ignorant, but he was right about one thing. I need shelter. It's foolish to travel any longer without having a place to rest safely. I'm running on embers. It won't be long before they snuff out and my body demands the sleep it so desperately needs. I'll be as helpless as Soren in a moment.

I'm not entirely sure what I'm looking for until I find it.

I enter a small clearing. A gap in the foliage allows sunlight to shine down, which must support the short grasses breaking through the rocky soil. The same type of tree that I saw supporting the boys' house stands at one edge of the clearing. I recognize it by the leaves, each one bigger than the size of my head. They're green along the edges but a deep purple in the center.

Soren said there were trees that didn't crumble after they were cut. This must be one of them if it's supporting a whole house off the ground. I let my pack fall from my shoulders, take my ax in my hands, and start chopping. The branches toward the bottom of the purple-leafed tree are thick and strong, each the width of one of my legs. I cut several from the trunk, trim them to size, and nick the smaller branches from off their sides.

I roll the logs over to the other side of my new space. Another tree, this one with an enormous, smooth brown-black trunk, stretches high into the sky. I prop the branches I cut against it, wedging them between the rocks on the ground, shaping the wood as necessary to get a good fit. When my little fort is long enough for me to stretch out comfortably within, I roll out my bedroll, throw my pack at the top to use as a pillow, and go in search of something to serve as a door.

It's not long before the perfect solution presents itself, for if there's anything to be found in the wild in abundance, it's wood.

A strip of bark, intact, strong, and wide, rests near a fallen log, having long since peeled from its trunk.

I lift it from the ground—it's heavier than I thought—and haul it over to my little fort. I squeeze myself inside, rest the bark against the opening, and fall onto my bedroll.

I'm out in seconds.

MY TIRED EYES CRACK OPEN. I'm not sure how long I slept, but by the crick in my neck and the desperate need to *go*, I suspect it was a very long time.

I'm surprised to still be alive. I thought for sure something would find me when I was asleep and vulnerable, that my attempt at a shelter would be useless against the wild.

But Soren was correct. The wood remains strong. My fort held.

After taking care of my morning needs, I place the bark back over the opening of my fort, hoist my pack over my shoulders, slide my ax through the strap on my back, and head for the stream I hear bubbling nearby.

I still have Soren's blood caked to my skin. I do my best to wash up in the freezing water with a bar of soap I brought from home. By the time I get the last of it out from under my fingernails, my hands are trembling from the cold. I refill my canteen and immediately start rubbing my fingers together for warmth as I find the road again.

Today I will look for the god. I put Iric's cynical words out of my mind and replace them with my sister's.

You will try, won't you? Promise me.

I promised. I will try.

I step carefully along the road, listening for cackles from the ziken, which are especially active during the day. I watch the ground for snaketraps. I avoid the agger vines that dangle over the road. One brush of the stinging leaves, and my skin will break out in itching hives. We have a few of the plants inside Seravin's boundaries.

An hour goes by, and all I can think about is how careful I must be. Today's mission is to find the god. No more. I must observe him, see if there's a weakness I can exploit.

I feel childish for even thinking it. He's an immortal god who has wiped out whole villages when they displeased him. If he had a weakness, someone smarter, stronger, or more skilled than I would have learned it by now.

The road continues toward the mountain. Another hour passes, and everything becomes so overgrown and just . . . wild. I don't think anyone besides Peruxolo has ever traveled this way before.

I can't see anything through the brambles and thick trees on either side of the road, if it can even still be called that. Tall weeds grow in the space between where the wheels would have rolled, though they're now bent. Even the lines where the wheels have trod are sporting smaller, now-crushed plants.

I wonder just how far away I am from Seravin. Maybe a two-and-a-half-day walk? I spent one whole day walking away from Seravin, then another running before I stumbled across Soren.

No one travels farther than half an hour into the wild. No one stays in it for more than a few hours.

And here I am. Alive for three days? Four? Still not sure how long I was asleep, but I'm certain I slept longer than one night.

And now I'm traveling alone on a road never trodden by a mortal.

I can't help but be afraid.

I've been walking for at least a quarter of the day, but finally the mountain's base comes into view. The plant life clears for about a hundred yards leading up to the mountain, replaced by rock-covered ground.

The road basically ends. The ground around the mountain is too broken up to be used as a road, despite the cleared greenery.

Which is probably why I find the wagons discarded here.

What's left of them, anyway.

Piles of broken wood line the base of the mountain. Seven piles, to be exact. I spot immediately which wagon carried all the precious stones, because the crumbled bits of wood still bear the weight of gems, as if the wagon just collapsed and the stones fell down with it. They're untouched. Unused. Out in the open where anything could claim them.

A man died because Peruxolo decided that pile of gems wasn't large enough, and he's left them here as if they were a trash heap.

But then, I guess he doesn't demand tribute from us every year because he needs anything from mortals. It's about keeping villagers scared and under his rule. Keeping us weak. Making us suffer.

My fear turns to anger, which I welcome, since it will be much more useful in ending the god.

Rather than stay out in the open, I cross back to where the line of trees and undergrowth will keep me hidden. I use the cover as I follow that line of wagons and then continue around the base of the mountain. It's possible the god went up, rather than around. But he's on foot. And the food, water, and everything else that was held in those wagons, save the gems, is missing. Granted, Peruxolo doesn't have to touch things to move them. So perhaps he floated them and himself up to the mountain's peak.

Either way, I'm not about to start the climb until I've thoroughly explored the bottom. I don't need anything sneaking up on me.

My efforts are rewarded ten minutes later.

I find an opening.

Right into the mountain. A seam large enough for three men to enter side by side. But of course I can't see into it. It's much too dark.

So I find a sturdy tree. I climb it, find a good spot to sit, and I wait. I watch. I listen.

Sometimes I convince myself I hear talking, but then it disappears like a rough wind. Sometimes I think I see flickers from firelight play along the walls of that opening, but those, too, are probably imagined. There's nothing prominent enough for me to truly believe I'm seeing signs of life.

Until a figure steps outside.

It's the same tall frame. The same black cloak and large ax strapped across the back.

It's him.

It's the god Peruxolo.

And his face is uncovered.

Even with the distance from my hiding spot up in the tree to the seam in the mountain, I can see the sharp angles of his face. He does have the face of a man, with hair the color of dark sunlight, held back in a band at the base of his neck. Thick eyebrows give him, well, a godly look. Thin lips are pulled into a straight line as he walks toward the tree line.

Toward me.

My muscles freeze as I try to think of what to do.

I can run, hope he doesn't catch me, hope he doesn't know I'm here. Or I can hold very still and hope he doesn't hear me breathing, hope he can't sense a mortal's heartbeat nearby.

But then, why would he head straight for me if he doesn't know I'm here?

I spend far too much time deliberating, and the choice is made for me.

I hold my breath when the god is directly below me.

Only then do I notice the well-trodden trail through the plants. Oh, he comes this way often. A beat of hope passes through me.

But the god pauses. Right. Underneath. Me.

My limbs start to tremble. My breath escapes my lips, despite my best efforts to hold it in. But amidst the fear, through the horror of being near the most terrible being known to my people, a thought creeps in. I imagine a course of action I could take right now.

If I could silently slide my ax from my back—if I could perch myself in just the right position on this branch—if I could angle my fall just right—and hold my ax just so—

Maybe I could strike the god?

Peruxolo turns in a slow circle, watching the surrounding wild with narrowed eyes.

My heart is in my throat. I try to swallow it back down. But the sound is so very loud.

Peruxolo doesn't look up.

And bless the goddess, he keeps walking.

When he's finally out of sight, my breath comes out in a whoosh.

I can't make rash decisions. I promised Irrenia I would try to come back home. Launching myself at Peruxolo without a plan is no way to achieve that goal.

And *I don't deserve to die*. Surely the goddess knows. Surely she knows the trial wasn't my fault.

Either way, I will do this the right way. Slowly, deliberately. When I have a plan, I will face the god.

When I'm certain he's long gone, I climb down from the tree. I walk on my toes as I head back for the road at a snail's pace, but I don't dare make a sound.

When I finally do reach the road, I run.

CHAPTER

7

I tire long before I make it back to my little fort, my pace slowed to a crawl.

I'm brought up short when I find someone inspecting where I slept last night.

Soren.

"Very impressive," he says, indicating my fort.

"How did you find me?" I didn't exactly go a great distance from their tree house, but the wild is thick and good for hiding things.

"Took me all day. I figured you couldn't have gone far with how exhausted you must have been. Got lucky with this place."

"What are you doing here?" I ask, somewhat irritated. Why did he seek me out? I'll have to move now. Find a new spot to build another fort to remain hidden.

"I brought you something." He nods toward a bucket I hadn't noticed before. I peer inside to find bright yellow berries piled to the rim.

"What are they?"

"We call them 'yellow berries.'"

"How original."

"They're very sweet. Iric and I lived off these until we were able to trap meat. Try one." He pulls a berry from the top and offers it to me.

I narrow my eyes at it. It's so bright. Surely it's poisonous if these are only found in the wild.

Soren shrugs and pops the berry into his mouth, chews, and swallows. When he doesn't start retching, I dare to try one for myself. I don't put the whole thing in my mouth, but rather take a small bite. It sends juice dribbling down my chin.

But the fruit is tasty. Sweet, with just enough of a kick to it to make it exciting. I put the rest of the berry in my mouth before wiping my chin off on the back of my hand.

"It's a small way to show my gratitude for what you've done for me, but I assumed since you're new to the wild, you won't know which plants are edible yet."

I grab a handful of berries and walk with them over to the tree opposite the clearing, the one whose branches I chopped to make my fort.

"How did you know these wouldn't kill you when you first tried them?" I ask.

"Well, I didn't," he says.

I peer over my shoulder. "You didn't," I repeat, confused.

"Iric was so hungry. We'd run out of food the previous day, and

I didn't know what else to do. I tried many things that day. In small quantities. I recommend avoiding the indigo-colored berries and the dark purple fruit. I won't scar your ears by telling you what happened when I tried those."

Apparently, putting himself in harm's way is something Soren excels at. "And I suppose you volunteered to taste everything in your path while Iric merely watched?" I ask.

Soren just shrugs.

Odd I decide is the best word. This boy is very odd.

"Thank you for the berries," I tell him.

"You are brave and wondrous with an ax," Soren says. "May the goddess grant you rest in her Paradise in the next life."

I force myself not to react to the words. I'd thought the two boys didn't believe in the goddess, but it would appear I was wrong. At least where Soren is concerned.

I nod, both a dismissal and my own show of gratitude.

Then I turn back to the tree in front of me. Grabbing a long and pointed rock from the ground, I press it to the bark firmly and scrape a line at an angle.

"What are you doing?"

I jump slightly. Soren's voice is close, and I hadn't heard him come up behind me. I assumed he would have taken my hint and left.

I face him, not bothering to hide my irritation this time. "Look, I appreciate the food. It was a kind gesture, but I have work to do. And it's really none of your business what I do with my time."

Soren looks perplexed. "You . . . want to be left alone?"

"Yes."

He's taken aback. "It's safer out here if we stick together. The only reason Iric and I have survived this long is because we have each other. Our shelter is plenty big for three people. The ziken can't climb. We're safe from them. Your fort is truly impressive, but if any beast discovers you're sleeping inside, it won't take much for them to break through. Especially the gunda."

I roll my eyes but don't bother telling him the gunda isn't real. It's not worth the energy. Instead I demand, "Why are you concerning yourself with my safety?" I don't like at all the way he's showing so much interest in what I do.

"Because I'm gallant and chivalrous."

I stare at him.

"Why are you looking at me like that?"

"Are you *flirting* with me?"

He grins. "I just think it should be pointed out that you're a fierce warrior woman and I'm a fierce warrior man, so we should spend some time together."

I cock my head to the side. "I found you broken and bleeding on the ground."

"I was ... having an off day. Give it time, you'll see what I'm really like."

"I have no interest in seeing *any* more of you." I wave a hand up and down his profile with the words, which I hope makes all meanings of the phrase perfectly clear.

Soren stands there for a moment, as though he doesn't know what to do next.

"The road is that way." I point in the direction I intend for him to go.

I turn back to the tree.

"All right. You want to be left alone. I understand."

I let out a sigh of relief.

"But there's a problem," Soren says. "You see, you saved my life. Now it belongs to you. I owe you a life debt. From now until I draw my last breath, I am your man."

I blink.

Damn.

I know of the warrior code of honor, of course. But it didn't occur to me that by saving this fool, I'd be shackling him to me.

Should have left him to die.

You don't mean that. Irrenia's voice cuts into my head, chastising.

Okay, I suppose I don't mean that, but I can't have this boy following me around all the time.

"I release you from your debt," I say. "Think nothing of it."

"You can't do that. That's not how it works."

I groan. "Please go."

He looks from me to the tree and back again. His lips purse. "Tell me what you're doing and I'll go."

I fix him with what I hope is a death glare, but he doesn't budge. If anything, he looks more determined than ever to stay.

Rock still in hand, I return to the tree, etching once more. "I'm mapping out Peruxolo's domain."

Silence from behind me. After finishing the mountain, I draw the thick wild off to the right, leaving a gap in the trees where I saw the trail.

I turn to the side of the tree and carve out a list.

FACE OF A MAN

BLOND HAIR

CARRIES AN AX

"You went to the god's lair?" Soren finally sputters out.

"I did." This boy is like an irksome fly that just won't leave me alone.

"Why?"

"You said if I told you what I was doing you would leave. Are you going to dishonor yourself by lying?"

"No, I'll take my leave," he says hurriedly. "Stay safe, Rasmira."

I listen to his footsteps as he retreats. I'm surprised Iric let Soren out of his sight after what happened last time. If it were my friend—

I stop that line of thought, because I realize I've never had a real friend, only a pretend one who sought to get me killed.

AFTER MUCH DEBATING, I decide not to pick up my fort and move camp. It's too much work, and I'm certain I could take Soren if it came down to it. Though for now, I'm convinced he's harmless. Annoying as hell, sure, but harmless. Besides, it would be terribly foolish of him to be out and about at night.

As I lie in my little fort that evening, sleep has a harder time coming. I'm not quite so exhausted, and blasted Soren has thoughts of the gunda going through my head.

Damn him.

Damn him and his cursed life debt. I don't know how he thinks he can possibly do for me as I have done for him. He's a banished warrior. He must not be very skilled with an ax if he was exiled.

But you were banished, a little voice reminds me.

That was different.

Not necessarily. You shouldn't be so quick to judge until you know his story.

I don't *want* to know his story. Just the thought of being near him again makes me uncomfortable. No more boys in my life. Never again.

I roll over and pull my blanket over my head.

THE NEXT MORNING, I'm quick and efficient. Lace up my boots. Place the bark strip back over the opening in my fort. Eat breakfast (which includes Soren's berries, but I determinedly don't think about where they came from). Haul on my pack. Grab my ax.

And then I'm on my way to the god once more.

I don't know if an immortal can be killed, but I do know that if I'm to learn more about this being, I need to get inside the mountain where he lives.

Though unbidden, I think of the last Payment I witnessed. Of the village leader who was killed without more than a flick of the god's wrist. If Peruxolo can kill that easily, what will he do to the person who attempts to take his life?

That's not important, I try to assure myself as I take up a steady pace down the road. My eternal soul is what is important. I don't know if it's truly in jeopardy, but I'm not about to take any chances.

To occupy myself on the journey, I utter kind words about my sisters aloud for the goddess to record in her Book of Merits. I stretch my arms, roll my neck, try to think of what I'll do if the god doesn't leave his lair and give me an opportunity to search it.

It's much too soon before I'm back in the woods across from the mountain. I climb the same tree I did yesterday, a tall number with yellow-brown bark and smooth branches, and I wait.

And I wait.

And I wait.

My limbs ache hours later, when I'm still holding so very still, staring at the dark seam in the mountain.

Then a blond head of hair finally steps out.

Peruxolo.

Just like yesterday, he walks right over to the tree line and starts following the well-worn trail through the undergrowth. This time, however, he doesn't stop when he's right below me. He passes by without pause.

Another day I will follow this trail and see where it leads, but for now, I want to see inside the mountain.

I shimmy down from the tree. Slowly at first, I step toward the seam. When nothing bad happens, I pick up my pace, no more than a quick walk.

But then I jog because the god is away, and I don't know how much time I have. And I can't believe I'm doing this. I can't believe these are the steps I must take to return home.

A jolt runs through me, and in the next instant, I'm falling backward. I don't catch myself in time, my backside connecting with the uneven ground.

What the devil?

I rise, look around me. There's nothing in sight. I look down. I felt as though I'd been struck. But all over. Like I ran into a wall.

The opening in the mountain is still a good ten feet in front of me.

I try approaching it again.

But after two steps, I'm brought to a crushing halt once more.

I raise my hands, hesitantly reach out in front of me with my fingers. I can't feel anything tangible against my skin, and yet, I can't move forward any more. It's as if my wrists are tied to the end of a rope that is pulled taut. They can't cross the invisible barrier.

The god has powerful defenses at work. Defenses that remain even when he is not present.

I back up just a couple of steps, select a rock from the ground, and hurl it toward the opening.

But unlike me, it meets no resistance. It sails right through the opening and lands with a soft *clack*.

Is it just me, then, that cannot enter?

I slide my ax from my back and hold it up to where that barrier lies. But it's like pressing it up against a solid wall. It won't break through the air.

My next thought is that perhaps no weapon can enter the god's lair. Maybe that is why I cannot enter. I drop my ax on the ground behind me and try to press against the barrier with my hands once more.

No such luck.

I return my ax to my back before carefully examining the mountain. Small grasses and trees grow along it. Otherwise, there is nothing but rock and ore—exactly what one would expect on a mountain. Inside the gap, now that I'm so much closer than I was before, I can see firewood stacked along the dark edges of the interior. Large animal skins line the floor, offering a soft carpet to walk on.

Luxury is exactly what I'd expect to see in the home of a god.

"What are you doing?"

I freeze in place.

I've heard that voice before. That deep rumble that makes the hair on the back of my neck rise.

I turn.

Peruxolo has returned, his hood now covering his head. He is some distance from me, perhaps fifteen feet or so, and I thank the goddess for that distance. If he were any closer, I might lose my footing for the fear coursing through my veins.

"I asked you a question," he says. "You'd better answer before I lose my patience."

My mouth has grown dry, but I somehow force my lips to open. "I came to see you."

"That was foolish."

This could be the end of my life right here. One flick of his wrist, and I'm dead. I cannot remain standing here as this scared girl. I need to be more. I need to think quickly. I need to be brave and wise.

Be a warrior.

"The way I see it," I begin, "my days are numbered as it is. The wild is no friend to mortals, and I figured my chances were better with you."

That sends his hood cocking to one side. "You came all the way here on your own? Which village are you from?"

I cannot give up the name of my village. What if he decides to take out my foolishness on all of Seravin? On my sisters?

"I have no village. Not anymore," I say. "They cast me out after I failed my trial."

"You were banished." He laughs, short and deep. "You over-estimated yourself greatly. You thought you could join the warriors,

99

be the only female among their ranks. Yes, I can see it now." He tips his head back, and I can spot closed eyelids, as though he's watching my fate pool behind his eyes.

"But you're alive. Alive for five whole days on your own, and now you seek me out. Why?" he asks.

"The ziken grow hungry. I know I cannot evade them forever. You could provide me with safety."

"I could," he drawls. "The question remains, what is it you could provide me with?"

The way he says it makes me feel dirty, and I take a step back, right up against that barrier.

Silence stretches between us, and I manage to turn myself so I have open air behind me, not that invisible barrier and the seam in the mountain.

At last, he lets out a lazy sigh. "No ideas? I've none, either. There's nothing you could do to serve me. I want nothing from you. Your journey was wasted."

I swallow, dare a step backward. "Are you going to kill me?"

"Only if you return here. Now go!" The last word comes out so loudly, I jump a good foot in the air. Then I'm backtracking, keeping my eyes on the god.

Movement comes out of the corner of my eye, and Peruxolo and I both turn our heads.

Rocks cascade down from the mountain, rolling, tumbling, hurtling toward the ground. I watch for a moment, confused by the scene, until I realize this is the perfect distraction I need.

I take quick steps backward, watching the god, watching the danger in front of me.

After a time, he turns away from the rockslide. The rocks

reach the ground, perhaps a hundred yards away from his home—no damage done there. Of course not. Perhaps he concentrated so carefully on the slide to use his power to control it.

And I wasted some of that time by watching it, too.

But now his attention is back on me.

"Is that as fast as your mortal legs will go?" he questions cruelly.

Peruxolo runs for me. He gains momentum quickly, while I stumble over my own feet trying to retreat. Just before I turn around, to put all my efforts into sprinting away from him, I watch him thrust his arms out in my direction. And that invisible force that I felt earlier—the god's power—

It strikes me, forcing me off my feet, flinging me backward onto the hard ground. I breathe out once, deeply.

Then I'm scrambling—running—fleeing for my life.

When at last I find the road, I dare a glance back over my shoulder.

Peruxolo sweeps his cape behind him before disappearing into the mountain.

CHAPTER

8

After a time, I think my lungs will burst if I do not stop running. I collapse onto the ground, my body quivering with exertion and fear.

I manage to skid off to the side a ways, burying myself into the thickness of the wild, out of the obvious sight of the road. Just in case Peruxolo followed.

Not that it matters. If he wanted me dead, I'd be dead.

I don't know how long I sit there, catching my breath, imagining all the ways I could have died, but it doesn't feel terribly long before I hear something.

Steps in the wild. Approaching from the god's direction.

I have the ax off my back in an instant.

I crouch behind a tree close to the road, watching, waiting.

When a figure comes into view, I pause, trying to make sense of it.

As it comes closer, I ready my ax, preparing to strike. And at just the right moment, I thrust the shaft toward the road, causing Soren to trip right over it.

He'd been running, and the fall sends him flying, crashing and skidding across the broken-up ground.

He curses as he stands, wiping rocks and mud and dried leaves from his scratched-up palms, his skinned knees.

I'm fuming.

"Did you *follow* me?"

"Did you trip me?"

What. The. Hell.

I hold my hands in front of me. They're shaking. I can't decide if I want to wrap them around Soren's neck or cover my face with them.

I almost died. And Soren is here. Why is he here?

I growl. "What's the matter with you? I told you to stay away from me! You promised you would! What are you doing here?" I'm a pot of water that's just set to boiling, and I'll burn anything that gets too close.

Soren, realizing this, takes a step away from me, brushing carefully at his bleeding palms. "I promised no such thing. I said I'd leave your camp, and I did. What are *you* doing here? Are you trying to get yourself killed?"

Of course I wasn't, but I say, "That is the purpose of our mattugrs, is it not?"

That brings him up short. "Your mattugr . . ."

"I've been sent to kill Peruxolo."

There it is. I said the words out loud. Now I realize just how hopeless they are.

"Which is, once again, none of your business," I add.

"Your life is my only business now. Do I need to remind you? I owe you a life debt."

"And just how do you think you're—" I cut off as I realize something. "The rockslide. That was you?"

"I tried to divert the god's attention so you could flee. Thank the goddess, he didn't think to climb the mountain and see what caused the slide."

"They're probably a regular occurrence near the mountain," I say, thinking aloud. "I doubt he thought anything of it."

"That's good for us."

"There is no us!" I shout. "I neither need nor want your help."

He doesn't want to help me. Getting close to me only serves his own ends, whatever they are. I know this. I know that people are only capable of thinking about themselves. I don't have any desire to find out what it is Soren wants. I don't care.

I will not make myself vulnerable like that ever again.

"It's not up to you," Soren says. "The goddess wills it. I will not disobey her laws. Will you?"

"You—"

A sound fills my ears. Something loud, like a rock falling to the ground. It comes again. And again. And again.

"What is that?" I whisper.

At first, I think I see one of the trees moving. *Moving.* But then I realize it's no tree. Its skin is the same color as the deep brown bark of the innas, a perfect camouflage. It's so very tall and large, over four heads taller than Soren and me. Four black eyes stare down at us, unblinking. They dilate simultaneously once they take in the two of us. I realize now that the loud, crashing sound is each of its steps across the ground, but I can't make sense at all of what I'm looking at.

But Soren must make something of it, because he says, "Run."

I TAKE OFF AFTER him down the road, Soren barely one leg stride ahead of me. And whatever that thing is, it races after us, bounding on two legs.

"What the hell is that?" I shout.

"The gunda," Soren says.

"The gunda isn't real."

Soren flings an arm behind him in the direction of the creature, an emphatic gesture.

Yes, I see his point.

I dare a glance back over my shoulder. Despite its large girth, the beast is *fast*, those legs taking longer, quicker strides than our own. What I had mistaken as the texture of bark, I now realize are actually tendons connecting to powerful muscles. The gunda doesn't have any arms, just toned legs to carry it. The beast doesn't have a neck, either. The main body thins toward the top, where all four eyes rest in a row. A tail snakes out behind it, balancing the gunda as it runs.

It doesn't make a sound, no cackles like the ziken, and somehow, that silence is even more terrifying. Where is its mouth?

"It's gaining on us!" I shout.

"We can't outrun it. Watch your feet," Soren says. Then he turns quickly, heading right into the thickness of wild.

Now I'm leaping over rocks and brambles and thick tree roots, running into low-hanging boughs and ferns. Snaketraps snap closed as we pass by them, our momentum enough to stimulate the plants' natural response, even though we haven't stepped into the leafy, teeth-clad mouths.

The gunda plunges in after us, but it has a harder time with its body. It can't fit into places we can, and it must take a less direct path in order to continue following us.

"Can it climb?" I ask.

"No, but that won't stop it from reaching us."

I rack my brain for all the stories I've heard about the gunda, trying to fathom how a beast with no mouth could be dangerous. But in the stories told to me as a child, the sheer size and many eyes of the beast were enough to frighten me. It was a creature said to consume men whole. Hunters and warriors would disappear, never to be seen again. But no one from my village has seen the creature in a hundred years. It's become only a myth.

And now it's chasing me.

The muscles in my legs are screaming at me to stop. I've already exhausted them once today by fleeing the god. My arms don't want to pump any longer. I'm not in good condition for the fight ahead.

Soren is spent, too. He slows considerably and barely catches himself when he falters on a loose rock.

"We need to stop," I say to him.

"We stop and we die," he says.

"Then where are we going? Do you have a plan?"

He doesn't answer as he suddenly puts on a burst of speed. Somewhere, I find the strength to match it.

We break through the foliage. The rough rocks turn into smooth pebbles, which angle downward into a small lake.

On the opposite side of the lake, a rise—a small cliff—extends over black water. It's a good ten-foot drop into fathomless water housing goddess-knows-what horrors.

"It—can't—swim," Soren says around heavy breaths. I want to ask him how he knows this, if he'll stake his life on this information—

But the gunda breaks onto the shore with us. So close. Too close.

"Axes out. Now!" Soren stops running and turns to face the threat, but his gaze isn't focused on those eyes up top. No, his attention is directed much lower. Toward the base, where the rough skin has started to *move*.

Tendons strain and muscles flex as a flap of skin rises directly at the front of the gunda, until it is parallel with the ground, just below all those eyes. Something falls to the ground from the interior—a tangle of white and red—

At first, I can't make sense of what lies beneath. Some sort of fleshy pink skin, coiled like a snake and held tight against its side.

But then that pink skin lashes forward, like a frog's tongue, and I realize that's exactly what it is, a tongue, ready to strike and catch its prey.

Soren dodges that forked tongue, rolling off to the side. When the tongue meets the ground instead, rocks stick to it, and they're drawn back into the gunda's body. That flap of skin lowers back down, trapping it all in place.

And that's when true horror washes over me. There were no teeth around that tongue, no mouth or throat. Just wet, sticky skin. If that thing catches me, it'll enclose me in darkness, hold me tight to its body, and slowly I will decompose, absorbed through the gunda's skin. I'll likely die from the lack of air first, but the thought of being unable to move, encased in wet, sticky darkness—it has me backtracking, nearly tripping over my own feet.

My eyes lower to the white-and-red heap on the ground in front of the beast, and I realize now what it is.

A carcass—the remains of its last meal.

The gunda quickly realizes it's captured nothing edible. The rocks and dirt clods tumble to the ground as that flap of skin rises once more.

I send a prayer up to the goddess. And when that tongue flings outward again, toward me this time, I throw myself out of the way.

Pain burrows into my side and clears my head as I strike the rough ground.

I've been cast out and rejected by my village. I've been sleeping on the ground in the wild. I have a ridiculous boy following me everywhere I go.

But I am a warrior!

I am Rasmira Bendrauggo, and I'm going to kill this beast.

I've made this decision, when someone else comes bounding through the trees.

Iric.

He already has his ax in hand.

"No," Soren whispers from beside me, and I take a moment to wonder why he would protest more help, before Iric speaks.

"What have you gotten yourself into?" Iric demands, and I'm certain he's talking to Soren. "Ziken wasn't your preferred method of dying? You'd prefer the gunda?"

"What are you doing here, Iric?" Soren shouts back.

"I couldn't focus on anything when I knew you'd gone after the girl again. You're lucky I spotted you cutting into the wild with the gunda on your heels."

"Get out of here!" Soren demands.

"Don't tell me what to do!"

After the gunda drops its newest mouthful of dirt clods, it turns in Iric's direction.

Soren reaches between his feet to grab a sizable rock and hurls it at the gunda. It strikes the creature solidly in the back, but it doesn't budge. Doesn't turn to see what disturbed it, provided it felt the impact at all.

So Soren charges it, ax held high. He only gets a couple of steps before I join him.

Opposite us, Iric dodges a tongue lash and attempts to bring his ax down on the thick muscle, but the pink flesh returns to its resting place much too quickly. The skin flap starts to lower as Soren and I make contact.

It's like striking rock. Only, rock crumbles eventually. But this, the skin of the gunda, it doesn't even dent.

I rear back my ax, taking a heavier swing, but all it does is send pain ricocheting up my arms. The skin is impenetrable.

We need to carry on with Soren's plan: drowning it.

"We need to get it up that ridge," I say. "To push it into the water."

"We need to get it away from Iric," Soren says. He darts around the beast, trying to get it to focus on him instead of his friend. I'm all for saving friends and family, but Soren's single-minded determination is a bit extreme.

The two of us are exhausted. But Iric? He must be fresher than we are, especially if he only walked the distance from the tree house to the lake.

"Iric!" I shout. "Run up the ridge over the water! Get it to follow you. We need to drown it."

Iric takes off running, heeding my command, and the gunda follows. Soren tries to hurry after the pair, but he's so spent. We scramble after the two figures curving around the lake.

The lake that's now rippling, I note. Deep green skin skims the top of the water. Nothing distinct for me to make out the shape, just enough for me to know that whatever lives in the water is enormous.

I hope it likes to eat gunda and not people.

Soren and I are practically crawling by the time we get to the base of the ridge overhanging the water. Iric is dodging the gunda's strikes as best he can. The gunda's tongue lands at the edges of the cliff, pulling rocks up and sending more tumbling into the water. I can imagine whatever lives in there circling in place, just waiting for something living to fall into the lake.

"Iric, get away from the edge!" I say as I force my legs up the incline.

"No problem!" Iric says sarcastically.

He runs in as much of an arc around the beast as he can, but the ridge isn't wider than fifteen feet. He just barely gets around the gunda before that tongue strikes, curling around Iric's foot.

Iric loses his ax, his fingers clawing against the ground as the tongue starts to drag him backward, slower than its previous retractions, due to Iric's weight.

I leap forward, ax raised high above my head, but Soren gets there first. He brings his own weapon down across that tongue, severing the tip from the rest of it. It frees Iric, who hurriedly pulls the wet flesh from his ankle.

"I'm going to be sick," Iric says. Then he unloads his stomach's contents onto the ground. Soren reaches Iric's side a second later, and Iric manages to kick the severed tongue over the cliff.

Meanwhile, the gunda is wriggling. It has no voice with which to scream, but it's clearly in pain. Flap open wide, tongue swishing aimlessly on the ground, blood trailing after the severed end.

I rush straight at it.

"What is she doing?" Iric asks, but I don't spare either boy a glance. I put my focus on the gunda. On that open flap and exposed skin. That soft skin.

Let's see if that's impervious.

I let the spike come free of my ax and ram it into the gunda at a full sprint. Flesh gives way, spike and ax points embedding deeply, and brown blood spurts right into my face. Blinking rapidly, I pull my ax free and swing again, this time from the side, letting one of the ax blades sink in even deeper.

That does it.

The gunda is swaying side to side on its two legs, ambling around like a bird with its head cut off. I leap over the flopping tongue.

The gunda backs up toward the cliff edge.

I ram it again with the point of my ax, pushing it the rest of the way.

The body falls first, the impossibly long tongue sliding after it along the ground.

A yell.

I turn.

Soren and Iric must have been coming to help me, because they're both much closer than I realized.

And the gunda's wriggling tongue end had found another target while it was sinking.

Iric's waist.

At a speed much too fast for me to do anything, he's dragged right past me and over the edge, joining the gunda in the depths of the lake.

CHAPTER

9

Soren and I both dash to the cliff's edge, watching the water settle into place. Whatever creature resides in the water dives down, its dark shadow fully receding below the surface after Iric and the gunda.

Soren shucks off his armor, and I realize that we've no hope of swimming while weighed down so heavily.

"He can't swim," Soren says.

"What?" I say incredulously, pulling off my second boot.

Soren doesn't answer; he drops the last of his armor to the ground and dives in after his friend.

When I finally get the rest of the metal off my body, I join him.

I can't manage a graceful dive like Soren did, so I leap feetfirst, taking a large gulp of air. A cool wind rushes past me before cold water engulfs me. It's not unbearable—we're in the summer months, and after a few seconds, my body adjusts.

The water is murky. I think it might be clearer if there weren't a disturbance on the bottom of the lake, churning up mud and plants. It's impossible to see much, but I swim down, because I know the solid body of the gunda would have sunk.

I see dark shapes mostly. The large solid figure that looks like a log must be the gunda, and something much bigger swims around it, as though waiting to pounce. I see a flash of white. Teeth.

That has me kicking backward until, there—

Two figures that look like they're wrestling in the water.

I swim for them, arcing my body down, fighting against the air in my lungs that tries to drag me up toward the surface. Bubbles float out of my mouth as I try to make myself less buoyant.

But after a few more feet, something changes, and I have no trouble reaching the lake's bottom. The weight of all the water above me is enough to keep me from floating back up, I realize.

I reach the boys. The tongue, I see, has already been discarded. Soren tries to pry the armor from the folds in Iric's clothing.

I swim toward Iric's legs to unbuckle his boots and slide out the armor covering his shins, while Soren works at the metal around Iric's forearms. It's difficult forcing metal to move across wet leather. My throat already burns. Though I know how to swim, I don't spend much time underwater. I've not practiced holding my breath for long periods of time.

And Iric, who's never even learned to swim—I can only imagine how he must be faring.

A force of water rushes past me, sending me spinning in a

full circle before I can right myself. A shot of ice runs down my spine as I realize it's from whatever lives in the water swimming past me. Just how big is it?

Soren reorients himself and swims back for Iric. I join him, despite my lungs begging me to go up for air.

We finally get everything undone. The two of us working together, Soren and I kick Iric to the surface. I'm breathing deeply, appreciating the feel of air in my lungs more than I ever have before.

Iric is coughing, clawing at Soren and me, panicking. He's trying to climb atop the two of us, and he pushes me under the water more than once.

Finally, Soren slaps him, which seems to calm Iric some.

We're so very close to shore when I feel something rough brush against my leg. I kick at it, using it to push me forward to a section of lake where I can actually touch the bottom.

I turn around, and that's when I see it.

The monster in the lake.

Toward the surface, where the water is much clearer, I see its profile. It's long and slender with bumpy, dark green skin. A long snout the length of my arm sports an army of teeth overlapping its lips. It dives down, maw gaping wide, presumably to take another bite out of the gunda.

I lose my footing, scramble on hands and knees to reach dry ground. As Iric finally finds his own feet, he races ahead of the two of us before collapsing far away from the water's edge. He falls onto his back, staring up at the sky, reassuring himself he's not trapped below water.

Soren bends in half to rest his hands on his knees. He lets out a warrior's victory cry. Now that the danger is past, the thrill of defeating the gunda burns through me, too, and I throw my fist in the air and let my voice call out toward the heavens.

But then we both notice Iric. His breaths come fast, too fast, and I think he might be having some sort of fit.

Soren drops down to Iric's side and awkwardly pats his shoulder. "It's all right. You're safe."

"Did you see it?" Iric asks between quick breaths. "The hyggja?"

Soren sits back, resting his arms atop his knees. "Only its shadow."

"The monster in the lake?" I ask. "I saw it." A shudder goes through me.

Both boys turn toward me.

"Yes, the monster in the lake," Iric says. "The beast I have to kill if I'm to return home. If I ever want to see Aros again."

His mattugr. He fears the water. He can't swim, and his village sent him to kill the water beast—the hyggja.

He's still breathing too rapidly. Iric seems trapped in his own mind, replaying horrors. His eyes flit across the sky wildly.

"Who's Aros?" I ask, hoping to distract him.

Iric turns. Blinks. "The man I love." His eyes stare to the right of me, as if he can't quite focus.

"When I have bad days," I say, "I think of my sister, whom I love more than anything. Think of Aros now. Focus on him, and if it helps, you can tell me about him."

I don't think he'll do it. He's shaking badly, and his breaths aren't slowing. But he grits his teeth, forces himself to take a deep breath.

"He's short," Iric says after a minute. "Shorter than even Soren. Dark hair. Strong hands. He's a hunter."

He gulps down more air. "He's funny. Loves to laugh and be outside. He never could stand to be cooped up indoors for too long. I really got to know him when I was . . . fifteen, I think. I was upset because Soren didn't—couldn't—return my feelings."

Iric's fitful body calms considerably as he talks, and Soren looks at me, relief for Iric's improving condition written across his features.

"I'd climbed one of the big trees inside Restin's boundaries," Iric continues. That must be the village they're from. The one tasked with providing precious stones for Peruxolo. "I wanted to be up high where no one could find me. Where I could be alone with my thoughts. And he was already up there. Aros. So we talked. We got to know each other, and by the time we were seventeen—" He breaks off, closing his eyes.

"You became more than friends?" I prompt.

"I realized I hadn't actually loved Soren. I admired him. He was my best friend. Our love for each other is the love between brothers. But Aros, I loved. Aros, I wanted to spend forever with."

He looks down at the ground. "But I can't. Because I'm trapped out here. Because I listened to him." He points an accusatory finger at Soren.

Soren seems to pull into himself. "I'm so sorry, Iric," he whispers.

This is an interesting revelation. I hadn't realized these two had such a complicated history. I'd thought them best friends.

"It's done," Iric says. "This is our life now. We live out here. We'll die out here. And that's the end of it."

"Wait," I say. "All you have to do is kill the hyggja? And then you can go home?"

"*All*? Yes, Rasmira. That's all. Simple thing, really."

I let out a short laugh.

Iric turns toward Soren. "What's wrong with her?"

"Do you know what I have to do?" I ask. I go on before he can answer, because he obviously doesn't know and will only have another snarky comment for me, I'm sure. "I have to kill Peruxolo. The god. The immortal who probably isn't even capable of being killed. But you? Your beast *can* be killed. Are you telling me that the whole time you've both been in the wild, neither of you has even *tried* to accomplish your mattugrs?"

Iric crosses his arms, angry now. I feel a little guilty for incensing him so close to a near-death experience, but not guilty enough to take back the words.

"I told you before," Iric says, "dying horribly is stupid. I don't believe in your goddess, and I will not get eaten by the hyggja because our village demands it."

"And you?" I ask, turning to Soren. I know he believes in the goddess. He's mentioned her before.

"I can't die. I have to protect Iric."

"What, do you owe him a life debt, too? Are you incapable of saving yourself?"

Soren glares at me. Good. I want him angry with me. Maybe he'll finally leave me alone.

"I do not owe Iric a life debt," he says, "but I am the reason he was banished to the wild in the first place, so I will keep him alive and help him survive. I won't risk my life by attempting my mattugr, and I'm not about to go home without him even if I did complete it."

I shake my head at both of them. These stupid, stupid boys. "Fine. You're both lazy cowards. Stay out here and die for all I care."

I wring out my shirt as best I can and head for the cliff to retrieve my ax and armor.

"Are you going to try to kill the god again?" Soren asks.

"Obviously," I say, not bothering to turn around.

Silence for a moment, and I can imagine perfectly what must be going through his head. He owes me a life debt and wants to help me, but he doesn't want to risk himself because he feels that he owes Iric.

Finally, he says, "I will help you."

I stop and spin around. "Do your own damn task! I don't need help from any boys!"

Iric's face curls down into a frown. I think he's decided that he doesn't like me, despite the fact that I saved Soren's life. "Hurry and put your armor back on," he snaps. "You're showing everything."

Then he turns on his heel and darts away, his last words no doubt meant to embarrass me.

I look down at my shirt. It's sticking to me like a second skin, and the chill—it's not helping to hide anything.

Soren glances over, as though his eyes are reacting to Iric's words before his mind has a chance to catch up to them. He looks away quickly and blushes.

Actually blushes.

"What are you, twelve?" I ask, crossing my arms over my chest. I scurry up the hill, gather my things, and return to my boy-free fort.

THOUGH I HAVE NOTHING to cook, I build myself a fire first thing upon arriving at my camp. As the flames heat my chilled skin, I remove my sopping clothes and hang them on a nearby branch to dry. I don one of the spare pairs of clothing from my pack and stare at the flames in front of me.

Dying horribly is stupid.

No, Iric. Losing all honor and doing nothing to get it back is stupid. An eternity of damnation is stupid.

Tomorrow, it's back to observing the god for me.

THREE DAYS LATER, I stand in front of the map I've carved into my tree. I use the rock to shape a hole at the end of the trail the god travels regularly, the one that wends below the tree I usually use as a hiding place when observing him. I was surprised by what I found at the trail's end.

A latrine.

It was unremarkable and disgusting, but now I know the god must eat and drink as a man does.

Once done with the drawing, I turn to the side and add to my list.

FACE OF A MAN

BLOND HAIR

CARRIES AN AX

CAN USE HIS POWER TO LIFT ME OFF THE GROUND

USES A LATRINE

On the other side, I have other details written down.

PERUXOLO'S DOMAIN:
I CANNOT ENTER
MY AX CANNOT ENTER
ROCKS CAN ENTER
STICKS CAN ENTER

I let the rock drop from my hand and clatter to the ground. I've learned a little, but I don't know what to try next. How are rocks and sticks going to help me?

"How's the god hunting coming along?"

I spin, my hand going for my ax, but of course, it is only Soren. "Could you wear a bell or something?"

"I think what you meant to say was 'It's nice to see you again, Soren.'"

"I cannot tell a lie."

"Someone's in a good mood this morning."

This time, I actually *do* reach for my ax.

"Now, before you get angry," he says, "you should know that I brought you dinner."

That's when the smell hits me. Juicy valder meat. Soren holds a skinned, roasted beast on a spit. He offers it to me.

I eye the meat, my mouth watering. I haven't had hot food since I was still in the village. Despite my irritation, I take the meat and bite into it. It's tender, and I chew slowly, savoring the taste.

"Thank you," I say once I swallow.

"I've seen you with your pack of supplies. You must be running out of food."

He's not wrong.

"So I brought you this," he continues, shrugging a large metal contraption off one of his shoulders. It's circular with metal spikes around the edges. A dried brown substance crusts the tips. Blood.

"What is it?" I ask.

"A trap for catching valder. Iric designed it. He's the most talented metalsmith I've ever met. Let me show you how it works."

The hunters from Seravin use traps, but they're all made out of rope. Nets that raise into the air when stepped in. I've never seen one made out of iron.

"I thought Iric was a warrior, like you," I say.

"He took the warrior trial, but he trained most of his life with the smithies."

"Why would he do that?"

"It's . . . complicated."

"Make it uncomplicated."

"It's not really my story to tell."

"Then what's your story?" I ask.

I don't know why I bother. Perhaps it's because I've been alone for the last few days with no one to talk to.

"If I tell you my story, will you tell me yours?" he asks.

"No." I don't hesitate before answering.

Soren looks down at his boots and smiles softly. "When Iric failed his trial, I failed on purpose so I could watch over him in the wild."

"That's very noble of you," I say.

"Not really. Not when it was my fault he was banished at all."

And that's the part he won't explain. But something tells me he didn't grab a decapitated ziken head and clamp it onto Iric's arm. How else could you cause someone to fail? If Soren willingly lost to protect his friend, then he couldn't have purposely made Iric fail, could he?

Soren lays the trap down by his feet. Spikes that can only be described as teeth make a circle around a metal lever in the middle. Soren explains how the device works, how pressure on the lever sends the sharp teeth clamping shut like a mouth, trapping whatever steps on it. He and Iric usually place a morsel of food on the trap to attract the valder. He recommends I set it up away from camp so that if something is caught, it won't alert ziken to the whereabouts of my camp.

"It's very clever, but why would Iric give me this?"

"It's his way of saying thanks for helping him out of the lake."

"I'm surprised," I say. "I thought he didn't like me."

"Well," Soren says, his lips pressing together in thought. "You're not his favorite person, but after some convincing, he agreed you should have it."

I let out a short laugh. "Then please do pass along my thanks to Iric."

He stills. Just for the briefest of moments. Then, "Of course."

"And thank you, Soren, for bringing it. It is much appreciated."

He beams. After a moment, he asks, "Would you take a walk with me?"

I'm taken aback. "Why?" Then I realize it doesn't matter. "No."

"It could be fun."

"I doubt it."

"Now that's hurtful."

"You'll recover."

Soren looks down at the toe of his boot, thinking for a moment. Then he says, "Could I show you where the yellow berries grow the thickest so you can pick them on your own?"

I scramble for an excuse not to come.

"If you learn where they are, then I won't have to come back here to deliver more to you," he adds.

He's good. Very good. I can't argue with that logic.

"All right, then. Lead the way."

If he wants to smirk over the victory, he's smart enough to hide it from me.

I don't walk beside him, but rather just behind him, so I can always keep him in my sights.

Soren pretends not to notice. Either that, or it honestly doesn't bother him at all. When he veers around a tree, he holds back the branches for me so I can cross without getting whipped by their needles. He takes me in roundabout ways to avoid obstacles, but I put my foot down when he jumps over a log and then holds out his hand to help me over.

"Do I look like a helpless child?" I ask.

"I was just being polite."

"I'm a warrior. Treat me like one."

"Sorry, I've never met a female warrior before. Didn't realize they preferred to be treated like men."

"That's not—"

I've always wanted to be free to behave like a woman, but Father never allowed it. But Father isn't here now, is he?

I think about what I want. How *I* would like to be treated. I don't want Soren going out of his way to make me more comfortable. That just seems silly. What I always wanted was to be free to wear what I wanted. To act how I wanted. Father would chastise me if I hugged my sisters in front of him, if I cried when I was little, if I whined or complained when I was injured.

But no more.

I am a warrior of the wild, and I can behave however I damn well please.

"I'd prefer it if you treated me as you would another warrior," I say.

"All right, then."

Soren leads me back to the tree house. He stops to open a shed I hadn't noticed before at the tree's base. Inside I see more traps, extra rope, chopped firewood, and buckets. It's one of the latter that he grabs.

Then he takes me along a well-trodden trail, one I'm sure he and Iric have made during their time living out in the wild.

Eventually, Soren comes to a stop in front of . . . brambles. Smooth vines with plump yellow berries grow like weeds. They're everywhere, the plants extending far into this section of the wild.

Soren puts the bucket on the ground and starts picking berries and dropping them inside. I hurry to join him. It seems the best way to say thank you for sharing this location with me.

"What village are you from?" Soren asks.

Since I can't see how it would hurt to tell him, I answer, "Seravin."

"I've heard of your leader. Torlhon is said to be one of the greatest warriors of his generation."

Just hearing his name turns my insides cold. His face is all I can see for a moment. Not the way it looked when praising me. When proud of me. When training with me. But the way it looked as it sentenced me to banishment. When it told me I was tasked with killing a god.

"He is," I manage.

"Did you know him well?"

I swallow. "Yes."

Soren pauses with his hands full of berries about to be deposited into the bucket. He stares at me, waiting for an explanation. But he doesn't ask, just leaves a space for me to fill, should I choose to. Not forceful, just open.

"He's—my father."

That sends his eyebrows shooting upward. He lets his load roll into the bucket, then wipes his hands on his hide-covered thighs.

"I'm sorry," he says.

"Why?"

"Because you are here instead of with your family."

And that word, *family*, has thoughts of Irrenia racing through my mind. My throat suddenly aches, and I feel the annoying presence of extra water in my eyes. I blink forcefully, keeping it at bay.

"What about you?" I ask. "Did you leave behind a family?"

"Iric's family raised me. My father died a warrior's death. He was on watch when the ziken tried to breach the borders. I was three."

"I'm sorry."

"Sickness took my mother the year after. I had no siblings. No living relatives at all. But Iric's parents were unable to have any more children, though they desperately wanted another child, so they took me in."

"I'm sorry," I repeat.

"Don't be. I don't remember either of them."

126

But he's here now, which means Iric's parents lost both of their boys after they took their trial. I wonder if they reacted the same way my father did. With such disappointment and sudden hatred.

"And Iric's parents are the kindest and most giving people I know," Soren says. "They'll have the biggest estate imaginable waiting for them in Rexasena's Paradise."

I suppose not, then. Perhaps it makes it harder, in a way, to leave them if they were loving up to the end.

"Do you have a big family?" Soren asks. "I know nothing of it outside of your father's fame."

The bucket is full now, but Soren and I pick berries and put them directly on our tongues. Neither of us moves to head back down the trail.

So I tell him about my five sisters. They, at least, are not painful to talk about, except for the small ache in me that longs to see them.

"Six daughters!" Soren exclaims. "Your father must have been so proud."

At first, I think Soren is jesting, but after a moment, I realize he's serious. He honestly believes that my father is proud of his large family.

"He would have been proud if we were all sons." I don't mean to say that aloud, but out it comes anyway.

"How can that be? After hearing you talk about your sisters, they all sound wonderful."

"They are, but my father is blinded by his legacy. He thought me his one chance to pass down the role of village leader and warrior. And then I disappointed him by . . ."

Failing is what I was going to say. But I didn't fail. *I was failed.*

"I'm sorry," Soren says. "It sounds like Torlhon is an excellent warrior, but a terrible father."

I'm surprised by the words, but they sit so right in my chest. "Yes, that is exactly the right way to describe him."

I look up toward the sky; the sun is fading fast. "It's time for me to head back. I don't want to be out in the open when it's dark outside."

"Are you sure I can't persuade you to come stay with Iric and me?"

I don't even try to let him down gently. "No."

For some reason, he seems to find my quick answer amusing. "All right. Well, don't forget your bucket." He nods to the one we've filled with berries.

"That's your bucket."

"Then you'd better bring it back after you've eaten its contents."

I can't help the small grin that surfaces. Well played, Soren. Well played.

CHAPTER

10

I have just enough time to set the trap Soren brought me and make it back into my fort before nightfall. I bring the bucket of berries inside with me so they hopefully can't be sniffed out by hungry vermin.

The next morning, when I go to check my trap, I find that the mechanism worked perfectly. A dead valder is crushed between the metal teeth. It probably died on impact.

I also note, however, that Soren's warning about placing the trap away from my camp was justified.

A ziken is already chewing the head off my catch.

"Hey!"

The ziken turns around and licks the blood from its lips. It raises its head and lets out a cackle. I slam a blade of my ax right into its gaping maw, cracking teeth and taking the top half of the head clean off.

Just to be safe, I sever the neck with another swing, then stare at the mess on the ground. I managed to dislodge a canine perfectly. I pick it up from the ground and stare at it. It's the length of my finger but much wider. The tip is sharp, but I don't dare test it by touching it. I'm sure the tooth is still coated in venom. If it were to pierce my skin, I'd be a wriggling, uncontrollable mess.

I pocket the tooth. It's a nice token. Maybe it will bring me good luck.

But my face turns down in disappointment as I stare down at my ruined meat. I open the trap, pull the small beast from it, and cock back my arm to chuck it into a tangle of ferns, but stop.

An idea for a better use of the ruined valder hits me. I tie it to my pack, move and reset the trap, then head to the god's lair for another day of observation.

FROM UP IN MY usual perch, I watch the god's lair. I've already relocated the valder I brought with me. At first, I worried the dead beast wouldn't be able to cross Peruxolo's barrier, but after I cast the throw, it sailed right through without meeting any resistance, landing just inside the dark opening in the mountain.

Peruxolo must not have heard the impact, because he hasn't come to investigate. I hope he's somewhere deep in his lair and well occupied.

What does a god do all day?

Count his gems?

No, wait, he never even took the gems from the Payment inside with him.

Maybe he relishes the pain and suffering he causes by robbing mortals of their necessities? That sounds far more likely.

I wonder if he feeds off our pain. If that is what strengthens his powers, I've no hope of lessening it.

In all my warrior training, patience was not something I excelled at. I tap my fingers along the bark, crack my neck from side to side, attempt to swallow the yawn that surfaces.

Maybe the ziken don't venture out this way? Maybe they've learned to steer clear of the god's lair. I doubt he tolerates any beasts in his wood.

As soon as the thought hits, my patience is rewarded.

A ziken has its nose tipped up, sniffing at the air. It follows the path I took earlier, right up to the god's invisible barrier.

I hold my breath as the beast . . . steps right over it.

When the valder crossed the barrier, I thought perhaps dead flesh wasn't a danger, and so the god had no such restrictions for it. But the ziken, a predator, steps right up to the mountain and even steps *into* the gap to retrieve the meat I've thrown inside.

My surprise is overridden by frustration. What does the barrier protect him against? If a dangerous beast can get through, but I *can't*, then what does that mean?

The only things that haven't managed to cross over are me and my ax.

Does the barrier solely protect against humans and their weapons, then?

I stare down at my body, glance from it to my ax.

Wait a moment.

I let myself down from the tree and stalk toward the barrier. I pause at the tree line when I remember the ziken is still inside. With my new idea pounding within my head, I wait for the beast to finish its meal and run off. I can't very well do battle with it when Peruxolo could overhear at any moment.

When it's safe, I take careful steps toward the god's lair. I watch my feet to ensure I don't overturn rocks or give any hint that I'm here. It's overkill, I'm sure. If he didn't hear the ziken chomping outside his threshold, he won't hear me. But I can't help it. I have no doubt that if he catches me, he will kill me. Mercy is not a concept Peruxolo has been known to show anyone, and he never breaks his word. I remember all too clearly what he promised if I returned to this spot.

When at last I step up to the barrier, I reach out. But this time I press my forearm flat against it and try bending my wrist in half. My fingers go over, but my arm stays firmly in place. I try the same tactic, this time with my torso, bending at the neck.

My head goes through, but not my body.

Not where I'm covered in armor.

In *metal*.

With two fingers, I find the seam on my forearm and slide the metal from the leather. One sheet from the top and one sheet from the bottom. Then I try pressing my arm against the barrier.

It goes through.

But I'm halted at the upper arm, where more armor rests within the seams of my clothing.

A small laugh escapes my lips. I slam a hand over my mouth, but as I look up to check the gap, I realize it's too late.

Peruxolo is already there, watching me. Either he can sense when my metal is near, or the timing was simply not with me.

Ice seems to wash through me, starting at my head and falling to my toes. I drop my forearm guards to the ground and take a slow step back.

"You again," he says. "Do you not remember what I told you would happen if you returned?" He takes slow steps toward me, and for every advance he makes, I mirror it with a retreat.

"I do."

"And you came anyway. Why?"

I cannot lie. The goddess forbids it. I can't risk her anger when I've already failed my trial. My options are to not answer or to answer truthfully. I have no doubt that silence will result in a speedy death. But answering—talking—it might distract him while I think of something.

"I have to kill you," I say.

A breath of a laugh brushes out of that hood. "You've been watching me. And I suppose the first time we met you were—what? Looking for a weakness?"

I hate how he says everything, as if reading the thoughts right from my mind.

"Did you find one?" he asks, and he somehow manages to make the question sound condescending, as if he knows I didn't. Or maybe he knows that he doesn't *have* one. Because he is in fact unbeatable.

"I've only ever killed to survive," I say. "I've killed animals to eat and animals that meant me harm. But I'm making an exception where you're concerned. You're my mattugr. I have to kill you if I want to go home."

At my last statement, Peruxolo throws back his hood.

It's the same face I've seen many times before, when I don't think he knew I was looking. Blond locks, high cheekbones, blue eyes.

"You dare to challenge a god?"

I wonder why he bothered to throw back his hood. Seeing his face only humanizes him, makes it easy for me to confuse him for an ordinary man, gives me courage I didn't know I had.

"I dare," I say.

He spreads his empty hands out wide. "Very well, then. Take your best shot."

I hesitate, not for fear this time, but because he hasn't drawn his ax. Something about striking an unarmed opponent feels wrong.

But then I remember the face of that girl who lay unconscious in the back of the wagon train. I remember how Peruxolo put his fingers on her face, turning her this way and that, inspecting her as one might a piece of jewelry before deciding whether or not to purchase it. I remember the hungry faces of the children in my village. The dead, bleeding village leader who couldn't scrounge up enough gems to satisfy Peruxolo's greed.

Those memories give me the strength to charge. Ax arced over my shoulder, ready to swing, I hurl myself at Peruxolo, sprinting full speed.

He doesn't move, doesn't cringe, doesn't blink as I get close and swing.

My ax connects with air, solid air, before ricocheting backward and throwing my balance off kilter. I barely manage to find my feet, to spin back around and take another swing, as if catching the god off guard might make a difference.

It doesn't.

My ax bounces off nothing. It doesn't even come close to striking the god.

"Pathetic," Peruxolo says. "The mortals sent a little girl to kill me. Though, if I'm your mattugr, they didn't expect you to succeed. They sent you to die. I won't play executioner at your village's behest, but I can hardly let you live after you've come here with the intent to kill your god."

"You're not my god. Rexasena is the true goddess over all the world. You are just some foul being who was granted too much power."

"I'm done with you now," he says, and he flicks his wrist in my direction.

I don't think, I just move. I throw myself off to the side as soon as I see the beginnings of the same motion he used on the village leader he killed with one sweep of his hand.

A *clink* to my right—the sound of his power striking against the rocks beside me in a very near-miss.

"Hold still," he commands, in a tone that still sounds almost bored.

I will do no such thing. I fling myself backward as his hand snaps from side to side unleashing . . . *something* at me. But I'm too quick, too unwilling to submit to his power.

But then my back collides with something behind me, and I dare a glance over my shoulder from my seated position.

The invisible barrier to the god's home. I'm trapped.

"Which village sent you after me?" he asks. "I will unleash my wrath upon them."

I don't answer, looking around for anything that might save me.

"You'll die here, regardless, but surely you'd like revenge on the village that sealed your fate?"

Revenge against the entire village? Because a handful of people betrayed me? I don't think so.

Peruxolo steps closer. "Speak now. I won't ask again."

My right hand curls against a fist-sized rock beside me. I remember the first time I came to find the god's lair, how I flung a rock, and it sailed right into the seam of the mountain when I myself could not enter.

I hurl the rock with as much strength as I have at Peruxolo. I watch as it sails through the air, hitting its mark with an audible *crunch*. Peruxolo raises a hand up to his cheek. When he lowers it, the sun glints off of red.

I made him *bleed*.

He stares dumbstruck at his hand for a few seconds, as though he'd forgotten what it was to bleed.

But then his eyes find me.

I realize now that the reason he lowered his hood is because he never intended to let me leave here alive. Why should he care if I see his face?

His hand darts inside his cloak, to his side. When it resurfaces, a long blade comes with it, the sun shimmering off a bright metal.

A silver dagger.

I barely process this as my gaze is still focused on the droplet of blood sliding down the god's cheek. By the time I realize his dagger somersaults through the air toward me, it is too late.

Then I'm staring at the hilt protruding from my gut.

Wretched agony shoots through me.

Torn flesh. A pulsing, sharp, burning pain spreads from the wound. Blood darkens my shirt.

I lower a hand, my fingers trembling over the handle of the silver blade. It split right through my armor. Left side of my abdomen. Below the heart, but I know there are other important organs within the human body. Irrenia would know what to do if she were here. I don't know if I should pull it out or—

I fall to my knees, my limbs suddenly going weak. Only then do I remember the god is still about ten feet in front of me.

"You have two choices," Peruxolo says as my eyes meet his. "You can pull out that dagger and bleed to death. Or you can wait for the ziken to smell the wound and come to devour you. Either way, you will die a painful death, and the world won't be disgraced by your presence any longer."

He gives me a disgusted scowl before making the walk back to his domain.

I fall onto my back, my breathing ragged. I don't think he punctured a lung. It's just that every time I breathe, the dagger is jostled, and it sends a fiercer wave of pain through me.

I'd rather die from blood loss than see the ziken have at me. But just placing a finger against the dagger's handle is—

A sharp intake of breath.

I can't do this.

The rocks below me dig into my skin, and my back rests uncomfortably on my pack.

My pack.

Irrenia's salve.

The muscles in my abdomen scream as I move my arms. I grunt, lower my arms back to the ground. Try again. This time a scream of pain rips from my throat as I try to unhook a strap from one of my shoulders.

My vision grows spotty. I might pass out if I try again.

And then I might never wake up.

Tears leak from the sides of my eyes.

This. All of this. Because I was deluded enough to think Torrin cared for me. Because my mother saw an opportunity to be rid of me forever.

I. Don't. Deserve. This.

My soul has worth, and I won't let it depart this world just yet.

Quick as I can manage, I shrug a shoulder out of one of the straps.

I gasp. My eyes roll upward.

And I'm out.

ARMS UNDERNEATH ME.

Rising off the ground.

Movement.

MURMURING. YELLING. SCREAMING.

"What happened to her?"

"She went after the god again."

"Did she know you were following her?"

"I don't think so."

"We have to get the dagger out. Where's that magical cure she used on you?"

"In her pack."

"On the count of three, I'm going to pull. You ready? One, two, three!"

My voice leaps out of my throat as fire rips through my middle.

BEFORE I EVEN REALIZE I'm awake, there's pain—throbbing rawness in the upper left corner of my abdomen. All my limbs feel sore. And my back aches from sleeping on it for goddess knows how long.

My eyes are crusty—from dried tears, I realize—and it takes some time to open them, but when I do, I realize I'm in the tree house.

I manage to lift my neck enough to see my bare midriff. No dagger. And my skin looks whole, but underneath I see a purple bruise. I don't dare try to sit up.

A glass window lets sparse light into the room, and I wonder where in the world the boys managed to find a window. It's cracked with a shard missing. They've stuffed a wad of cloth into the opening, but the window does its job, giving me enough light to see by. A small table and two wooden chairs rest below it. Empty boots look hastily cast aside against the wall, which means—

I turn my neck in the other direction.

There are the boys.

They sleep on top of hides hastily sewn together and stuffed with feathers, their torsos and feet bare. Thank the goddess they kept their pants on. They're sharing a blanket, and a pang of guilt spreads through me. I must be sleeping on Soren's mattress and blankets. They're sharing Iric's bedding.

I try to make sense of what happened. But after getting

wounded, everything is hazy. When did they cut half my shirt off? And where's my armor?

I made Peruxolo bleed.

The memory surfaces, and I remember my discovery that his power deals with metal. Despite the pain, a bud of hope blooms within my chest.

If a god can bleed, surely he can die.

As delicately as I can manage, I probe the wound. There's a small lump, and it's sore to the touch. They must have administered Irrenia's salve to me, and while it healed the surface, my injury is deep. There's some bleeding inside.

Will it still kill me?

A deep exhale is followed by the rustling of blankets. Soren rolls over, his eyes already open. They meet mine.

"You pulled through."

"Was there any doubt I would?" I ask.

"You lost a lot of blood when we pulled the dagger out. Took us forever to clean it up."

"Us?" comes a new voice. "You mean me. *I* had to clean it up. You wouldn't leave her side." Iric sits up from the mattress and rubs at the back of his neck.

"How did I get here?" I ask.

"I carried you," Soren says.

"How did you find me?" Another murky memory surfaces. I think I heard the two of them talking. "You followed me. You've *been* following me."

"He hasn't done any of his chores since you saved him from those ziken," Iric says. "He follows you every day until the sun goes down."

My neck snaps in Soren's direction.

"Are you really going to be upset about it when I was able to save you?" he asks.

I roll my neck, preferring to stare at the wall than let Soren see me attempt to compose myself. I want to be angry. I am angry. I told him specifically to leave me alone. But mostly I'm angry that I didn't notice him tailing me.

Instead, I control my initial irritation. "Can you help me stand?" I ask, hating how I have to rely on them for help.

"You're better off resting until your wound fully heals," Soren says.

"And how, pray tell, am I to perform basic bodily functions if I remain resting until my wound fully heals?"

He looks away from me, and I imagine him mentally rebuking himself.

Soren stands, and I get a full view of his muscled torso.

I cannot tell a lie.

He is impressive.

All warriors are well built, but with his sapphire eyes, long jaw-line, and unruly hair, most girls probably wouldn't be able to look away from him.

But me?

I stare at my toes until Soren pulls on his boots and shirt and stands before me. He reaches both hands down to me, and I hold up my own hands to meet him.

His calluses cover my calluses. They're in the exact same places as mine from so much ax-wielding. But I can't help but think of how similar they feel to the only other boy who has ever held my hand.

Soren hauls me up to my feet in one smooth motion. He doesn't let go of me right away, like he wants to make sure I'm steady first, but I yank my hands free.

His eyes widen marginally at my reaction, but he seems to shrug it off in the next instant.

"We'll lower you down the same way we got you and Soren up the tree," Iric offers. He opens the door in the floor and ties a loop at the end of the rope hanging from the pulley already positioned there.

I look from one boy to the next. "Thank you," but I don't really feel the words. I'm too concerned about what is about to happen, how there will be nothing between me and a fifteen-foot drop except two almost strangers.

If they'd wanted to hurt you, they would have done it when you were unconscious, I assure myself. It doesn't make the discomfort go away.

I suppose there's something to be said for pain. As soon as my full weight is pressing into the loop, I forget all about my fears. I can't think of anything except the pulsing bruise below my heart, the rope digging into my thighs.

When my feet blessedly hit the bottom, I untangle myself from the sling. Two more sets of feet hit the ground as both boys join me.

"Do you already have a spot?" I ask, certain they must.

"Down that trail." Iric points. "Can't miss it."

"Will you be able to"—Soren gestures below my navel—"by yourself?"

My face heats up. "I'll manage."

I stride down the trail, and behind me I hear a smack.

"Did you really just offer to help her piss?" Iric whispers loudly enough for me to hear.

"No! I was just making sure she could. Why would you hit me?"

"Because you're behaving like an idiot."

I miss the next exchange because I'm too far. I find the latrine. Any sort of bending is extremely painful, but I manage to relieve myself without getting anything on my clothes.

When I make it back to the house, Iric and Soren are still having a quiet argument. They cease as soon as I'm in view.

"Something wrong?" I ask.

"No," Soren says at the same time Iric says, "Yes."

I wait for an explanation, but neither boy is forthcoming. Soren is watching Iric, and Iric is grimacing at the ground.

"I doubt you're about to start helping with the chores again anytime soon," Iric eventually says to Soren, "so I'd better get to it. You stay here to play manservant."

"That's not necessary," I say. "I'll leave as soon as one of you retrieves my armor and ax."

"All right," Iric says, before pulling himself up the branches leading to the house.

But Soren yanks on his foot and pulls him back down to the ground. Iric barely manages to catch himself on his other foot.

"We talked about this," Soren says to him.

"Fine," Iric says with a sigh. He turns his gaze to me. "We'd like to invite you to stay with us until you heal."

Was that the cause of their argument? Soren wants me to stay but Iric wants me gone? Well, then. I'll make it easy for them. "Thank you, but no."

"Rasmira," Soren says, "if you lie down, you won't be able to get back up again, and you need someone who can monitor your wound. Let us help. Please."

He's asking me to trust them. To willingly put my safety in their hands. I don't like it. I don't like it one bit. But he has a point. I won't make it on my own. Not if I can't get up to feed myself.

Soren has been nothing but kind and even helpful despite everything. Iric, I haven't seen nearly as much, but he seems tolerable. Logically, I know staying with them is the smart thing to do, but I can't change how I feel. The desire to take my chances on my own is almost overwhelming.

But physically, I'm spent.

Even now, standing and moving have taken their toll on me. My abdomen throbs, and I feel light-headed, ready to collapse again.

"Maybe one night," I finally say, trying to sound stronger than I really am.

"Great," Iric says, and his voice doesn't quite match the word. "And I'm off. Since Soren is feeling so extra helpful today, I'll let him get you situated." Iric shoots a glare at his friend before taking off down a trail—one that leads in the opposite direction as the latrine.

Soren rolls his eyes after him.

CHAPTER

11

"The floor is fine," I say once Soren gets me back up the tree.

"Nonsense, take my mattress. Iric and I can share."

"You've saved me as it is. I don't need to steal your bed."

"You'll heal faster this way. Don't you want to be on your way?"

He couldn't have said anything that would cause me to take the bed faster. I manage to lower myself to my knees and then flop onto my back. The impact sends a gasp of pain through my lips.

"You're not one to ask for help," Soren notes.

"You've just now realized this?"

A small smile brushes his lips.

"What was all that about back there?" I ask, jerking my thumb toward the window. I pull a blanket over my naked abdomen. It's not like both boys haven't gotten a good look at my bare midriff, but I feel more comfortable covered.

"All what?"

"The arguing. Iric's strange behavior."

"Iric has opinions."

"Many people do," I say.

"Sometimes he gets caught up in his own problems instead of thinking of others."

"And I'm one of those problems?"

"You're not a problem. It's just that, well, you're a girl."

"Noticed, did you?" A ball of irritation forms in my gut. "And Iric doesn't think a girl should be a warrior, is that it?"

"What? No! That's not it at all."

"You're not explaining very well, then."

"I just don't think you'll like the answer."

"Tell me anyway."

Soren sits on the other mattress and laces his fingers together in his lap. "All right, let me explain it this way. Iric has already mentioned Aros."

"His man back home."

"Yes. He hasn't seen him in a year, but they still exchange letters. Aros leaves him one every time he goes out with the hunting party. I've tried to tell Iric he needs to end it. He's banished, and he'll never see Aros again. Dragging it out like this will only cause him more pain."

"I fail to see how this has anything to do with me." I do feel sorry for Iric, though.

"It's only ever been the two of us out here, but now a girl has joined us in the wild. Iric thinks that because you're the only option for me and I'm the only option for you that we'll end up . . . together. We'll get together, and he'll still be alone."

Huh. That, I didn't expect.

Maybe I would feel some sympathy if I had any faith in real relationships, but I'm certain they don't exist.

I say, "You're assuming I like boys."

This finally brings his eyes back to mine. "Do you?"

I don't know the answer to that. In one way, it's simple: I am attracted to men. That is what Soren is asking. But right now, with my broken heart and trust, I don't see how I could like another boy ever again.

So I say, "I did."

After a beat of silence, I add, "It's a ridiculous notion."

"That's what I tried to tell him. We wouldn't get together because we're the only options for each other. We'd get together because you're a wickedly talented warrior woman who doesn't let anyone get close to her, and I love a challenge."

He laughs at the look I give him. "I'm kidding! Sort of. Okay, mostly not, but would it really be so terrible to give me a chance?"

"Yes."

"Why? What happened to you?"

Ziken cackling. Sharp teeth. A flash of red. Torrin's and Havard's laughter—all of this flashes through my mind in the time it takes me to blink.

"You can tell Iric," I say, "that he has nothing to worry about. Besides, I won't be here long. Just until I'm healed."

Soren watches me for a moment, and I can tell his mind is turning, thinking . . . something. I think he comes to some conclusion, and I really hope it's him accepting the fact that we are not a possibility.

"Won't we at least see more of you now?" he asks.

"Now?" I repeat.

"Now that we're friends."

I scoff at the word.

"Surely we're at least friends now, Rasmira. You saved my life from the ziken. We faced the gunda together. You jumped into the hyggja lake with me to save Iric. Either we're friends, or you're really just the most selfless person in all the seven villages."

I'm a warrior. I've always done what warriors do. We protect others.

And now Soren wants to be friends because of it.

That's how things started with Torrin. First, he was my friend. Then he pretended that we could be something more. But Torrin's end goal was to get me killed.

Soren wants to help. Because he owes me a life debt. A boy who is so honor-bound could not have dark intentions. And if he does, I cannot fathom what they would be. Romantically, I have no interest in him, but . . .

"You saved my life. For that, you may call me your friend," I say at last, even if I'm uncertain I could consider him mine.

"Good," Soren says. "I'd like to have at least one out here."

"But you have Iric."

Soren shakes his head. "We are together for survival's sake. But we are not friends. Not anymore."

I have so many questions for my...friend. But even now my eyes weigh as heavy as stones.

"Get some rest," Soren says, as though I need the encouragement.

WHEN I WAKE AGAIN, it's to the smell of something delicious cooking.

Iric has moved one of the chairs over by the fireplace, and he turns valder meat over on a spit as he stares at the flames.

I don't know why, but I feel compelled to make conversation with him, so I try to think of something to say.

"You've—" My voice comes out as a croak. I cough and try again. "You've built a very nice life for yourself out here. I'm impressed by your home. I didn't think it was possible to survive in the wild."

Iric doesn't turn at the sound of my voice, but he answers, "It became easier once we learned more of the wild's secrets. In the villages, the people are isolated. They only have access to the plants and animals nearby. There is more that grows deeper in the wild. There are trees that remain strong long after they're cut. There are new metals not found in our mines. There are plants that are edible. Beasts that are more dangerous."

"About the plants—Soren mentioned sampling them to learn which were edible."

Iric's head lifts from the flames. "He did, and back then, I was far too angry to care if he lived or died."

"I tried asking Soren what happened at your trial."

"And?"

"He said it wasn't his story to tell."

"Soren," Iric mutters, "ever so loyal. Sometimes he makes being angry with him very difficult."

"Will you tell me what happened?"

Iric chews on the inside of his lip. "How were you banished? You are clearly a competent ax-bearer."

"I asked you first."

"Sometimes you have to give before you can receive."

"Why am I the one who has to give first?"

"Because you're in my house and I'm cooking food for you."

I try to shift my weight to relieve all the pressure on my back. All I manage is to make the pain in my abdomen intensify.

"You are a riveting conversationalist," Iric says when I don't comment.

I try for a leading statement. "Soren can't be the reason you're banished, surely."

"You weren't there. You wouldn't know."

An image rips across my vision. Torrin holding a ziken head, red on its lips, a cruel smile on Torrin's.

Maybe it's because I don't feel threatened by Iric. He doesn't like girls. He doesn't have any sort of agenda with me. He's not trying to befriend me or do anything to help me. He tolerates me because Soren owes me a life debt, and maybe it's because Iric is so upfront in how he feels about everything, but I suddenly don't care if he knows what happened to me. Part of it, anyway.

"Did he take a decapitated ziken head and use it to pierce your skin?" I ask, hardening myself against the memory.

Iric fumbles with the spit for a moment. "No."

"That's what my friend did to me. He only pretended to be my friend so I would trust him. Then he waited until the right moment to betray me. To get me banished."

"Why would anyone do that to you?"

"Because I was supposed to be the next village leader. I was raised on a pedestal, praised and cherished above all others. And he hated me for it, as if I could somehow control it." Or even wanted it in the first place.

It is a relief to get the words out, but it is shortly replaced by vulnerability. When people know your secrets, they can use them to hurt you.

"I don't know you well," Iric says, "but I can already tell you didn't deserve that. You are kind. You are strong. And you're not entirely dull, either."

I laugh, but it turns into a groan as my wound throbs.

Iric holds out the spit in my direction. "It's done."

I manage to reach out an arm with minimal strain on my stomach and bring the meat to my lips. The grease still sizzles. It burns my lips. But I take a bite anyway and hand it back over.

Iric watches the flames while he eats. "You were wronged. I was stupid. That is the difference between our two trials. You see, I wanted to be a smithy my whole life. I learned the trade from my father, who is still the most skilled in all of Restin."

"What changed your mind?"

"Soren."

I should have known that was coming.

"Aros was my world. And the thought of ever losing him—it was the most terrifying thing I could ever imagine happening. We were in our favorite spot, up in the tree where we first met. We often went there for privacy." A pause. "Did you know he is what gave me the idea for building iron traps? He'd tell me about his hunting trips. They venture out into the wild, find a good spot, and wait. They hold absolutely still, hardly daring to breathe, just hoping for a valder to cross their path. Then they have one shot, a single throw of a hatchet. If they miss, the animal moves out of sight before another throw can be attempted. And I thought there had to be a more efficient way to catch them."

Iric can't help but get pulled into the memory. I don't say anything for fear he won't tell me the rest of the story.

He pulls himself back and says, "Aros had great respect for the warriors. While we were up there in that tree, a group of them came into view, passing beneath us. I still remember how he looked at them. Wielding an ax makes them so fit, and Aros was admiring them."

"Surely you don't blame him for looking?" I ask. "And a smithy is just as fit from pounding metal all day."

"I know Aros loved only me. I know he was only looking, but still, it needled at me. I couldn't get it out of my head. For weeks I was in a foul temper. And Soren finally asked me about it."

Suddenly I see where his story is going, and even though I already knew it had an ugly ending, now I'm realizing the scope of it.

"I told him. Soren wasn't at all surprised. He went on about how all the ladies wanted to marry warriors. Why wouldn't Aros?"

"He didn't."

Iric looks at me now. "He did. Looking back on it now, I realize Soren wanted to spend more time with me. We were practically brothers. I spent most of my time in lessons, and any spare time I spent with Aros. But if I became a warrior instead of a smithy, Soren would see much more of me. He used my insecurity with Aros to convince me to switch specializations. He tried to convince me I had a talent for it. I knew it was a lie. I was passable with an ax at best, but I certainly had no special skill for it. But I didn't care. I thought Soren could get me through the trial, and then Aros would never even think of leaving me."

"And you failed your trial?" I ask.

"I was bitten within the first minute."

"And then Soren was overcome by guilt and failed on purpose," I say, remembering what he told me.

"He knew I wouldn't survive in the wild alone, so he bounded headlong into a group of ziken and let them have at him."

"So Soren actually has some skill with an ax?" I ask.

"He was the best in the village."

"That so?"

"The ladies practically hung off him."

"Did he also have someone special?"

"No. He liked all the attention. Didn't want to minimize it to only one girl."

"I see."

"Oh, the wild has changed him. I doubt anyone would recognize him if he ever did make it home. He's not nearly so arrogant or selfish. But I'm afraid he's still attracted to anything female."

The door in the floor opens with a slam, and Iric and I jump. We'd been so engrossed in our conversation, we didn't even hear Soren climbing the tree.

Iric and I are being entirely obvious with our silence and the way we're staring at Soren.

"Were you talking about me?" he asks.

"No," Iric says at the same time I say, "Yes."

Iric doesn't believe in the goddess, so lying doesn't faze him, but I still cringe at the sound of the lie. Obviously, Soren believes me.

"Only good things, I hope?"

"Yes," Iric says at the same time I say, "No."

"Have you been harassing her?" Soren asks Iric.

"She's the harasser!" Iric says. "She keeps pestering me about information from our home and our trial."

"That's what normal people do," Soren says. "They talk. Make conversation."

"We're not normal people. Normal people don't have to try this hard to stay alive." Iric holds the spit out to him.

Soren takes it and blows onto a portion before tearing into it. A week ago, I might have been disgusted by sharing a spit with two boys. But there's a sense of camaraderie, of *togetherness*, that I haven't felt since leaving home. Oh, how I miss Irrenia.

"My sister's salve," I interject suddenly. "Where is it?"

Soren looks down at the spit. "We had to use the last of it on you. Your wound was deep, and the blood pumping out of the injury kept washing the salve out. I had to apply generously."

"Do you still have the canister?" I ask.

"Of course." Soren hands me the spit and fumbles through a pile near Iric's mattress. Eventually he comes away with the empty container.

Having taken a bite, I pass the spit back to Iric before receiving the canister from Soren.

"It might be silly, but—" I start.

"There is nothing silly about wanting something of your sister's out here," Soren interjects.

Iric points to his mattress. "You see that blanket? The gray one covered in holes? It's practically useless for keeping warm, but my mother made it."

I nod, glad they understand, and press the canister against my heart.

"I want to go home," I say.

"It's not so bad out here," Soren says. "The food is good, and the fires are warm."

"The company leaves something to be desired, though," Iric says.

Soren rolls his eyes.

"I will never be content out here," I say. "No matter how comfortable you've made living in the wild. I told my sister I would try to return home. I intend to keep that promise. And I will not risk my soul by dying any other way than by attempting my mattugr."

"Not this again," Iric groans. "Don't be in a hurry to die. Your life is not worth so little."

"I'm not in a hurry to die," I argue. "I'm in a hurry to defeat Peruxolo."

Iric scoffs.

"I made him *bleed*," I say. "And I've learned more about his power. I think I'm getting close to learning how to defeat him."

"You made him bleed?" Soren asks. "I missed that part."

"I threw a rock at him. It struck true."

"Well done," Iric says. "You can stone him to death. And somehow manage to do it before he kills you with his power."

"You're very unhelpful," I snap.

"You nearly died. If Soren hadn't been there, you'd be a pile of picked-clean bones outside the god's home. And you want to get excited over a couple drops of blood?"

"Well, I don't see you making any progress. You haven't even bothered to learn how to swim. That's just sad."

"But I'm alive and well. At least I don't have strangers offering to help me piss in the woods."

"Alive and well. And a coward bound for hell."

"Whoa, now," Soren says, stepping in. "Let's stop with the insults and—"

"Oh, shove off," Iric says. He thrusts the spit into Soren's chest, smearing grease against his shirt. "I'm not hungry anymore. You can stay here with your new beau."

Iric slams the trapdoor on his way out.

Soren sighs. "That wasn't good."

"Is he always so argumentative?" I ask.

"Are *you*?"

"Hey, now. I'm in the right. You know I'm in the right. You know the goddess's will."

Soren hands the spit over to me. "You may know what is best for you, but you have no right to say what is best for someone else. Iric has his own beliefs. Don't try to take those away from him. You would not appreciate someone trying to dissuade you from believing in Rexasena and her teachings."

And with that, Soren follows his friend down the trapdoor.

I scowl at the closed door long after Soren climbs down the tree.

I don't know why I thought Soren would take my side. He's known Iric far longer, and no one ever bothered listening to me inside my village. I shouldn't have thought things would be different outside of it.

I may have been groomed for leadership, but I am clearly terrible at it. I can't make others follow my example. I can't get them to listen to me. I never could garner respect.

And why should Soren and Iric respect me? I may have saved Soren's life, but because of that life debt, he's followed me into danger more than once. I also helped when Iric fell to the bottom of the hyggja's lake, but since then I've done nothing but argue with him and belittle his beliefs. It may not be entirely one-sided; Iric has done plenty of arguing and belittling of his own—but I have entered his home, have upset his way of life. I am the newcomer, and Iric has been kind enough to welcome me, in his own way.

There are only two other people living in the wild, and I've managed to upset both of them.

Well done, Rasmira. Well done.

I need to fix this.

Regardless of his belief in the goddess, Iric wants to return home. He wants to see Aros again. Soren wants to see Iric safe and happy. The way for everyone to achieve what they want is for everyone to complete their mattugrs.

I have learned much of the wild and its dangers, but the thing that has become the clearest is this: Survival is more likely if we stick together.

The two times I faced the god, Soren was there to help. When the gunda came after us, Iric helped us defeat it. When Iric came close to drowning, it was Soren and I who saved him together. We can do impossible things if we work together, I'm sure of it.

And I need their help. I can't go into the god's lair while wearing my armor, yet I can't risk another encounter with the god without protection. Soren said Iric is a talented smithy—perhaps he would have an idea? But I'm not about to ask without offering something in return. I can teach Iric to swim. Hell, I'll jump in the lake with him again to defeat the hyggja, if that's what it takes.

Both boys are angry with me. I need to make things right with them, and then, *somehow*, I need to convince them that we can accomplish our quests. We can go home and make everything right.

It may take time, but I have nothing better to do while I heal.

CHAPTER

12

When the trapdoor opens later that evening, I pretend to be asleep. It's not the right time to broach the topic of our quests. I should let them both sleep off the argument.

I hear boots discarded on the floor, clothing rustling, then two bodies falling onto the other mattress.

"She's a deep sleeper," Soren whispers.

"You really shouldn't take a liking to her," Iric says.

"Why not?"

"She's determined to go after Peruxolo again. She won't be long for this world. I don't want to see you hurt."

Soren lets out a brief exhale of incredulity. "Since when don't you want to see me hurt? You've made it your mission to keep me miserable out here as payment for getting you banished. And I don't think Rasmira is going to get herself killed. She's more determined and skilled with an ax than anyone else I've ever met."

"And now she's out of her magical cream. The next serious injury will kill her or you if you persist in following her around."

Soren doesn't respond.

"Honor is going to get the both of you killed. You two are quite the pair."

"We're not a pair. Not yet."

"Shut up so I can get some sleep."

THE SUN WAKES ME. I've gotten used to my fort in the woods, the trees blocking out most of the light. But the window in the tree house faces east.

The boys are still out cold, so I pull down the blanket covering me to inspect my injury. I think the bruise has gotten lighter and the raised skin is not so pronounced, but perhaps that is only wishful thinking. Either way, at least the wound doesn't look worse. My skin is pale, but it was like that yesterday.

I try sitting up and promptly fall back onto the mattress.

I won't be rising on my own today, that's for sure.

My eyes take in the sights outside the window, as I attempt to entertain myself while waiting for the boys to wake. Fat lizards rest against high-up tree branches. They're hard to spot as their bodies blend into whatever they're standing in front of. I watch them lie in wait for birds to land close enough. Then their tongues dart out, quick as lightning, snatching up their food. Minutes later, they'll spit out a mouthful of wet feathers.

It's both oddly fascinating and disgusting.

They're like miniature versions of the gunda.

I shudder, grateful the world is rid of that hideous beast, at least.

There's a break in Soren's even breaths, and his eyelids flutter before opening all the way. His first move upon waking is to swivel his neck in my direction.

Does he fear I expired in my sleep?

I've never seen someone so worried about my health aside from Irrenia. It's . . . nice.

"Soren," I say, careful not to wake Iric, "what is your mattugr? I never did get a chance to ask you."

He throws an arm over his eyes to block out the light. "Starting with the easy questions this morning, I see." He sits up in bed and stretches his arms over his head. "In Restin, our mattugrs are given to us based on our greatest fears. Iric fears water and never learned to swim, so they demanded he retrieve the hyggja's head and bring it back to the village."

"And you? What do you fear?"

"Have you heard of the beast that lives at the top of the god's mountain?"

"No."

"We have a legend in my village about the otti. A bird with a wingspan the length of five men, a razor-sharp beak, and talons that can slice through the thickest armor."

"You have to kill it?" I ask.

"No, I have to pluck a feather from its skin. But as I said, this is only a legend. The bird could not even exist, which would make it a truly impossible task."

"What does this have to do with what you fear?" Does Soren have a problem with birds?

"When I was a child, I was afraid of heights. It went away as I grew older, but I don't think the village elders knew that."

"If you've overcome your fear, then why haven't you tried to seek out the otti?"

"Because it doesn't matter if it exists. So long as Iric remains in the wild, so will I. I'm not going home or risking my life when he needs me."

Soren isn't the one who will need convincing to complete our quests, then. It's Iric.

"Would you two kindly take your conversation outside?" Iric mumbles against the blankets. "Some of us have work to do today and would like to get some more rest first!"

Soren dons a shirt and boots before helping me up. He even helps me down the tree single-handedly.

I take care of my morning needs as quickly as possible. Unfortunately, it's not any easier to squat in the woods than it was yesterday. Walking, at least, seems more doable. My mind and muscles appear to have finally gotten the rest they so desperately needed.

Once I return back to the tree, Iric has joined Soren at its base. It would seem that I once again have interrupted a conversation, likely about me.

"I thought you were trying to get more sleep," I say.

"I was, but you've woken me up all the way. Falling back asleep is impossible now. You are not on my list of favorite people for today."

"Sorry, Iric," I say. "And I'm sorry about yesterday. Everything I said to you was unfair and rude. You've done me a great service, and

I'm doing a poor job of thanking you for it. What can I do to help this morning with the chores?"

Soren looks to Iric and smiles, as though he just won the argument they were having before I showed up.

Iric straightens. "I'm heading to my forge this morning. You could come with me."

"I'd like that."

"Or," Soren hastily adds, "you could come with me to check the traps for meat."

I look from one boy to the next. Are they really making me choose?

"I'll go with Iric," I say. He's the one I need to warm up to me.

Iric says, "Oh, don't be so obvious, Soren."

I find the second boy with his shoulders slumped, but he quickly rights them at Iric's words and glares at him.

"All right, then," Iric says. "This way, Raz. Mind the traps."

Iric takes me down yet another trail. A group of Iric's metal traps line the front, guarding the tree house from ziken, I realize. I leap over them and grunt from the pain that lances up my middle from the impact.

"Raz?" I ask when we're out of Soren's hearing.

"Your name is a mouthful. I'm shortening it."

"And should I call you *I*?"

"That just sounds stupid."

"And *Raz* doesn't?"

"Well, the name should fit the person."

"Is that supposed to be funny?"

His shoulders shake the smallest bit as I watch his back. He's laughing silently. "I thought it was."

"You don't like me," I observe.

"That's not true. I insult everyone. Don't take it so personally."

"Tell me, Iric, are you letting me tag along because you want me to ooh and aah over your forge or is this some master plan to keep me from Soren and prevent our inevitable romance?" I remember what the boys argued over yesterday. I wonder if today's argument was over the same topic.

"Both. Now be sure to step over this trap here on the trail."

I cease talking long enough to veer around the trap, not letting any metal touch me.

"You needn't worry," I continue. "I have no interest in Soren that way. Romance is the furthest thing from my mind out here."

"The longer you are away from home, the lonelier you will get. Soren's been here a year and now look at him. He's practically throwing himself at your feet."

"He's trying to repay a life debt!"

Iric shrugs. "Sounds like an excuse to be near you, if you ask me."

Oh, what would he know? Iric doesn't concern himself with honor. But I want him to like me, so I'm not about to say that aloud.

"And if, say, I had been a tall and handsome man instead of a plain-looking girl, what would you have done?" I ask.

"I don't need something pretty to look at. I have my letters with Aros."

Yes, good. This is the turn I want the conversation to take.

"How much do you love him?" I ask.

"More than my own life."

"And what would you be willing to risk to get back to him?"

Iric halts suddenly, and I nearly run into his back. He spins around, brows raised. "I know exactly what you're trying to do, Rasmira, and it's not going to work. I already told you, I have no desire to die. If you're trying to save my soul without my realizing it, you underestimate my intelligence."

I throw my hands up in defense. "I have no interest in getting you killed, I swear it."

"Then spit out whatever it is you want to say. Let's get it out in the open right now so we need never talk about this again afterward."

To the point. I like it.

"I want to help you get home," I say. "I want to teach you how to swim. I want to be in the water with you when you kill the hyggja."

Iric blinks but says nothing. Then he turns around and keeps walking.

"You're a brilliant inventor," I say as I follow him. "If anyone can come up with a weapon to kill the hyggja, it's you. The only thing you lack is the ability to swim, and that can be learned! I'm not saying all of this because I want you to die and reach Paradise. I'm saying it because I think it can be done, and I can help you get home to Aros."

"We're here," Iric says. "Mind the circle of traps. Keeps the beasts from running off with my tools."

Iric said he had a forge, but I wasn't picturing something quite so large. He's carved himself a stove out of rock, shaped a chimney out of metal. I spot a bellows made from animal hides and heaping buckets of coal off to the side. He has his own anvil, tools of all shapes and sizes, molds for casting, several good-sized hammers. It's a full smithy, right here in the wild.

It's beyond impressive, but if he thinks it will distract me from our conversation, he's wrong.

"Iric—"

"Why? Why do you care whether I go home or not? Why bring this up at all?"

I try to think of a truthful response that doesn't make me sound selfish, but one isn't forthcoming. "Because I need your help in return. I can't get into the god's lair while wearing my armor. You're a smithy. I thought perhaps you could help me build something that wasn't made out of metal."

"Ah," he says.

"But don't you see? Normally, those who are banished aren't exiled in pairs. You and Soren have had an advantage, and that's why you've survived so long. I'm only alive because of you two. If we all want to go home, we'll need to help each other."

"I don't think our villages would take kindly to us helping each other."

"There's nothing in the rules that forbids it. So long as you're the one to decapitate the hyggja, Soren is the one to pluck the feather from the otti, and I'm the one that ends the god, who cares who else is involved in the planning?"

Iric doesn't look convinced. I add, "I think we can do it. You must know I'm serious. I'm willing to put off killing the god to help you complete your quest. I can't die in any other way than completing my mattugr in order to be greeted into Rexasena's Paradise. I wouldn't take this risk unless I thought we could pull this off. I'm not trying to manipulate you. I want to trade. My help in exchange for your help."

Iric grabs a hammer, examines it as though he suddenly finds it fascinating. "And what about Soren?"

"What about Soren?"

"You would have me complete my quest, help you, and then leave him out here alone?"

I thought they weren't friends anymore. Iric blames Soren for his banishment. He acts as though he hates him some of the time. Is it all an act?

"If Soren wishes to help us, then we can help him in return as well," I say. Provided he can find a way to make himself useful to me and my mattugr, that is.

Iric nods. "I will . . . think on all of this."

He will?

Inside, I'm exploding, but I keep a smile from my face. "All right."

Iric returns the hammer to the table.

"I can't believe you've made all of this," I say, taking in the forge again. "How is it that you trained to be a smithy your whole life, but then the elders let you take the warrior trial?"

"How do you do it in your village?" he asks.

"At the age of eight, we pick a trade. We train for that trade until we're eighteen. Then we take the trial."

"Ah. In Restin, we do not need to declare a trade until fifteen. We're permitted to try all the trades, to train with any we might consider while growing up. We can switch at any time."

"That doesn't seem like it would produce adults talented in anything."

Iric gives me a look like I'm stupid. "Raz, it produces adults with some talent in *everything*. How else would Soren and I have survived if we didn't know how to hunt, how to build, how to make our own clothing?"

"You're right. That was a careless thing to say." After all, I was groomed for leadership for most of my life, and I was always terrible at it. "Where did you get all of these? Surely you couldn't have made all of this in the wild?"

"No. There's a trash heap outside of Restin's borders. Each time I go to retrieve one of Aros's letters, I stop by and look for anything useful."

"Is that where the window in the tree house came from?" It would explain why it was cracked.

"Yes. I've been able to repair most of the damaged tools I found while picking through the waste. I discovered a coal deposit not far from here, which serves as steady fuel for fire. Remember, I've had a year to make all of this. It didn't happen overnight."

"Doesn't matter. I think it's brilliant."

"We'll see how brilliant you find it after I've got you hammering for an hour."

I can't actually help with any of the hammering. Just gripping one of the tools has my stomach protesting. I had never realized how connected everything is to the abdomen. Breathing. Walking. Even holding things.

But I watch Iric work. I learn. Iric heats up metal until it is glowing red. He pounds it into shape. He pulls buckets of water from the nearby stream to the forge to cool the metal quickly.

It's fascinating work to watch.

Honestly, I believe it is a shame that Restin is being deprived of such a talented smithy.

CHAPTER

13

Either Soren doesn't do nearly as much work as Iric does around here, or he's suddenly become much quicker at doing it, because he always seems to finish first and find time to come bother me.

Sorry, *keep me company.*

"Are you hungry?" he asks a few days later.

I look pointedly toward the bucket of berries next to me. "No."

"Are you cold? I can get you another blanket."

The sunshine from the window warms my cheeks, and a small fire in the hearth keeps the tree house a perfect temperature. "No."

"How's the pain? Do you need—"

"Soren!"

He sits up straight. "What?"

"Don't you have work to do?"

"I've already finished. I'm at your disposal."

I consider telling him I'm tired and wish for quiet, but while the second may be true, the first is a lie. So I settle for a brutal truth. "You're hovering. It's driving me mad."

"It is?"

"Yes."

He ponders that a moment. "When I was ill, I loved it when Pamadel fussed over me." That must be Iric's mother.

"She must do it better than you do."

He gives me a wide grin.

I can't even make him go away by insulting him. Apparently, I'm too funny about it.

"All right, then," he says. "What am I doing wrong? How would your mother fuss over you?"

Suddenly my chest feels heavier. My face grows hotter. "She wouldn't. If she could get away with it, she'd lock me in a room without food or water and let nature run its course."

That, at least, shuts him up, but it only lasts about a minute.

"Did she have something to do with your banishment?"

I would have thought Iric would have told him what happened, but it would seem he hasn't shared our conversation. I only told him about Torrin, but if Soren is asking what happened, he doesn't know any of it.

"Yes, she had a hand in my banishment."

There's a hole somewhere under my skin, where Peruxolo's blade opened me up, but thinking of my mother is a far worse pain. And having shared that pain with Soren? A discomfort so rich shoots up and down my body, making me want to squirm from it.

Why did I tell him that? I'm not at my best, injured as I am. I must keep my thoughts to myself. I don't want his pity or his sympathy or whatever else he'll likely say.

Soren bends at the knees until he's crouched in front of me, meeting my eyes. "When you kill Peruxolo, think of the look on her face."

There's something about the sincerity and *fervor* in his eyes that makes my stomach tingle. Something in my mind shifts, and suddenly I'm not in such a hurry to get rid of Soren anymore.

When, he'd said. Not *if*, but *when*. He believes in me. He's still set on helping me.

We stay like that for a moment, each of us intently watching the other. It isn't until the trapdoor opens with a *bang* and Iric climbs through that we look away.

I'M STUCK ON THE floor of that tree house for a week before I can finally rise on my own. In all that time, I don't broach the topic with Iric regarding our mattugrs again. And I let up on Soren and his fussing over me.

Despite being able to sit up and lie down, I know that I can't strain the injury. Running or swinging my ax could open me up again. The bruise on my abdomen has faded to yellow, and the bump has gone away, but the last thing I want is to start bleeding internally again.

So instead of leaving for my fort, I stay with the boys.

"I made you something," Soren says when he arrives home after finishing his chores. He handles something bulky in front of him.

"What is it?" I ask. I hope the question isn't rude. Am I supposed to know what that wad of hides is? Some sort of blanket? It looks far too coarse for that.

"I've sewed some hides together but left an opening right here." He points to one corner of the fabric.

All right . . .

"It's a mattress for you. I've started hunting the birds we'll need in order to stuff it with down—only edible ones, of course, so nothing goes wasted. Whether you stay with us or move back to your shelter, I thought you'd want something of your own to sleep on."

I can't speak for a moment, I'm so touched by the gesture. "Soren—thank you."

"It's nothing," he says, a broad grin stretching his cheeks.

"You're very kind. May the goddess take note of it."

"And may your back never ache again," he jokes awkwardly.

WHEN I'M BETTER ABLE to move around, I fall into more of a routine with the boys. I spend my mornings checking the traps for food, helping Iric in the forge, picking berries from the bushes, or chopping wood. In the afternoon, Soren and I run through stances with our axes, while Iric cooks dinner. In the evenings, we all talk. We laugh. We get to know each other better.

Without even realizing it, I've somehow come to think of both boys as my friends.

One morning, I'm helping Iric out in the forge. I hold a long sheet of metal steady while Iric pounds at it. He's making me new guards for my forearm, since I lost those two sheets when experimenting with Peruxolo's barrier.

I shake out my right foot. I'm not yet used to the silver dagger I keep in my boot. Soren helped me make a sheath for the weapon Peruxolo tried to kill me with, and now the blade rests against my lower calf and ankle. Someday, I hope I will get to return the weapon to Peruxolo.

Preferably by putting it through his eye.

Suddenly, Iric halts his pounding and turns to me, startling me out of the thought.

"When you teach me to swim, will you make fun of me during our lessons?"

The question comes out of nowhere. It's something he's clearly been thinking about for some time.

At last my patience is rewarded.

"Likely," I answer honestly.

A slow blink. Deep sigh. Another pound with his hammer. "Fine."

"Fine?"

"I want to learn how to swim. Will you teach me, Raz?"

I try desperately not to show how deep my elation runs. "Of course. We'll start tomorrow."

He nods. "And I will start thinking about how to make you armor that isn't made of metal."

"Thank you. You will also want to come up with a way for us to be on more equal footing when facing the hyggja. We can't kill it with our axes. We will need something else."

"I've been thinking about that. I already have some ideas, but it's all moot if I can't swim. I won't be able to force myself near that lake if I can't feel more comfortable around the water."

"Do not worry. You will learn how to swim. It is not difficult. Your body floats on its own. You just need to learn how to hold it."

Iric doesn't look entirely convinced, but he's committed. Tomorrow, we start swim lessons.

AFTER BREAKFAST THE NEXT DAY, Iric and I head out together.

"Where are you going?" Soren asks. "That's not the way to the forge."

"We're bound for the pools," I say.

"Why? It's not wash day."

I look to Iric. Let him tell his friend what he wishes to.

Iric pauses such a long time, I think he won't answer. Then, "Rasmira's . . . teaching me how to swim."

Soren actually takes a step back at those words. "I've been offering to teach you to swim for the last year."

"And I've been telling you for the last year that I don't need your help. I don't want anything from you."

Tension ripples between the two boys. I'm not sure if I should step in or stay out of it.

Soren is the first to look away. "I'll come with you. Keep watch from the side."

"We don't need your protection," Iric insists.

I ignore him. "We'd be grateful to have the extra pair of eyes watching our backs."

Iric turns his disgusted look on me, but I don't back down.

"Don't be an idiot," I tell him.

I understand Iric's frustration. It's hard to allow others to see you at your weakest. I had to experience this firsthand while the boys were taking care of me. But I also know that true strength comes from being willing to fail in order to progress. That—if nothing else—is what I have learned from my mattugr.

Iric's whole body tenses up, and I wonder if he will change his mind about the entire venture.

He surprises me by continuing toward the pools. I hurry to his side, and Soren drops back behind us.

"Hope you brought an extra shirt," Iric grumbles out of the side of his mouth so Soren can't hear. "You'll want to double up, else Soren will lose his eyes as they bug from their sockets."

He's baiting me, angry that I'm letting Soren tag along. It's not going to work.

"I've an extra shirt in my pack," I say.

"Oh, excellent. And I'll be doubling up on pants." He smirks.

I snort. "I saw *nothing* that day you fell into the lake."

He blusters for a moment. "A man is not at his best when submerged in cold water," he says defensively.

"If you say so."

"I do!"

"What are you talking about?" Soren asks from behind us.

"Nothing," Iric says. He has his arms crossed angrily in front of his chest, while I try to hide a smile.

A twenty-minute walk from the tree house brings us to the pools. They're a series of freshwater springs. Time has eroded the rocks, and some of the pools are several dozens of feet wide and reach depths well over our heads. Each pool runs into the one next to it. Little streams trickle off to the sides.

Another perk to living with the boys for the last couple of weeks has been discovering the pools they use for bathing. (They're much preferable to the stream that runs by my shelter; I'm certain it's ice-cold runoff from the mountain.) The pools are clear with very little plant growth. One can see straight to the rock-covered bottom of each one. Most importantly, they're safe. Nothing deadly lives in them. Each pool is too small.

I lead Iric to one of the moderately deep pools. It'll come up to about my chest. Deep enough to swim, but shallow enough to touch.

We shed our boots and armor and then lay our axes down to the side of the pool where they can't get wet.

I enter the pool first, the cool water sending goose bumps prickling along my arms. Soren lowers himself to the ground and sits on crossed legs. He's not at the edge of our pool. Rather, he's distanced himself from us by a good forty feet, between us and the foliage of the wild. He pulls out a whetstone and takes it to his ax, his back to the thick expanse of trees.

I shout, "Won't you be more effective keeping watch if you turn around?"

He ignores me, keeping himself pointed toward Iric and me, and I wonder what exactly it is that he came here to see.

"I was right," Iric says as he steps into the pool with me. "I'm always right. Sometimes I hate being right."

"What are you muttering about?"

"Nothing. By the goddess, the pools are especially cold today."

It's a poor attempt at changing the subject, but I let it slide. It was probably only a reference to Soren's and my "inevitable" romance. I stifle an eye roll. Iric can be so deluded at times.

"Well, what's the first step to learning how to swim?" Iric asks.

I think for a moment. I've never actually taught anyone how to swim. It's something I learned at my family's private bathing pools.

"Place your hands on one of the sturdy rocks lining the edge of the pool."

He listens.

"Now I want you to hold yourself flat at the top of the water on your stomach. Kick with your feet and see how you do keeping your body afloat."

I realize too late that I didn't think that through very well. With the first kick, Iric drenches me, sending water into my eyes and hair.

I hear a snort and turn around. Soren's looked up from his ax, but he quickly turns his gaze back to the weapon.

I change positions, moving toward the rock Iric is gripping so I'm not in the direct line of spray.

"Okay, stop," I say.

Iric halts. "How did I do?"

"Well, there's significantly less water in the pool now."

"You said to kick. I kicked."

"You're like a rock splashing repeatedly into the pool."

"Well, I stayed afloat, didn't I?"

"Except for the part where you let one of your feet touch the bottom. Don't think I didn't notice that."

Iric has the decency to look guilty. "My head was about to go under."

"It's all right if your head goes under. You can hold your breath, can't you?"

"I can, but I don't like to. I can barely stand it when bathing."

"Watch," I tell him. I perform the same move I told him to do, only I let my feet kick gently at the water, under the water, so minimal splashing results. "Like that. Gently. Your body will float. Take a big gulp of air, and let it out slowly as you kick. I want you to release your air with your head under the water and only come back up when you need another breath. Can you do that?"

Iric tries again.

If anything, there's even more splashing. And letting his chin sink below the surface doesn't count as breathing out underwater.

"How was that?" Iric asks.

"Keep practicing."

As Iric continues kicking, I watch Soren out of the corner of my eye. At first, I thought he was watching me, and I thought to be self-conscious about my poor lessons. But after a while, I realize his eyes are on Iric. Watching the friend who he helped get banished to the wild. The friend who wouldn't take him up on his own offers of swim lessons. Iric is a proud man, and Soren is a bit of a broken man. He's here because Iric won't let him help, and all he can do is watch from the side as I do what Soren has been wanting to do.

I wave an arm at Soren, ushering him over. He returns his ax to his back before jogging up to me. Iric takes a deep breath and dunks his chin back in the water, kicking once more. If he notices that Soren has joined us, he says nothing of it.

"What should I have him do next?" I ask.

"He needs to get over his fear of having his head submerged. Have him dunk under the water."

Iric stops kicking and puts his feet on the bottom of the pool so he can stand. "Rasmira is teaching me. Not you."

"He has a point, though," I say. "You need to be comfortable with your head under the water."

He grits his teeth. "I can do that." He takes a breath so deep one would think it was his last and goes down. The hair at the top of his head dunks under for not even a whole second before he comes up again. He wipes the water from his face. "See. I did it."

"Do it again. Count to five and then come up," I say.

Iric arcs back an arm and connects it at just the right angle to send a huge spray of water into my face.

"Hey!" I shout.

"You're here to teach me to swim. Not make me do tricks!"

"It's not a trick. You need to learn to hold your breath. How else are you to face a water beast?"

Iric stomps over to the edge of the pool, preparing to haul himself out.

"Wait."

He pauses, but I can tell he's already about to decide to ignore me. I place a hand on his arm. "Come here."

Grudgingly, Iric lets go of the edge and walks with me back to the center of the pool. I take his hands in mine. "You're not alone in this. Remember that. We'll do it together."

He looks down at our joined hands. Resolve takes over his features, and he nods. "All right."

On the count of three, we both bend at the knees and go down. Iric's fingers in mine turn into a death grip, but I don't let go.

I cut him a break, and only count out three slow seconds, before tugging him back up. He doesn't need any extra encouragement.

I beam at him, proud of my student. "How did he do?" I ask, turning to Soren.

Soren is looking at me so strangely, the smile falls from my face. "What?"

"I've never seen you smile like that before. You have a lovely smile."

Lovely.

That word has my throat tightening, bile threatening to come up.

Even with the cut, you're still lovely. How do you manage that?

Another boy once called me lovely. A boy who regarded me as an insect, offering me food to draw me in with one hand while preparing to squash me with the other.

"That's enough swimming for the day," I say, the words coming out flat. I haul myself out of the water, grab my things, and plunge into the wild.

WHEN THE BOYS RETURN from the lake, I've already changed and braided my hair out of my face. I open the door in the floor, staring down at the two boys that are still very wet. I wonder if Iric pushed Soren in.

"Stay where you are," I say as Iric tries to grab a branch.

"Why?" he asks.

I've thought about this the whole time I walked back alone to the tree house. I had to think of *something* to keep my thoughts away from Torrin.

"We're going to complete our mattugrs," I start, but Soren butts in.

"We are?"

"Yes, you missed that conversation. But we are. And if we're going to help each other, we need to trust each other. Right now, Iric, you don't trust Soren. Or at least you're still holding too much against him."

Iric shoots an incredulous look up at me. "Of course I'm holding things against him! He is the reason I'm banished!"

"No," I argue. "You got yourself banished. You should have trusted Aros and taken the trial for the profession you wanted."

Iric's glare is murderous. "Just like you trusted your friend?"

Oh, that one hurts. I trusted Iric with what happened at my trial, and now he's throwing it in my face.

I slam the trapdoor shut and sit on it.

"What are you doing?" Soren asks.

"Neither of you is coming up here until you talk through your problems!" I shout.

"She can't be serious," Iric says.

I'm dead serious. Earlier today, Iric needed a gentler hand to help and encourage him while swimming. But this? This is something he needs to face head-on. And I don't care if he's angry about it.

There's pressure against the trapdoor as someone tries pushing against it. Probably Iric.

At the angle he has to shove, he's not moving the door anywhere.

"Dammit, Rasmira! Move it!"

"No!"

"Get out of the way or I swear on your goddess that I won't make you new armor!"

"Iric, you idiot! I'm doing this *for* you. You want to go home. We all do. You're not going to accomplish that if you keep holding so much over Soren's head."

"You expect me to suddenly forgive him because you won't let me inside my own house?"

"No, I expect you to talk. What happens after that is up to you. But I won't let your problems stand in the way of us going home."

He growls up at me, but I don't move. Eventually, I hear the sounds of Iric climbing back down.

"Soren, make her let us in!" Iric screams.

"What do you expect me to do?"

"Flash that winning smile or bat those long lashes or something."

"First, she wouldn't see me bat my lashes from here, and second—"

"This is your fault! You brought her here, and now she's stolen our home!"

They quiet as they hear me moving about the house, hauling things around.

"Is she—" Soren starts.

"She's moving the mattress over the top of the trapdoor! You are *not* keeping us out here all night long, Rasmira."

"That's entirely up to you," I say, plumping up my pillow before finding a comfy position.

"What do we do?" Iric asks. "Shatter the window? Or we could wait her out. There's not that much food up there. She's got to piss sometime."

A beat of silence. "Is the idea of talking to me really so unbearable that you're suggesting we lay siege to our tree house?" Soren says gruffly.

"You know what? Fine. FINE! Soren, I forgive you. There. Happy, Rasmira? I said I forgive him. Now let us up."

I don't bother responding to that pathetic attempt.

"That's not enough for you?" Iric demands. "You need me to mean it, too? I can't force that. That's not how it works!"

I don't know why Iric thinks he can reason with me at this point, but he keeps trying.

"I told you what he did! He made me think I could be a warrior! He made me believe I could have Aros forever if I took the trial with him. He promised he'd have my back during the trial, and you know what? He didn't. How do I forgive that?"

I can imagine Soren wincing after every accusation. After a beat of silence, he says softly, "Iric, I'm so sorry. I can't fix it. I did what I did. I was confident. Too confident, and I got us both stuck out here. I did the best I could after the fact. I failed my trial on *purpose* so you wouldn't be left alone out here. You're my brother, and from now on, I swear to always have your back."

"How can I believe that? How can I trust you?"

"Because I've changed. Because I've spent every day in the wild looking after you, excluding the fact that I now owe a life debt to Rasmira. But she's our friend now. She's on our side. And she's changing things. She's helping us go home. Is a whole year of penance on my part not enough for you? What more can I do?"

More silence, and I find that I'm holding my breath.

"I want it to go away. All of it," Iric says. "No more struggling to stay alive. I miss the village. I miss our family. I just want things to go back to the way they were."

"I do, too," Soren says.

"I've spent so much time being angry."

"You don't have to be angry. Not anymore. Now we have hope."

Iric is quiet for so long, I wonder if perhaps he left. Then quietly, so quietly I can barely hear it, Iric says, "I'm sorry, Soren. I'm sorry I've spent so much time hating you instead of being your brother and helping us go home."

And with those words, I move the mattress back to its former position. The boys come up top. Iric starts shucking his wet clothes and throwing them at me. I'm torn between averting my eyes and catching the heavy garments before they strike my head.

When Iric is turned, Soren mouths, *Thank you.*

I fall asleep with the most profound sense of contentment. I wonder if this is what it feels like to be a good leader.

CHAPTER

14

Iric's swimming lessons take precedence over all else. We still have to feed ourselves, of course. The wood gets chopped, the traps get checked, the berries are picked—but with that done, it's off to the pools. Day after day after day.

Soren continues to come with, though he mostly serves as a silent guard off to the side.

"You know," Iric says, "I can't tell if Soren comes to watch me or to watch you."

We're both in the water. Iric is flat on his back, and I've got my arms held out in front of me, tucked under him, helping him float.

"You, of course," I say. "He wants you to succeed. He's here to support you."

"Or to see you in sopping wet clothes every day."

"Iric, I will drop you."

"Come on, Raz. You know I'm kidding." He reaches up a hand and ruffles my hair with it, sending droplets down my face. "I think he comes because he likes seeing you in your element."

"My element?"

"You know, bossing people around? Kidding again! I mean, leading. Teaching. You're a born leader. Didn't you say that's what you were training to be? The next leader of Seravin? It shows."

"Yes, but I was never any good at it. Nobody ever listened to me. I never had the respect of the trainees back home."

"Did you treat them the way you treat us?"

We reach the end of the small pool, so I turn Iric in a half circle and start walking toward the other end. "What do you mean?"

"Well, did you encourage them? Offer to help them in the areas they were lacking? Did you give out quick and efficient orders whenever you were in a crisis? Like we were with the gunda."

I try to swallow past a sudden knot in my throat.

No, I didn't do any of those things. When the boys made mistakes, I pointed them out. When they were horrible to me, I put them in their places. During training exercises, they never listened to my instructions, so I stopped giving them. Instead, I took the lead and expected them to follow my example.

"I didn't treat them the way I treat you and Soren. They weren't ever kind to me the way you are."

Iric tries to turn his body toward me before he remembers he's supposed to be holding still and floating. "Maybe they needed you to be the bigger person and make the first move to change things."

"I'm not so sure about that. Could we talk about something else?"

Iric looks up at the cloud-covered sky. "Sure. Oh! Want to get a reaction out of Soren?"

"What?"

"Pull me closer."

I bend my elbows, tugging Iric near my chest. He gives me a devilish grin before reaching forward and tucking a strand of my hair behind one ear.

At first, the motion sends goose bumps along my skin—and not pleasant ones. Torrin would touch my hair this way and—

But then there's a sound, and Iric and I both turn our heads. Soren has dropped his whetstone onto the rocks. He bends down to retrieve it, and when he looks back up, he's got a glare fixed on Iric.

Iric lets out a low laugh. "Priceless."

"That's not funny," I snap. I take my arms back and cross them over my chest.

"Just because Soren and I are working on things, that doesn't mean I don't get to provoke him. Besides, he knows you're not my type, so the fact that he's getting worked up only makes it funnier!"

"You are a horrible person and—" I break off as I realize Iric is drifting away from me. "You're floating."

"What do you think we've been doing for the last half hour?"

"No, you're floating on your own!"

"I am? I am!" Iric fumbles for a moment, as though knowing I'm not there suddenly throws him off balance, but he quickly rights himself, and continues floating. "Soren! I'm floating! Look!"

But shouting seems to have been too much for Iric, for he goes under in the next second. I step through the water as quickly as possible to reach him, but Iric gets his feet under him before I get there.

When he breaches the surface, it's to hear Soren laughing at him.

Iric pulls himself out of the water and flies at Soren, tackling him with his soaking body. Then he's pulling on him, trying to force him into one of the pools.

"Raz, I could use some help!"

We're supposed to be learning how to swim, but what the hell.

I get myself behind Soren and push.

"No!" Soren shrieks.

Too late. We fling him into one of the midsized pools, armor and skins and all. He was smart enough to drop his ax before it got too close to the pool.

Iric was able to let go in time, but me? Soren clamps a hand down on my arm and pulls me in with him.

I kick to the surface and glare at Iric. "This is what I get for helping you? You abandon me?"

"I have swimming to practice," he says innocently before taking off for the pool we'd been using.

Soren stands next to me, the water reaching up to our shoulders. Good thing, since he still has all his armor on. A calculated decision on Iric's part, I'm sure. He didn't want to drown his friend, only drench him.

"Traitor," Soren says to me.

"I don't owe you any loyalty."

"I saved you from Peruxolo! That doesn't earn me any loyalty?"

"No." I raise my arm and send a wave of water crashing onto his head.

He glares at me for a moment, before watching Iric try to float in the far-off pool some more. I'm amazed and proud of Iric's confidence in the water alone.

"I've never seen him like this," Soren says. "It's a nice change." With a smile on his lips, Soren turns from Iric to me.

With Soren standing so close to me, I remember just how close in height we are. Our eyes are on par with each other. Our noses.

Our mouths.

I'm startled by the thought. Where in the world did it come from? Soren has always had a mouth, obviously. But now I'm noticing it as an individual entity.

His lips look so soft, a stark contrast to the rest of his muscled body.

If Soren notices a change in my demeanor, he doesn't show it. No, he sucks in a big gulp of air and goes under the water. I watch his body closely, trying to figure out what he's doing. A hand darts in my direction, and I realize too late—

I'm sucked under.

I send a punch Soren's way. It doesn't gather much force underwater, but it's enough to make him release me.

We both breach the surface.

"You ass."

He laughs again.

I jump, get my hands on either side of his shoulders, and push back. He might have been stable enough to withstand me without the armor, but with?

His armor drags him down.

He sinks rapidly to the bottom. It takes him some time to get his feet under him to drag the extra weight to the surface. He rubs water from his eyes, which are no longer filled with mischief.

The smallest of smiles rests at the corner of his lips, and I realize then that I'd almost forgotten what it was to have fun. Strange that Soren, a boy from the wild, should help me to remember.

"Truce?" he asks.

"For today." I return to Iric and monitor his progress.

IN ANOTHER WEEK, Iric is swimming. He's by no means a strong swimmer, but he knows how to float both on his back and stomach. He can paddle himself through the water and even manage big strokes above it. The most important improvement, however, is his confidence.

That lack of fear, his ability to put his head under the water and hold his breath without worry, it bolsters him. Gives him a sense of freedom he didn't have before.

Despite the improvement, I don't let up on our practices. Swimming muscles need to be exercised regularly, until they're strong. Iric gets tired out far too soon, but I will make a strong swimmer of him yet.

My wound is essentially healed, but I've made no plans to return to my little fort in the wild. There seems to be little point when I spend my days helping Iric and Soren, especially when there's room for all of us in the tree house.

It surprises me how much I've come to trust them, but I remind myself not to get too attached. We're exchanging services. I teach Iric to swim, and he helps me with new armor so I can enter the god's lair. It's a trade-off, and when all is said and done, Iric and Soren will return to Restin, while I will go home to Seravin. Assuming the villages really do welcome us back home and don't treat us as forever outcasts.

When Iric insists that he needs to start spending more time in his forge, I let him. There are traps that need mending, and Iric needs to work on my armor.

So as not to be a distraction, I spend the time with Soren. The summer months won't last forever, so we need to start stocking up on firewood for winter—just in case we're not returned home by then.

"Don't dull your weapon by using your own ax on the firewood," Soren insists.

"But the other axes have wooden shafts," I say, staring at the tools Iric designed. I'm still not used to the idea of long-lasting wood, despite having lived in the tree house for the last few weeks.

"They won't break," Soren says. "I promise." He grabs a piece of wood, places it on the stump in front of him, and takes a hearty swing.

I sling my ax on my back and stare warily at the axes Iric has made for chopping. Eventually, I decide to give them a try. Even so, I start off by making kindling, grabbing smaller pieces of wood and placing the ax carefully to cut the pieces lengthwise into even thinner segments.

"Coward," Soren says playfully. "What do you think is going to happen? The ax head will go flying?"

"Yes!"

He rolls his eyes at me. "Sounds like an excuse to get out of doing work."

"I am not afraid of work."

"Says the privileged village leader's daughter."

"You know what? I'm going to outchop you," I say. I grab a large round of wood, chop it in half, then cut those halves into quarters.

"Fat chance," Soren says. He throws down his ax to grab a heavy piece of wood and place it on his stump.

I focus on my own wood pile for the next minute, cutting through segment after segment.

After a while, Soren says, "I think we need to place some wagers. Make this more interesting. Whoever gets through their pile last has to wash the winner's clothes for the next week."

I drop my ax to the ground, place my hands on my knees.

Breathe. Just breathe.

Is there anything that won't remind me of Torrin?

The trial blazes behind my eyes. Our competition to see who could kill the most ziken. And after that—

He—

I shut my eyes as tightly as they will go, as though I can will the memories away. I don't want to think of it. Torrin won that day at the trial, and he keeps winning every time I think of him in the wild. Every time I feel like I can't do something because it reminds me of him.

I will *not* let him win anymore.

"Rasmira, are you all right?"

I open my eyes, focus them on Soren's face.

I'm with Soren.

Not Torrin.

Soren is banished with me, and he will help me because he also wants to go home. He's not setting me up. He's not going to betray me.

I've let Torrin win long enough.

"I'll be fine," I say. And though it hurts me to say it, though everything in my body screams at me to run away, to strike out on my own and not trust anyone, I add, "You're on."

I pick up my ax and resume chopping. Soren watches me for a moment, as though he's unsure what he should do.

"Do you have a strong desire to do my laundry, Soren?"

He smirks before returning to his own ax.

When I chop through my last piece of wood, I look over at Soren's pile. He still has five large rounds to get through.

I won.

I beat Soren.

And I beat Torrin's memory.

I'm getting my life back.

"I'll just add my clothes to your dirty pile, then," I say with a grin.

Soren stares at my mouth for just a beat longer than necessary, but before I can do anything about it, he says, "Or maybe we could just slip everything into Iric's pile."

"Are you kidding? Iric hasn't laundered his clothes in weeks."

"Good point," Soren says. "Fine. You win this time, but next time we're raising the stakes."

"Loser does laundry for a month?" I ask.

"Laundry *and* cooking."

"Better sharpen your ax before then."

"Oh, I will."

Soren and I stack the wood in the storage shed, until the large space is fit to bursting. There's something so satisfying about staring at the work I've done and knowing how it will keep me alive for the next several months.

Just as we finish loading in the last of it, Iric races up one of the trails, holding long metal rods in his hands. "I've done it. I know how we're going to kill the hyggja!"

"Are those *spears*?" Soren asks, eyeing the weapons.

Iric comes to a stop in front of us. "Yes! I've just finished them."

"How is falling back on flimsy weaponry going to help us?"

"We can't very well kill the water beast with axes! We'd never be able to throw or swing them through the water. But spears can be thrown from above the water. They can impale things beneath it! They may be older weapons, but they have their purposes!" Iric points to a space on one of the spears just beneath the sharp tip. "We can attach the end of a length of rope here, so after we cast a throw, we can haul the spear back to us and throw again."

Iric looks from Soren to me and back again, a boyish hope spread across his face.

"I think it's brilliant," I say.

"But spears?" Soren asks.

"If you don't like them, you don't have to help us with the hyggja," Iric snaps. "Raz and I can go home, and you can climb the mountain on your own."

"Fat chance," Soren says. "I'm in, but I have no idea how to use a spear."

"Good thing we have nothing but time out here to practice."

IN THE WASHING POOLS, we hold our breath under the water, challenging each other to see who can withstand the longest.

Surprisingly, Iric always wins. But then, he is the one who has the most riding on this.

We practice with Iric's spears, throwing them both while above the water and while in it. It's different than throwing an ax or throwing a rock. While the ax was meant to turn end over end when thrown, a spear is supposed to cut through the air like a bird. Straight, unwavering.

It's difficult. My wrist always wants to snap at the last moment, and I have to force it to be still, to let my fingers release the rod while holding my arm straight, but after a while, I get the hang of it.

Soren, however, is abysmal at it, and he has no problem letting his frustration show.

"These things are ridiculous!" he says after a throw that sends his spear straight into the ground a short distance away.

"You're just not used to being terrible at handling a weapon," Iric says. "Try again."

Soren rips his spear from the ground. "Flimsy, skinny, useless. People were not meant to kill things with these!" He turns his angry gaze on the spear. "You're an overly large eating utensil!"

"Try throwing higher," Iric suggests.

Soren throws again. The spear goes farther, but he somehow manages to make the wrong end strike the ground first.

Iric clutches his stomach while he laughs, and Soren looks ready to traipse over and bash him over the head with his fist.

I step in before he can turn those thoughts into actions.

"Here," I say, handing Soren my spear.

He grips the shaft, and I wrap my hand over his. Being pressed so close against him is odd, and thoughts of Torrin threaten to surface, but I put my focus into teaching Soren.

"Arc back, swing forward, and release. That's all. Don't bend your wrist," I say. We mimic the motion together, going through the steps without releasing the spear just yet.

"Good," I say, stepping back. "Now don't be so concerned with throwing it hard. Focus on throwing it straight first. Speed and strength can come later."

Soren stares at a point in front of him, taking aim, I think. He puts his arm through the motions we just practiced, and at the perfect moment, he releases.

The spear goes sailing, thudding satisfactorily into a tree trunk some ways away.

"Whoop!" Iric hollers, slapping him on the back.

"Well done," I say.

Soren walks off to retrieve the spear, a new spring in his step. As he does so, his left hand rubs over his right. Just not in the spot where his skin was touching the spear.

He rubs where my hand made contact with his.

PART 3

THE
MATTUGRS

CHAPTER

15

The lake is just as I remember it: massive, eerie, and surrounded by smooth stones. The water is clear in some places and murky in others, where plants cover the ground and mud is churned up by unseen critters.

I step up to the edge of the lake, staring out across the water. It looks so peaceful right now. One would never know a deadly beast lies hidden within.

Iric takes an especially long length of rope and ties it sturdily around the base of one of the thick trees. He then begins uncoiling the rest of it in the direction of the lake's edge. When he reaches the water, he drops the rest of the coil right on the ground.

Once we catch the hyggja, we'll need a way to get it out of the water. Iric's already thought of that.

The lake is quiet save for a few bubbles that breach the top. I think they're too small to have been caused by the hyggja.

"We have the advantage so long as we can stay on land," Iric says. He's already told us this multiple times on the trek to the lake, but I think he needs to say it again to reassure himself. "We throw our spears at the beast until it's weakened, and then we haul it on land, where I'll deliver the final blow. We do *not* go in the water."

Teaching Iric to swim was a precaution. Should anything go wrong, he needs to know how to swim, and he needs the extra confidence while standing near the water's edge.

"Do you suppose the hyggja has finished off the gunda's corpse yet?" Soren asks. "Maybe it won't be hungry."

"If that's the case," Iric says, "it might not leave the bottom of the lake. Then we'll have to come back later."

I do not like the sound of that. I don't want to wait to continue my task of killing Peruxolo. I *can't*. I need that armor.

Soren makes a face. "If anyone falls in, they'll be swimming in rotting gunda guts."

"I could have done without that image in my mind," I say.

"Just don't drink the water."

I gag.

"Enough," Iric says. "Let's get this over with." He reaches down, picks up a round rock, and casts it as far as his arm will reach. It sends up a great splash, and we watch until the rippling water stills once more.

"Maybe it's sick," Iric says. "Gunda didn't sit well with it."

Soren grabs his own rock, selecting a round, flat one. He casts it from his side, and we watch as the rock skips across the water's surface. One. Two. Three. Then it plunks down below, just a ways farther than where Iric's landed.

I grab my own flat stone, size up the water, and cast it. One. Two. Three. Four. Five.

"I was just getting warmed up!" Soren insists.

"Everything doesn't have to be a competition," I say.

"No," he agrees, "but it's far more fun that way."

He throws a second rock, and we count the bounces. One. Two. Three. Fou—

The rock barely hits for the fourth time before an enormous body launches out of the water, attempting to catch the rock in its jaws. All three of us stagger backward from the shock of it, instinctively putting more space between the hyggja and us.

It's easily three times the length of a man from head to tail, though only twice as wide. One would expect something flat like a fish, but no. If two men were to lie on their stomachs, one atop the other, it would be similar to the hyggja's shape. It has fins placed where a four-legged monster would have legs. They're thick and membranous, and I think it must use them to help swim and maybe move along the lake's bottom. But there's no way it can use them above the surface.

It cannot leave the water.

The hyggja's skin is a dark green, like grass under the pale glow of moonlight, but it doesn't bear scales. No, the texture is wrong. It's bumpy and hardened, just like the rock-strewn bottom of the lake.

And its mouth—

Oh goddess, its triangle-shaped mouth seems to go on forever. It's partially open with a row of top and bottom teeth peeking through the gap.

I see all of this in the second it takes for the beast to fall back down into the water.

"This was a terrible idea," Iric says into the silence that follows. I look to find him already turned around, heading away from the lake.

"Wait a moment!" I call after him. I follow him at a run, not stopping until I've cut him off.

"You saw that thing!" Iric says. "Nothing can kill it! It's practically made of teeth! And did you see how far it jumped out of the water?"

"Not far enough to reach us on the cliff. We'll be safe up there."

"No, we're safe back at the tree house." Iric tries to get around me.

I move with him. "You've come all this way. Iric, you made us spears! We have a good plan. We can't leave before we've even tried. What harm will a few throws be?"

Soren steps up beside me. "She's right, Iric. Let's give it a try first."

Iric wraps his arms around himself. "I can barely stand the sight of it. That beast has haunted my dreams for the last year. I hadn't realized just how big—"

"It doesn't matter how big it is," I say. "Nothing can survive with its head cut off. You said the plan yourself. We weaken it. We drag it on land. You saw those fins—it will be useless on land. Then you deliver the killing blow."

"You can do this," Soren says. "We're not leaving you to do this alone."

Iric rubs his arms before dropping them. "Fine. One throw."

"Each," I say. "One throw each. Then we can discuss our next move."

Iric agrees, and he leads us up the small cliff face. We each carry our own spear, the length of rope attached to it coiled around one of our shoulders. We come to a stop in a line along the edge, and we carefully place our ropes behind us, so that when we cast our throws, they will unspool without trouble.

"Let's do this," Soren says, the prospect of a battle exciting him.

I nod. "For Iric."

"For Aros," Iric says quietly to himself. "For Mother and Father. For *us*."

Iric begins pulling the sheets of armor from his clothing, and Soren and I follow his lead. It feels so wrong to go into battle without armor, but I know it is a necessity. Should we fall into the water, we can't be burdened down, and armor will not stop the hyggja should anything go wrong, anyway. Though I can't help but wonder which death would be less painful, drowning or being eaten by the hyggja?

Would it bite a person in half? Or would death be more slow and painful? Perhaps I should not indulge in such thoughts.

From up here, I can see the hyggja. The skin of its back skims the top of the water, and the rest of its outline is easily discernible below the surface. Its eyes are located at the top of its head, and I swear I see them watching us.

As soon as we approach the edge, the water beast swims toward us, moving in circles below the rise.

Definitely watching us.

Iric holds his spear at the ready. He sizes up the beast. "The water plays with the eye. You'll want to throw just ahead of where it looks like the hyggja is."

"How do you know that?" I ask.

"Aros," he says, and he throws.

The spear moves too quickly to track it, but I know it hits

home because it halts when it's halfway submerged in the water, and a gurgling growl, unlike anything I've ever heard before, surges upward. It's the kind of sound that instinctively makes me want to run.

"I hit it!" Iric gets his hands on the rope at his feet. He holds tight as the hyggja starts swimming in a mad jumble below us. Red turns up with the bubbles. "Hurry! Someone else cast!"

I take aim and throw, but the hyggja is moving too disjointedly. My throw misses by a foot, and I hurry to reel my spear back in.

In the next instant, Iric's spear dislodges from his quarry, the hyggja's pulling finally freeing it from the weapon. "Damn!" Iric says as he pulls his rope end over end to go for another throw. A small chunk of flesh comes up with the spear's tip.

I gag again.

"Soren, throw before it swims off!" Iric bellows. He rearranges the rope at his feet so it will unravel easily with his next throw. It somehow managed to get mixed in with my spear's rope as the two of us reeled them in. We scramble to separate them. Meanwhile, Soren pulls back his hand to his ear and launches his spear forward.

Soren whoops. "Got it!" he says over the top of another deep growl from the beast. Soren's hands go to the rope near his feet.

"Good!" Iric says. "Whatever you do, don't let go. We've almost got this sorted out." Iric and I finally have our ropes separated, but we have to wind them carefully on the ground so they will unravel with our throws.

"It's trying to swim away," Soren says with a grunt. He takes a couple steps forward to keep his hold on the beast.

"Let it go," I say.

"Do *not* let go!" Iric says.

"Soren, drop it now!" I shout.

"It's too strong!" Soren says.

"Don't you dare let go of that rope!" Iric yells.

"Shit."

The hyggja yanks Soren clean off his feet, and I watch in horror as he's pulled right over the edge of the cliff. He lands in the water, flat on his stomach.

I whirl around. "Why would you tell him that?" I scream at Iric.

Iric's frozen to the spot, staring where Soren disappeared.

"We have to move!" I tell him. I pick my rope coil from off the ground and throw it over my head and shoulder; then I grip my spear firmly in one hand.

"No one goes in the water," Iric mumbles weakly.

"Too late." In the next second, I take a deep breath and jump.

The shock from the cold only lasts a few seconds before my body adjusts. The water here is murkier than the washing pools, so I can't see as far ahead as what I'm used to when we practiced.

I don't know how much visibility I have. Seven feet? Maybe ten? Everything looks so different when underwater. Even still, I'm certain I don't see Soren or the hyggja. I kick my way to the surface and look.

There.

Water churns up maybe twenty feet in front of me. Panic sets in as I worry it might be Soren getting eaten alive. I kick my feet right for the spot, and when I'm closer, I dive back down.

The hyggja tumbles in circles, trying to shake off the spear, meanwhile Soren holds on for dear life to his rope's end, some ten feet from me.

A sound hits the water behind me, and I pray to the goddess it's Iric joining us in the water and not anything else foul living in the lake.

Before I can reach Soren, the hyggja manages to dislodge his spear. The weapon sinks to the rock-covered lake bottom as Soren swims to the surface for a breath.

I watch the hyggja turn to the side, so one of its large eyes is pointed directly at me—its prey. But rather than swim at me, it turns tail and swims in the opposite direction.

Unsure of what else to do, I swim after Soren to get another gulp of air.

"Where is it?" Iric's voice from behind us.

"It swam off," I say.

Soren gasps from next to me, still holding on to his rope. While he treads water, his arms pull at his rope, attempting to reel it in. He makes a face.

"What's wrong?" I ask.

"It's stuck on something." Before I can tell him otherwise, Soren breathes in quickly and goes back under.

Damn him.

I get a mouthful of air before joining him.

Soren tugs on his rope, using it to pull himself down to wherever it's stuck. Bubbles fly out of him as he goes. His head must be pounding from going down so deep.

I swim after him with Iric at my side.

The sinking feeling in my gut has nothing to do with how far I'm traveling under the water. The hyggja didn't turn tail and run. It's doing *something*. I'm sure it's not used to anything fighting back with any sort of success in this lake, but all creatures have instincts.

The instinct to eat is more powerful than the instinct to flee for a predator that's never had to fear for its life.

When I reach Soren's side, I see it. Not the hyggja, but the remains of the gunda. Its head is still mostly intact, though its eyes are glossy. But the middle area, where that mouth was, is gone. Nothing but bones with faint remains of stringy flesh left to see. Bile threatens to rise in my throat as I think of what I'm swimming in.

Instead, I turn my thoughts to Iric. My friend. I'm doing this for him. He deserves to go home to his family, and we can make that happen.

If we don't die first.

Soren reaches his spear but has to untangle it from some thick grasses. Iric is next to him, helping.

The hyggja disappeared in a direction over Soren's and Iric's heads, and I watch that spot with a critical eye, my lungs starting to grow uncomfortable.

I'm struck with a thought all of a sudden. The need to turn around and look over my shoulder becomes so strong, I can't help but listen.

And when I spin, it's to find jaws open wide, only feet from my head.

I throw my spear up on instinct—not horizontal as if aiming before a throw, but vertical to get it between those jaws—and thrust upward with as much strength as I can muster while underwater. Teeth barrel into me. There's a quick sting in my arm as I lurch backward, the force of the beast's swimming propelling me through the water. Something strikes me from behind, and I think I might have slammed into one of the boys, but I can't be certain. The beast still pushes me through the water.

Eventually the hyggja changes directions, and the stinging in my arm heightens before I feel teeth dislodging. I tumble backward in a reverse somersault through the water, and a noise comes out of me as my head cracks on the rocky bottom. I don't see stars, which must be a good sign. There's only pain in the back of my skull.

But then I feel the hyggja's fins skimming over my stomach.

I scramble, my eyes closing momentarily as mud and plant refuse are churned up by the beast skimming the lake floor.

I claw my way to the surface. A small burst of red adds to the water as I go, and I look down at my arm. There's a thin but deep gash, made from a line of teeth, just above my elbow on my forearm.

Below me, Soren and Iric are both spinning to the side as if they'd been knocked askew. But Soren has his spear unstuck, and he manages to get the rope over one of his shoulders.

My head finally clears the water, and I take several deep breaths before plunging back into the fray.

The hyggja is shaking its head from side to side fiercely. Its body spins around, and I get another good look at those teeth. It manages to chomp down on the spear, but instead of breaking the weapon, it sends it all the way through the roof of its mouth, the rope still attached to the tip and now stringing through a hole in the beast's flesh.

Brown-black blood clouds into the water around the hyggja, and the beast tries to swim off, probably in an attempt to sneak up on us again. All that does is pull my spear taut lengthwise against the top of the hyggja's snout. And with my rope still wrapped around my shoulders, it pulls me with it.

Feeling the rope through its skin, the beast becomes distracted and changes plans, now trying to free itself.

Soren and Iric take full advantage of that.

They swim right up to the beast, plant their feet firmly on the ground, and thrust with their spears. The hyggja shrieks, turning over, trying to get away, but all it does is tangle itself in the thick ropes, providing more leverage for Soren and Iric, who hold on to their ropes with all their might.

The water fills with mud and blood as the beast turns up the lake's bottom. It becomes impossible for me to see anything.

I take another break for air, dropping my coil of rope from my shoulders in my haste.

I breathe deeply, yet rapidly, a few times before submerging myself once more, frantically searching for the boys.

After swimming lower, I find Iric trying to direct the hyggja toward the shore, a task which he's having little success with. He's embedded his spear deeply into the beast's stomach, pulling with all his might.

Soren is nowhere to be seen, so I think he's likely gone for air.

Why hasn't Iric done the same?

The hyggja still squirms, but its movements have slowed. I manage to grab Iric by the arm and pull. At first, he's reluctant, shrugging out of my grip, but the second time I reach for him, I think he finally takes stock of the air left in his lungs.

He hands me his rope and propels himself to the surface; the hyggja drags me every which way, rolling, turning, scraping against the bottom. After another tumble, its front fins are sufficiently pinned under layers and layers of rope, and it begins to rely solely on its tail for movement.

Soren shortly joins me, finding the end of one of the other ropes and holding fast.

The hyggja starts to turn toward him, finally getting the sense to go after him instead of keeping at its futile attempts to free itself from all the rope.

I don't think so.

Hand over hand I pull myself along the rope as quickly as I can until I reach where it connects with the hyggja's body. I wrap my legs against its body, and inch upward, closer and closer to the head.

More and more blood seeps from the creature, slowing its movements even more. It's the only reason I'm able to reach those jaws, to wrap my arms around the snout and pin it firmly closed.

Where the hell is Iric?

My question is answered a moment later, when Iric appears back in the water, holding yet another length of rope. It's the one he attached to the tree along the lake's edge. He swims right up to the beast—you'd think he'd never shown any fear about it earlier—and ties the end of the rope around several layers of the coils already pinning the hyggja's fins down.

With that done, he kicks for the surface once more. I motion Soren after him.

It will take two of them to hoist Iric's prize toward the lake's edge.

CHAPTER
16

The boys groan from the weight of the hyggja, but I can barely hear it over the sounds of my own breathing. That last round in the water had to have been at least a couple minutes. Either my eyes are watering or the lake water runs down from my hair.

The beast is only halfway out of the water, its right side exposed to the air, while the left is buried in the lake. Without the buoyancy of the water aiding us, the hyggja becomes far too heavy to manage.

I turn my body around, holding the jaw closed while getting my feet on the ground in front of it and pushing.

But it doesn't make a difference. The hyggja isn't going anywhere.

The beast tries to wriggle from side to side. I don't let go. If the snout gets free, it will still be lethal.

Iric and Soren stare at me.

"Do something!" I snap.

An airy growl spits out between the hyggja's nostrils, and I look pointedly at Iric.

He retrieves his ax from the cliff, where he left it with his armor, hoists it over one shoulder, and treads for the hyggja. With Soren at the tail and me at the head, we attempt to hold the beast steady as Iric's ax hovers over the beast's neck.

He swings.

The neck is so thick, it takes him three tries to cut through the width of it. Each swing sends red-brown water flying through the air, drenching me all over again.

But I'm finally able to let go. I sprawl onto the ground and just breathe. Nothing else in the world is so important as breathing. Though my limbs are exhausted, triumph pulses under the surface, and I relish the feeling.

Iric did it.

And so did I.

I'm that much closer to defeating Peruxolo.

I let out a scream of victory, and Soren joins me, the two of us whooping into the air. When Iric doesn't join us, we go silent, eyes fixed on him.

"What the hell was that, Soren?" he demands.

"What?" Soren asks.

"What was the one rule? Do *not* go in the water. Soren! I thought you were dead!"

So quiet, I can barely hear it, Soren says, "You said not to let go. I listened."

"I didn't mean to let yourself get dragged into the water! Why would you do that?"

"I owed you. I got you banished. I hoped I could help make things right between us again."

"You didn't need to put yourself in danger for that. Soren—" His voice drops. "Rasmira was right all along. You were not to blame for my banishment. I was, and I knew it. It was so much easier to be angry with you rather than myself, but I've already forgiven you." Iric reaches over and puts a hand on Soren's shoulder. "You didn't need to prove yourself to me or make up for anything that happened in the past. We're good, brother. We're good."

By the look on Soren's face, I think he might be ready to cry. Instead he coughs. "Thank you."

"So don't do anything that stupid again or else I'll take off your head just as I did that beast's!" Iric says.

"Do me a favor and manage it in one swing, won't you?"

"I'd like to see you hack through that mass in one swing!"

Soren grins, and the boys fall silent, too exhausted for words again.

I bask in the feeling of utter exhaustion, yet utter triumph. I wonder what my father would think if he saw me now. If he saw how I pointed these boys in the right direction, encouraged them to complete their mattugrs, and even helped to take out the fearsome hyggja.

And what would my fellow trainees think?

I'm surprised by the sudden desire I have to see them. Those who don't openly hate me still kept their distance from the girl who would lead them one day. They barely tolerated me.

But I've learned so much, and this feeling I have right now, of accomplishment, of reveling in another's success, I want to experience it again with the men back home. I want to be this kind of leader for them.

I want to go home and make things right.

After several minutes, my skin grows itchy from drying in the sun. I roll over and find Iric staring confusedly at the severed head.

"You did it," I say. "You can go home. Why do you look so troubled?"

"It doesn't feel any different," Iric says.

"You just did something amazing," I say. "You made these weapons and came up with this plan. You dealt the killing blow. You earned this. You don't feel accomplished?"

"It's not that," he says. "I am proud of what I did and so grateful to you two for helping me achieve it. But I thought I would *feel* different. I lost my honor, my place in Rexasena's Paradise the day I was banished. And the only way I could reclaim it was to kill the hyggja or die trying.

"But it doesn't make any sense. Nothing about me has changed. I'm the same person I was an hour ago. All I did was kill this thing. How does that act suddenly redeem me?"

"But—I thought you didn't believe in the goddess," I say.

"It's easier to choose unbelief when the alternative is eternal damnation."

Soren offers, "You failed your warrior's test. You had to prove yourself as a warrior. You have done that now. You've proven your skill and redeemed yourself."

"But that test was against ziken," Iric says. "I'm still not very skilled at defeating them. I killed an underwater beast. The two aren't even related. How is this the goddess's will? The mattugr was given by men. How do they know her will? Shouldn't I *feel* redeemed if this is what she wanted of me?" Then quietly, "Maybe she truly doesn't exist."

Iric's words are troubling. Is this how I will feel if I kill the god? Will I have done nothing?

"I think you'll feel differently," Soren says, "once you walk back into Restin and see the faces of your mother and father."

"Perhaps," Iric says. He rolls onto his feet. "But I'll have to wait to find that out. First, I have some armor to make."

Iric holds out a hand to me. I take it, and he helps me to my feet.

"Let's go get cleaned up. We all stink."

THE WASHING POOLS ARE our first destination. Once done, we return to the tree house and change into dry clothes, hanging up our now clean ones to dry. Iric bandages the bite above my elbow before walking off with the hyggja's head in a leather sack slung over his shoulder. He mutters something about finding a way to keep it preserved until returning to the village. Leaving him to it, Soren and I get started on supper.

I feel as though I haven't eaten in days after all the toiling in the water.

My stomach groans as I add more kindling to my growing fire. Meanwhile, Soren prepares the valder meat for the spit. He keeps pausing in his work and looking over at me, as though he has something he wants to say. In the end, he keeps looking away and focusing on his task.

I think to call him out on it, but then I wonder if I don't want to hear whatever it is.

As Soren sets the spit over the fire, he finally speaks. "I can't thank you enough for what you've done for Iric. You did for him what I could not. He wouldn't let me teach him to swim. Wouldn't hear anything I had to say about our quests. And honestly, we couldn't have killed the hyggja with only two people. We needed a third.

"Iric's banishment has weighed on me for a year. It's all I could think about. That guilt was never-ending, and now . . ." He looks at me, and though our eyes have met many times in all the while we've known each other, this time is different. My stomach tightens, heats, and I feel as though we're saying things just by holding each other's stare.

"Thank you," he says. "You didn't just save Iric. You saved me. In more ways than one." And before I know what's happening, he leans down and leaves a kiss on my cheek. He pulls back and stares down at my mouth, then at my eyes.

Torrin's face flashes across my vision. How long ago was it when he kissed my cheek rather than my lips as I so desperately wanted? I've decided that I won't let him win anymore, but that doesn't mean I can suddenly control when he enters my thoughts.

And though I've decided Soren can be my friend, I haven't had a chance to think of him as being anything else.

So I don't encourage him. I look away and step back. "You're welcome, Soren. I did what any friend would."

Perhaps saying that word was a bit much, but Soren gets the hint. "I'm going to check on Iric. See if he found something to do with that head for safekeeping."

He bolts down the trapdoor faster than a hare running from a fox.

I let out a held breath as I think of Soren. Soren and his nice lips. Once, all I wanted was to know what it felt like to be kissed. And now the thought of kissing brings a bitter taste to my mouth.

I hate that. I want to think of Soren that way. I want to wonder why he wants to kiss me. If it's because he still thinks of me as his savior, or if he really sees me, beyond the warrior. I want to puzzle through our time together, want to figure out the moment when maybe things started to change for us.

But I can't.

The more I try, the more his face mottles into Torrin's. I see Torrin holding that ziken head with my blood smeared across its teeth. I see the smile he had at my expense when he succeeded in his plan. I see him by Havard's side, the two of them relishing the moment as the venom takes hold of me and sends me sprawling on the ground.

Silent tears fall from my eyes. I wipe them away hurriedly.

Girls cry. Warriors don't cry.

Dammit, Father. I'm a person. I have feelings. I was so screwed over, and if I want to cry, I'm *allowed* to.

Once I give myself permission, a weight seems to grow light and float away from me.

I don't care what my father thinks of me anymore. I loved him, and he abandoned me the moment I didn't suit his purposes.

No one commands me out in the wild. I will behave the way I want to. I will be who I am, and I won't hate myself for it.

I was taught to be respectful to my parents, because it was part of Rexasena's teachings. It is one of the many things we must do to gain access into her Paradise. But will she forgive me if I don't believe everything my parents have said or done to me?

Instantly, warmth floods through me. I feel light as air, capable of doing anything, and most importantly, loved. Whether it's my own imaginings or the goddess herself strengthening me, I don't care.

"Thank you, goddess," I whisper, grateful for the comfort, wherever it comes from.

OVER OUR WELL-DESERVED hot meal, I ask Iric, "What did you decide to do with the head?"

He swallows the bite of meat he'd been chewing. "I buried it in enough salt for it to keep until I'm ready to head back to Restin."

"And when will that be?" I ask.

"I haven't forgotten our deal, Raz. Besides, I'm not heading home until Soren gets that damn feather."

Soren's body stills, his cup of water suspended over his lips. After a moment, he lowers his hand to the table. "You would . . . wait for me?"

"We're all going home. That was the deal. And I think I know the best way to do it."

"Do share," I say, my stomach now full of warm food. I feel ready to sleep a week, but we should discuss our next plan.

"It's safe to say that I would be useless climbing the mountain with Soren," Iric starts. "My skill doesn't lie in fighting, but in building." He turns his next words to Soren. "You and Raz should climb the mountain together. Meanwhile, I'll stay here and build that armor I promised Rasmira. It makes sense for us to do Rasmira's task last when there's so much we have to prepare for it. But you, Soren? You can battle a bird."

"We don't even know if the otti exists," Soren says.

"All the more reason for you to take Raz up there to check it out."

"Rasmira has no obligation to climb the mountain with me," Soren says. "You two had a bargain. Swimming lessons for armor. I can't offer her anything in return for her help."

I'm about to silence Soren's reasoning. I don't need anything in return for helping him climb the mountain.

But then I slam my mouth shut. I would never have even thought of offering my help a few weeks ago. I have my own task to tackle. Why would I risk my place in the goddess's paradise if Soren's not giving me anything in return?

Because I like him.

My cheeks warm without my permission.

But just as quickly, panic sets in. Liking Torrin is what got me banished to the wild. I *can't* like Soren.

But I do.

I hadn't realized it before, but now it's so obvious.

I like him. I want to help him, but I also have a promise to keep and fears to worry about and—

I put my focus into breathing and thinking. Breathing and thinking. That's all I have to do.

I don't want Soren to climb that mountain alone. I don't want him to die. But I also need every move I make in the wild to draw me closer to killing the god.

And then I get an idea as I realize something.

It would never be enough to walk back into the village carrying Peruxolo's head. He has the face of a man. No one would believe it was the god's. If I'm to return home, I have to publicly kill Peruxolo.

My father has to see the god's powers and see me defeat him. Somehow.

But would Peruxolo come if I issued such a challenge? What if he laughs it off? What if he visits his wrath on the villages instead?

But then I realize—

He can't. He wouldn't.

Not if I tell him all the villages have been invited to watch the battle. He'd want to come and show off his powers. He'd want to put me in my place for all the people to see. Instilling fear and awe in mortals is what Peruxolo enjoys most. Surely he wouldn't skip out on such an opportunity.

I only hope that I can find a way to come out on top.

"Soren," I say, cutting off the boys' argument, which I really hadn't been listening to anyway. "When I'm ready to challenge Peruxolo, I'm going to do it publicly. I want all seven villages to witness the battle. But I can't do that on my own. I'm forbidden to set foot in any village, but if you complete your task, you could deliver the invitations on my behalf. I will climb the mountain with you if you will travel to each of the seven villages and invite them to the battle."

Silence.

"That's not a terrible idea," Iric says.

"You'd be traveling through the wild alone," I say. "It could be dangerous—"

"I'll do it," Soren says. "It's a deal. When do we leave?"

"First thing tomorrow?"

"Works for me."

"Actually," Iric says, "I'm going to need your help tomorrow before I can get started on Rasmira's armor."

"What are you going to make it out of?" I ask. "The god's power deals with metal. Our iron armor can't get through the barrier, but we haven't had a chance to test other metals."

Iric grins proudly. "I wasn't planning on building you armor out of metal."

"If you think you're going to get away with making me wooden armor, you—"

Iric starts laughing. "I'm not going to build it out of wood, you impatient twit. I'm going to build it out of ziken hides."

I'm taken aback. Ziken hides. That actually—"That's brilliant!" I say. It's durable. Strong. No metal involved. And—"Do you think it would heal itself after being struck?"

"Only one way to find out."

"Iric, you are a genius."

"I'm not sure whether to be touched, or offended that it's taken you this long to realize that."

"Touched," Soren offers.

CHAPTER

17

The next morning, Soren and I pack for our trip up the mountain. It doesn't take long. My few possessions are always in my pack. It's mostly a matter of gathering food and blankets.

Then it's catching ziken for my armor.

"Typical," Iric says after the three of us have wandered for a quarter of an hour. "The beasts always show up when you don't want them to, but the moment you actually *need* one they're nowhere to be found!" He pauses after a few hundred yards to hack off the head of a snaketrap that's grown into the path and casts it aside. He does this every time he comes across one.

"Hasn't been able to stand the sight of the things after twisting his ankle in one," Soren whispers to me. "Happened after the first month we were banished."

I don't blame Iric in the least. The plants are vile, and the smell of a slowly digesting and rotting snake is hardly something one could forget easily.

Eventually, a ziken does cross our path. It's chasing some rodent through the undergrowth, but it stops as soon as it sees us. Soren, being the closest, decapitates it with two swings. One to knock it off balance and one to sever the head.

"Good," Iric says. He looks between the dead ziken and me. Looks me up and down. "I'll need two more to cover her in hides. Just in case."

By the time we catch two more ziken and drag the carcasses to Iric's forge, we've lost most of the day. Soren and I aren't about to start the climb when the sun will set soon, so we postpone a day.

Soren doesn't seem bothered by the delay. I would be beyond frustrated, and I'm impressed by his patience.

First thing tomorrow morning, we will start the climb.

AFTER A FULL NIGHT'S REST, Iric sees us off. "Don't die. I will be very put out if I go through all this trouble to make you armor only to have you snuff out of existence before you get to try it on."

I hide my grin. "Don't worry about me. I'm good at staying alive."

"Keep Soren alive for me, too."

"Of course."

Soren scoffs. "You're talking as if I'm useless with an ax."

"Nah," Iric says. "I'm only worried you'll be too distracted to keep an eye out for danger."

Soren darts a glance in my direction and grins. "I'll be fine."

Iric looks between the two of us. He sighs. "Also, if you two want to, you know, be together, you now have my blessing."

I blink several times before I can form words. "What are you talking about? We're not *holding ourselves back on your behalf.*"

"Whatever you tell yourself, Raz. Do whatever you like on the mountain, just do *not* tell me about it when you return. Oh, and do hurry. Some of us have our own romantic attachments we'd like to get back to. Have a lovely time! I'm off to the forge."

Iric spins on his heel and disappears down a trail. I'm left spluttering in his wake.

An awkward silence fills the space between Soren and me after that, so I start walking toward the road.

"You could have said something," I say as Soren falls into step beside me.

"Like what?"

"I don't know. At the very least you could have smacked him upside the head."

"I was so sure you were going to."

"I was too stunned to do anything. He's gotten cheekier."

Soren actually grins at that. "He gets that way when he's in a good mood. He's excited to see Aros soon. Won't you be in a good mood once you kill the god?"

"I don't know how I'll feel." I sidestep a dangling branch and leap off a tilting rock on the ground.

"Me neither. I've spent so much time worrying about Iric, I haven't had a chance to think about what completing my mattugr will mean for me."

We veer around a tree so large, its base is twice the width of the tree house.

"Iric said you used to be different," I say.

There's a hitch in Soren's stride. "What did he tell you?"

"You were arrogant and good at getting into trouble—and getting out of it. You were the best warrior in your village and the most sought after. Ladies hung off you."

Soren drags a hand down his face. "Ladies did not hang off me."

"No? What, then?"

"Well, they were there . . . It's just . . ."

"I'm beyond amused watching you fumble for words."

"It wasn't like I was with a different girl every night. I had a lot of friends who were girls, and they hung around, and—"

"So they did hang off you."

Now he glares at me. Actually glares. "And I suppose men didn't flock to you back in Seravin?"

"Are you joking? A girl acting in a man's job? One who wasn't delicate or feminine or pretty? They wouldn't come near me."

He huffs out a breath of air, as if waiting for me to turn it into a joke. Then he realizes I'm serious. He searches for the right words, and I'm suddenly mortified to think he's trying to make me feel better.

"A man who finds his masculinity threatened by a powerful woman is no man at all," he says. "You want someone who lifts you up, not tries to bring you down."

I don't know what I was expecting him to say, but certainly not those words. "I like that. Let me know if you find any men who fit those requirements."

He's smiling at me, as if I've been left out of the joke. "There are men from Restin who fit those requirements."

"I believe it. I rather like the two I've met so far."

The thick foliage opens up into the clearing at the mountain's base. Whatever Soren's reply might have been, it's cut off as he cranes his head back to take in the full height of the mountain.

"Just how long is it going to take us to climb this?" he asks.

"I don't know. I've never climbed a mountain before. Let's find out." I take a step into the clearing. The god's lair is far from here; I made sure we came out of the tree line nowhere near it.

We don't climb straight up, but rather zigzag so as not to be so winded by the incline. It's not terribly steep, but I imagine that after a few hours, we'll really start to feel it. The trip is painfully slow. Every other step sends a sprinkling of rocks tumbling down after us, and Soren and I slip frequently, catching each other before tumbling head over feet. Despite the distance we've kept from his lair, I fear we will draw the god's attention with the noise and tumbling rocks.

Eventually, we hit a patch of trees, and I relax because Peruxolo will no longer be able to spot us now that we have cover.

Soren, I notice, keeps glancing behind him. Not at the ground, exactly, but more like he's looking in the direction of the tree house.

"What's wrong?" I ask.

"This might have been a bad idea. We shouldn't have left Iric alone."

"You're worried about him."

"He's not a warrior. Anything could happen while we're gone."

"He's smart. He has his traps placed all around his forge and the tree house. He'll be fine."

"But what if something happens while we're gone?"

I reach out a hand and touch his shoulder, stilling him a moment. "You're a good friend to be concerned about him, but I think you've spent too much time worrying about Iric and not enough worrying about yourself."

"Worrying about Iric is all I've done for the last year."

"I know. You're a selfless person. May the goddess take note of it, but it's all right to take care of yourself as well. Iric forgave you, but you need to forgive yourself, too."

Soren glances at my hand on his shoulder before meeting my gaze.

"Thank you," he says. "I think you might be right, but it's hard to change."

"It's something you have to work at. I know better than anyone."

Soren reaches for my hand on his shoulder, and he threads our fingers together. "I like the changes you prompt in me."

I stare at our clasped hands, unable to move for a moment. I wait for Torrin to surface, wait for his mocking laughter to whisper in my ears and the phantom pain of the bite to take root in my arm.

But they don't come. Soren's hand in mine grounds me in the present.

A bad thing happened to me back in the village. There's no point in trying to pretend otherwise. I've spent so much time trying to forget. I put all my focus into killing the god, into helping Iric and Soren, because I couldn't deal with what came before.

But it's why I'm here. The goddess saw fit to test me in this overgrown, dangerous place. My own kind betrayed me, but I have survived nonetheless.

I'm glad I was banished.

The thought startles me, but I realize at once how true it is. If it hadn't happened, I wouldn't have met Iric and Soren, who have come to mean so much to me. I wouldn't have learned so much about myself and what I can do. I wouldn't have learned about teamwork and survival. I wouldn't have learned so much about the god.

I may have lost much.

But I have also gained much.

And I am better for it.

Acceptance settles within me, and I finally look up.

"Are you all right?" Soren asks. "Is this okay?" He gives my hand a little squeeze so I know what he means.

"When we first met, you asked me if I had a boy waiting for me back in my village. I don't."

He grins at me, and we continue climbing, this time hand in hand.

EVENTUALLY, WE CONNECT WITH a thin stream of runoff during one of our cutbacks. We both pause to drink deeply from our canteens, then refill them.

"Where there's water, there will be animals nearby," Soren says.

He's not wrong. We pass by no fewer than three goats in the next crossing. They have great, sweeping horns that jut over the tops of their heads, but they give us no trouble, hopping away as soon as we're spotted. They have incredible strength in their back legs as they leap at least ten feet in the air to climb up ridges in the mountain.

"I wish I could jump like that," Soren says.

"And what would you do with such an ability? Jump over everyone's heads?"

"I'd make it up the tree house a lot faster."

"Just think of how much more you'll get done every day with the extra four seconds you save climbing the tree house."

He smiles, but then his eyes catch on something over my shoulder. Soren launches himself at me. We both go down on the ground, hard. At least he gets an arm beneath my head so it doesn't crack on the rocks below. Still, his weight nearly knocks the wind out of me. My armor clinks against the rocks, so if we're hiding from something, I have a hard time believing we did a good job.

Soren puts a hand over my mouth, but one look at my incensed stare has him lifting it off and using that hand to take some of the weight off me. After several seconds, he dares to peek over the fallen log I now notice is blocking us.

His head shrinks back down almost as soon as it clears the wood.

My heart beats rapidly at the unknown danger. Is it the god? Could he be up here?

And then I notice just how close Soren is to me. I can feel every point on his body lined up with mine as he's lying on top of me.

Soren isn't looking at me, though. He takes another look over the log, and I push against his stomach, trying to get him off me.

He doesn't budge, and a second later, a blur of brown vaults over the log we hide behind. I catch a glimpse of the underbelly. Tree-bark skin like the gunda, but unlike the gunda, it has four long legs that end in clawed paws. A tail whisks out behind it. It hits the ground several feet ahead of us and takes off running. Another goat ahead looks up from the stream in time to see the enormous cat and bolts with the feline close at its heels.

When they're both long out of sight, I say, "Next time, get off me so I can help you fight it."

"Sorry, I was too busy thinking about how I would get my ax off my back without it noticing."

I shake my head. At first, I think to be angry with him, but then I realize I would have done the same thing. I would have protected whoever was next to me first.

It's a warrior's instinct.

"I vote we put some distance between us and that thing." Soren stands and reaches a hand down to me.

I take it.

"Did you know cats could get that big?" he asks.

"No," I answer. There are a few kinds in the wild, but they're small, preying on rodents and valder. Some would even dare to come into the villages at night. They're harmless to people unless they feel threatened.

As we take to hiking once more, Soren looks over his shoulder frequently.

"If it caught the goat, it will be detained for some time, I'm sure."

"It's probably not the only cat on the mountain."

Seemingly without even thinking about it, Soren reaches for my hand.

And this time, there is no overthinking. This time, there is only a rush of heat where our hands meet.

With Torrin, everything was new. My skin tingled at his touch, a giddy sensation would take over my stomach. I was so eager to experience everything for the first time.

But Soren . . .

He put his own life at risk to help me get away from the god. He brought me food when he knew I must be close to running out, even showed me how I could obtain more on my own. He recognized that I didn't like accepting help from others, and he challenged me.

I like that.

I like him.

It's not about giving in to the first boy who ever acted interested.

It's about being interested in the boy who is finally worth it.

Soren was interested in me from the first time we met. He made that clear, but once he realized how that made me uncomfortable, he stopped. He found less obvious ways to be near me, to help me.

And now I find myself wanting to be for him what he is to me.

CHAPTER
18

As the day grows later, we decide to stop and figure out how we're going to best survive the night.

"Climbing up a tree won't help us this time," Soren says. "Cats clearly love heights."

Eventually, we find a section of the mountain so steep, it's practically a wall, and it serves as an excellent cover for our backs.

"This will work great," I say.

Soren and I get to work on building a fort similar to the one I first built in the wild. We use our axes to cut and shape tree branches. We prop them against the rock wall, leaving a small hollow underneath. It takes only an hour to get everything just right, piling on the branches so thickly that very little light can get in. It will certainly keep any animals from spotting us. A thick strip of fallen bark serves as a makeshift door. Bless the wild for all the sturdy wood.

I cover the rough ground inside our shelter with as many leaves as I can find, using only the ones from trees I recognize to be safe. Some leaves in the wild sting to the touch. Others give off an aroma that attracts bugs. And some release their pigment and stain the skin. Since none of that is ideal, I stick to what I know.

Even after that, the ground is still so very hard.

"Maybe we should lie atop the blankets," I suggest.

"The night will grow too cold." Soren pauses. "We could share. Put one blanket below both of us and the other on top."

"All right."

We eat a dinner of dried meat and berries outside before turning in for the night. Our lean-to is cozy. There's barely enough room for us to lie side by side. It's so much more practical for us to share the blankets than for us to each have our own.

We squish our packs and axes down by our feet, and then Soren pulls the top blanket over the two of us. I'm scooted over just far enough that there's a small gap between Soren's body and mine.

Even then, I'm far too aware of his body. His hand is only an inch from mine. He smells of pine and freshly churned dirt, which I wouldn't have thought would be intoxicating, but it is. I sense the rise and fall of his shoulders as he breathes, hear him shift as he tries to get more comfortable.

Despite the uncomfortable sleeping arrangements and Soren's presence, I drift off eventually, but sometime in the night, I wake, shivering. The elevation has brought with it a distinct chill.

But at my side, I can feel a wave of heat radiating off Soren. He's like a fire. How is that even possible?

I try not to wake him as I scoot over, pressing my front to his back. Heat curls into my arms, and I sigh at the warmth.

But I think I woke Soren.

A slight hitch in his deep breaths is the only outward sign.

He doesn't say anything, so I ask, "Is this okay? Sorry to wake you, I'm just so cold."

He rolls toward me, and I back up against that rock wall, giving him room to move.

"Come here," he says when he's facing toward me. I'm unsure at first, but the promise of warmth is too much to resist.

"Turn around," he says, and I realize why as soon as I do. We fit so snugly with my back pressed to his front. His legs curve against mine. One of his arms rests under my head, giving me a pillow, while the other wraps around my front to press me even closer to him.

"Better?" he asks.

"Mmm," I say. I'm already starting to drift off, I'm so comfortable.

There's the lightest pressure on the back of my neck. His lips, I think. But I'm already so far gone, I can't be sure.

AN OBNOXIOUS LIGHT DARTS across my eyelids. I open them only to be momentarily blinded. A small gap in the branches allows a beam of sun right into my face. I adjust my neck, trying to get my head at a better angle, when I realize what's in front of me.

Soren.

I must have rolled over in the night. His face is inches from mine, our breath mingling. His lashes are draped over his eyes, his face completely relaxed in sleep.

I realize just how much I like that face, once I'm free to look at it so openly. The scars from warrior training suit him, giving him a roguish look. He has a heavy brow, a smooth forehead with brown locks falling across it, a nose that might be a bit too small for his face, but it's hardly noticeable with such perfect-looking lips.

I'm struck with the desire to trace them with a finger, which surprises me. Must be because it's morning—a sleep-addled brain clouds judgment.

I pat Soren on the shoulder instead. "Wake up. We should get moving."

He doesn't move, so I hit him a bit harder.

He jolts awake, sitting up too fast. His head smacks against one of the branches overhead.

"Ow," he says, rubbing his head.

"Sorry. You were out like a rock."

"I . . . had a hard time falling back asleep."

That would be my fault. "I shouldn't have woken you last night."

"It's fine. Now we'll know how to start out tonight. Then you won't have to wake me."

My cheeks warm at the prospect. I shove aside the makeshift door of our lean-to and stretch in the morning air. It is still cool, but the morning is already alive with movement. Lizards up in the trees snort. Birds in the distance call to one another. Against the rock wall, I barely catch sight of camouflaged moths, the only giveaway being the outline of their gray wings overlapping the slate. It's a beautiful day already, and it's easy to fool ourselves into thinking there is no real threat on the mountain.

After we eat breakfast and pack everything back up, we resume our climb, this time with sore muscles.

It's impossible to tell how much longer it will take to reach the peak. More and more trees cover the mountain the higher we climb. I can neither see the top nor the bottom.

The ground grows less rocky, more solid and stable, and the trees grow thicker. Animals that I've never seen before dangle from the trees by their knees. Unknown plants with bristly yellow leaves grow out of the ground. The wind carries scents from new trees that prefer the higher altitude.

When I first entered the wild, I remember being afraid of every unknown sound and creature. But here, everything is exciting, tinged with a sense of adventure. One that I'm happy to be taking with Soren.

He walks at my side, our strides perfectly matched. I catch sight of his hand swaying at his side. Before thinking twice about it, I reach out and grab it.

Soren looks up from his feet and fixes a boyish smile on me.

Blessedly, the rest of the day is mountain cat free. We climb as far as we dare before setting up camp once more. We find a good spot to build another lean-to, this time against a tree with a trunk so wide it might as well be a wall.

"Might rain tonight," Soren comments as we finish. "Good thing we found a tree for extra shelter, but let's lean some leafy branches across it just to be safe."

The extra time we take turns out to be well worth it after we climb inside. While I can hear the light rain outside, not a drop reaches us.

Soren stretches out across the blanket while I situate the packs down at our feet. When I'm done, he holds open the top blanket—and his arm—for me to crawl inside.

I'm turned into him this time, my forehead pressed against his chest. His hand moves in circles across my back.

"You don't have to tell me," Soren says. "I've asked you this before, but I thought maybe now you might want to answer. Did someone close to you break your trust?"

I swallow. "Yes."

Soren pulls me closer, his other hand never letting up on its soothing motion at my back. He's quiet, letting me fill the space, should I choose.

I'm surprised to find that I'm ready to share my whole story with someone.

"There was—is—a boy back in my village. His name is Torrin." There is something about talking, about saying his name aloud, that is so freeing. I tell Soren the whole story. I tell him about my misplaced trust. About my mother who betrayed me at the first opportunity. About how my father turned on me so quickly.

Soren's cheek rests against the top of my head as he holds me against him, letting me finish.

"If I've seemed so single-minded in my desire to kill the god," I say, "it is because I have so much to set right. I want to be with my family again, but I also need to reveal the wrongs done against me. I want to go back to Seravin and truly earn the respect of my fellow warriors by behaving as a leader should."

I breathe deeply, relishing the feeling of sharing the burden of my story. Finally.

"Thank you for telling me," Soren says. "I'm so sorry you had to go through all of that."

"I'm not. Not anymore. Not when I think of how the wild has changed me. I'm better for it."

"I know what you mean. I think I'm better for my own banishment, too. And better for having known you. I hope you know—I'm not like this boy-child, Torrin. I don't—"

I lift my head up so I can see his face and press a finger to his lips. "I know you're not."

Instead of lifting my finger, I leave it there, letting it trace his lips. I don't know if I feel brave because it's dark or because Soren now knows everything and he's not shying away from me.

There's a shift in his body. His hand returns to my back, ghosting up and down my spine. The fort gets hot. But not uncomfortable. Though perhaps unbearable. In a good way.

And just as I realize I want him to, he kisses me.

My breath leaves me. I wasn't prepared for the gentle pressure, for the sensation that shoots down to my toes. It's more delicious than I could have imagined, the way his mouth moves against mine. Kissing is a bit wetter than I expected, but after a while, I don't even notice. Soren smells like all the good things in the wild: the freshness of a morning after it has rained, newly cut branches, crushed pine needles. His thumb at my cheek strokes in time to his kisses.

As soon as I understand the right motions to make, I take control of the kiss, pressing my lips just a little more roughly over his, moving them faster.

His response is immediate. He matches my tempo without hesitating. His hand goes to the lowest part on my back to draw me closer. My hands are wedged against his chest, but I want to feel more of him, so I slide them up his neck, across his cheeks, into his hair.

Oh, I like having them in his hair. Not only are the strands so smooth, but I can better move my lips when I can keep his head just where I want it.

He surprises me when a soft wet pressure goes to the seam of my lips.

His tongue.

I'm unsure what he wants, but I open my mouth to him and—

Now there's even more sensation as his tongue strokes against mine, and it's so glorious. I'm drowning in him, yet I feel engulfed in flames at the same time.

Being wanted. *Knowing* that I am wanted is the most glorious feeling in the world.

And I do know he wants me. I feel it in his kisses. Feel it in his arms wrapped around me. And lower, where one of my legs is caught between his, where my stomach is pressed so tightly against him it would be impossible not to feel just how much he wants me.

He pulls away for a moment, his head flying upward so he can breathe. "Rasmira," he chokes out. "I need a moment."

And I realize then that unless I want things to go even further, I need to let him compose himself. I debate for a second. Do I want to go further?

Not yet, I decide.

I pull my lips away, try to detach myself from him, but he holds me in place.

"Don't go," he pleads, "just hold still a moment."

I listen to his rapid breathing. Feel his heartbeat pounding against my own. He presses his forehead against mine, and I revel in the closeness. I desperately want to close that distance, but I wait, my body nearly shaking from wanting, my lips feeling swollen but eager for more.

He wraps his arms around me, tucks my head under his chin. "Sleep," he says.

"Are you joking?"

He laughs. "We have another busy day tomorrow. Maybe we'll even reach the mountaintop."

"Sleeping is the last thing I want to do," I whine.

"Good," he says. "But I think it would be safer if I only kissed you during the daytime."

"Safer? You mean easier."

"Perhaps."

"I thought you liked a challenge."

"I have a feeling you'll be challenging me a lot."

I smile, even though he can't see it. "Of course."

He kisses me again.

I WAKE TO FIND Soren already watching me. His lips curve into a smile as soon as he sees I'm awake.

"Good morning," he says.

It only takes a second for last night's kisses to come back to me. I go warm *everywhere*.

"Morning," I say.

"How did you sleep?"

"Aside from the fact that I got less of it than I did yesterday, rather well."

"Not me. I slept way better."

He won't stop looking at me. My eyes flit everywhere. Everywhere but at him. The discomfort is astounding after how nice last night was.

"Rasmira, look at me."

I manage it.

"Do you regret what happened now that it's daytime?" he asks.

"No," I say hurriedly. "You just keep looking at me."

"I'm staring. I'm sorry. It's just—"

"What?"

He leans down and presses his lips to mine. "Now that I've kissed you, your lips are all I can think about."

Despite our less-than-comfortable sleeping arrangements, it would be far too easy to stay in this lean-to with him all day.

"I think I have a solution for that," I say.

"Let me guess, climbing?"

"You're so smart."

Today's trip is less productive. Soren trips more than once because he's looking at me instead of the ground, and I laugh at him.

Then there's the fact that our climbing keeps getting interrupted with kisses.

I could blame Soren, but it's not always him. I put a halt to our progress just as often by pushing him up against the nearest tree.

At one point, we stop to refill our canteens. Soren is bent over the stream while I take in the scenery below the mountain.

"I can see the villages from up here. There's Seravin. And Restin is only a bit more north, right?"

"Yes."

"So there it is. Then there's Mallimer and the rest sprawling northward. And the wild! It goes on forever. Come look, Soren!"

"I may have overcome my fear of heights, but I don't think I should see just how high up we are. I'll settle for listening to you describe it."

"The trees grow thicker more to the north. And—they're

241

greener. I wonder what we'd see on the other side of the mountain! Do you think the wild continues on in an endless expanse or would we see something new?"

"When we discover the otti bird to be only a myth, we'll have all the time we want to explore it."

My heart drops a moment. What if Soren is never allowed to go home? What if he is doomed to stay in the wild forever?

I won't let that happen.

I pull Soren to me in a fierce hug. "You won't be stuck out here alone. I will earn my place back as my father's heir, and I will change things. I will find a way to bring you home."

He returns the embrace, and we stand like that for a while, just holding each other.

But over his shoulder, I see a hint of movement. It blends in almost perfectly with the surrounding trees. If it weren't for its open eyes staring fixedly at us.

I whisper, "Don't move."

My hands go to the sheath at Soren's back. So very slowly, agonizingly slowly, I begin to slide the ax upward.

The mountain cat doesn't blink as it watches Soren and me. I wonder if it's the same one from before. Perhaps the goat got away and it followed our trail until it caught up with us?

Its haunches sway back and forth, steadying, readying to pounce. In a decisive move, I rip the ax the rest of the way from the sheath and sidestep Soren. I feel pressure on my back, but I ignore it. Because as soon as I decided to move, so, too, did the cat. It leaps forward and sprints the few yards to us, before leaping again, this time with the intent to pin me.

My mind works at an impossible speed. I should dodge the strike and go for one of the clawed legs, but sidestepping leaves Soren open. If only I had my ax, I could activate the spike and get the cat in the neck as it lands.

Instead, I shove Soren's ax straight ahead of me and brace myself for impact. The two tips of Soren's double blades pierce the cat's chest, but only just. That thick skin holds against the force of its own pounce. Its back legs land on solid ground, but the front—

They go to my shoulders and dig in.

At first, I think my armor will hold, but there's a *chink* sound, and then needle-sharp pain. The cat bends at the neck, trying to bring its gaping jaws closer, but I hold my arms steady, letting the weight of the cat dig deeper against the ax. My arms tremble from the force of it.

Out of the corner of my eye, a slice in the air, a blur of a blade.

My ax in Soren's hands.

He embeds it deep in the cat's back. Trapped with my blade beneath it and Soren's above it, it can do nothing except extend its claws, digging them deeper into my shoulders.

I set my teeth, let a wisp of air snake through, as I hold back a scream.

Soren dislodges the ax, and the cat releases me, backs up so it can take us in, readying to strike again. Brown-black blood drips from its chest onto the ground.

Everything darkens all of a sudden. Out of the corner of my eye, I can see a shape blocking part of the sun. Not a cloud, something nearer and swifter. I'm torn between not taking my eyes off the cat and seeing what the blur of movement is.

It's growing closer. Growing bigger.

It's coming right for us.

I can't help it.

I look.

Blue and white, a mixture of cloud and sky. A perfect camouflage—just like everything else in the wild.

As if the otti bird needed the extra advantage.

Razor-sharp talons that match the azure of its underbelly stretch out, each one the size of an arm. They clamp firmly over the middle of the great mountain cat. The feline didn't even hear it coming.

A mighty growl lets loose, but it's nothing to the shrieking *caw* of the victorious bird. It takes off in flight, the great cat clutched in its talons. Wings flap against the ground, sending rocks tumbling over themselves. I waver, nearly knocked over from the wind gust. Soren reaches a hand out, whether to steady me or himself, I don't know.

And we watch as the bird and cat disappear from sight.

With a grin, I turn to Soren. "It's real."

CHAPTER
19

"Don't just stand there," I say. "Let's go. It went that way." Soren still stares at the last point he saw the bird before it disappeared. I wave a hand in front of his face. He blinks and finally turns his head away.

"I didn't think we'd actually find it!" he shouts. I step back at his loud exclamation, one composed of sheer shock. "Sorry," he adds.

"We did. And it's getting away."

"It's already gone."

"But the trail is fresh, you idiot. Let's go!"

He finally finds his feet and starts upward again, trailing along to the right, the direction the bird went off in. It was definitely going toward the peak, but from a slightly different angle.

Soren leads this time, his motivation escalated by the sight of the bird that could be his salvation. I trail behind, not saying anything. My excitement grows as I watch Soren's grow. He picks up the pace, his breathing frantic, but knowing how close we are seems to give him more energy.

I'm staring upward, trying to guess how much farther until we reach the top, when I hear Soren stumble.

He must have fallen onto his back, because by the time I see him, he's moving himself to a sitting position.

"What happened?"

"I must have run into something?"

He says it like a question. Up ahead, clumps of enormous boulders lie about the area as well as some trees, but they're too far away for Soren to have stumbled into.

I step past him, thinking perhaps he stepped into a hole in the ground and stumbled, but I can't see how that would have sent him falling backward rather than forward.

I connect with something solid and teeter backward, but I manage to catch myself. I look back at Soren on the ground, whose expression is just as puzzled as mine. He watched me the whole time, saw that I ran into . . . nothing.

I reach out my hands in front of me.

They connect with solid air at the wrists.

"It's just like the god's lair," I say. "This is exactly what it felt like when I tried to enter."

"Could he be close?" Soren whispers, eyes flitting about our surroundings.

"Or he doesn't want us approaching this part of the mountain. Perhaps it's part of his domain."

We wait, not daring to move, in case the god is nearby.

But after a few minutes of not being struck down by inhuman forces, we relax.

"You said the barrier keeps out metal?" Soren asks.

"Yes, but we can't very well leave our armor and axes behind to climb the peak. Not after our mountain cat attack. We'll circle this area. Maybe there's a break. Peruxolo's power can't encompass the whole mountain or else we wouldn't have made it this far."

With one forearm pressed against the invisible wall, I start walking in a direction parallel to it, Soren trailing behind me.

Only about twenty feet later, my arm falls through the nothingness with no resistance.

"It's gone," I say, turning toward the peak once more.

We start the upward incline, but it's only seconds before we run into another wall.

"What the hell?" Soren says.

Our frustration growing, we walk along the new wall until it disappears, then continue the climb upward.

Our path turns into an invisible maze as we avoid the god's power. We backtrack, zigzag, go in what feels like circles—just so that we can find a path that isn't blocked by the invisible wall.

"We'll never find the bird like this," I huff after running into yet another barrier.

"We're making progress," Soren says.

"Barely."

"Before you arrived, I'd never even set foot at the base of this mountain. This *is* progress. Don't give up on me now."

That stops my complaining instantly. I'm doing this for Soren, because I want him to be free to return to the villages. And I need his help to publicly face the god. We can do this.

But all these barriers—it's like the god is taunting me. Does he know I'm alive? Why is he protecting this mountain peak?

A bird's call draws both our gazes upward. We can't see the otti. Not from where we stand.

But that sound—it's *close*.

Soren flies up the mountain with me right behind him. We're met with the god's power only once more before we halt and drop to our stomachs.

We lie at an incline, our heads just barely grazing over the tops of the rocks. Up ahead, a nest made of branches and weeds is perched atop a circling of rocks. The nest itself is half the size of the tree house. And inside, a mess of little squawks and fuzzy blue heads.

A tail flicks upward, not that of a fowl—but the large mountain cat that had been caught less than an hour earlier. The hatchlings are tearing through it. I now make sense of an assortment of other noises. Swallowing and ripping. I cringe.

"Where's mama bird?" Soren asks.

From our hidden position, we try to take in all the surrounding trees and cliffs, but the great otti isn't in sight.

"Will one of the hatchlings work?" I ask.

"They're too small; they haven't grown feathers yet."

Right.

"She can't have gone far," Soren says. "Let's wait her out."

"What's your plan?"

"Well, she's a bird. At some point, she'll come sit in her nest. I'll sneak up behind her and take a feather."

I whip my neck in Soren's direction. "You want to approach her while she's in her *nest*? She'll be the most volatile then! And, what, you think she'll just let you walk away after yanking out one of her feathers?"

"Do you have a better idea? No matter what, she's going to be volatile!"

I think for a moment. "What supplies did you bring?"

"Other than food and a change of clothes?" He pauses. "Actually, I did bring a net, but it's far too small to fit over the giant bird."

"Let me see it."

He frees the net from his pack and hands over the tangle of ropes. I stretch it out on the ground behind us. I shrug my pack from my shoulders and pull out a coil of rope. With a knife, I cut it into four strips, then tie each strip to one of the corners of the net, lengthening the ends and giving us better handholds.

"It won't cover her wingspan," I say, "but perhaps her head and back? If we can just pin her long enough, you can get close enough to grab a feather."

Soren looks from the net to me. "That's a much better plan. Let's do it."

UP IN THE TREES, I stand on two separate branches, holding the net, waiting for Soren's cue. As I watch him kneeling behind a boulder, waiting for the otti's return, I want to laugh at him.

His master plan was to just sneak up on the bird and take a feather.

Honestly, how did he even survive before I was banished to the wild?

I don't think he's ever excelled at thinking before acting. No wonder Iric said he used to get into trouble all the time.

One of my legs starts to cramp, so I attempt to stretch it out without toppling out of the tree. It would be so much better if we could set the trap on the ground and rig it to spring upward and catch the bird when she steps on it—but with those sharp talons, she'd shred through the rope in seconds.

This trap has to be sprung from above, and Soren needs to be on the ground, ready to pluck a feather once the great bird is caught.

If only she'd bother to show up.

The hatchlings still take their time with their meal. A fuzz-covered head lifts into the air with a chunk of meat held between its beak. It uses gravity to help force the hunk of mountain cat down its throat.

My eyes swivel back to Soren's hiding place, only to see that he's no longer there.

He's creeping toward the nest.

"Soren, what are you doing?" I ask in a loud whisper.

"Speeding things up."

Something sinks low in my chest, and I have the burning urge to rush to him as I watch him advance toward the nest.

Idiot. He's out in the open.

But I hold my ground. He's going to lead the otti to me, and I have to be ready.

But my throat closes off as I watch Soren draw closer.

During Iric's mattugr, there was fear for him, fear for all of us—but now—

This is different. Nothing can happen to Soren. I couldn't bear it. I feel the seconds tick by like a hammer against my heart.

When he's ten feet from the nest, the wind picks up, sending Soren's hair over his shoulders.

At five feet from the nest, there's a loud chirp as one of the hatchlings eyes Soren warily. There are five hatchlings in total, and the others soon spot Soren. The sounds of eating cease. Earsplitting chirps ratchet up from the nest, clear sounds of distress. The birds rise onto their toes, each one as tall as Soren's arm.

A faint whooshing sound stirs the air.

"Soren, she's coming!"

I can't see her yet. The sky hides her too well, but Soren must spot her, because he suddenly darts toward me.

My heart races as he clears the tree line, and the otti finally comes into view. She lands on the ground just before the trees, her wings sending the branches swaying. Soren, breath heaving, comes to a stop just below where I wait with the net, and we both watch the bird. She tucks her wings to her sides and hops a step forward. Talons crunch against rock as she leaps her way around trees and over boulders, drawing closer and closer, her mouth open, releasing angry caws into the air.

Soren backs up slowly when he's sure the otti will take a straight path to him. She seems to gain both confidence and speed the closer she gets to him.

"Now!" Soren yells.

I drop the net, watch it land over the otti's head, back, and tail feathers, before climbing down the tree as quickly as I can to help.

Soren grabs the front two ends of the net, holding down while the bird rears her head. I scramble behind her to grab the back ends. She tries to buck, swivel her tail feathers, but with her talons pinned beneath her, she can't free herself from the net.

"It's all right," Soren intones. "We'll let you go in just a second. I need something first."

The otti turns her head to the side, sizing him up with one black eye. She tries to push her beak through a gap in the net.

And succeeds.

She snaps at Soren, who just barely manages to dodge it. With both rope ends clasped firmly in his hands, he sidesteps the bird, joining me in the back. The otti's neck turns with the motion, pinning her head against her side.

"She won't hold still," Soren says. He stumbles beside me as the otti attempts to raise her wings. "Damn."

He holds both of his ropes in one hand and reaches for one of the bird's long tail feathers.

There's a whisper of sound as the feather comes free, and I watch the bird's eyes dilate.

She flaps her wings madly, not in an attempt to fly, just to clear us away from her, and I lose my grip on the rope in my right hand.

"Soren!"

The otti gets a leg free with the opening I've given her, and she rises on that side, talons trying to find purchase on the ground.

Soren grabs the remaining rope in my hand, while I try to leap onto the bird's back for the end I let go of.

She bucks again, her freed leg finally finding purchase, and I tumble down her back before landing on the hard ground.

"Rasmira, are you all ri—oof!"

I crank my neck to see Soren pulled forward as the otti finds her other leg. She spins around and hops toward the opening in the trees.

And then—seeming to think better of it—

She launches herself in the air.

With Soren still dangling by the ropes.

What is it with that boy and not letting go?

Branches and twigs rain down on me as the otti forces her way through the canopy. Soren shrieks as he's yanked after her.

On the ground, I find the feather Soren pulled from the bird. I throw my pack over the top of it so it won't blow away. Then I race out of the tree line to find Soren.

The shrieks make him easy to locate.

He has his eyes firmly closed, and he holds on for dear life as the bird flies through the air. They dart left, sway right, drop a few feet—Soren gets dragged every which way as the bird tries to throw him and the net off.

Thank the goddess she's tucked her talons under her body for flight. Else Soren wouldn't be long for this world.

They're perhaps thirty feet in the air, far enough that Soren could sustain serious damage were he to fall. They sail over the nest of little birds, who chirp at the sight of their mother.

The otti is more weighed down on her left side, where two ends of the net are still firmly grasped in one of Soren's hands. They twirl in circles for a moment, before plummeting a couple more feet.

I'm chasing them down, flinching every time I think Soren's about to lose his grip. His legs kick uselessly in the air, the ax on his back worthless with his hands on the ropes.

The two figures cross over another grouping of trees, and I follow after them, plunging into the undergrowth. Through gaps in the trees, I can just barely make out Soren's kicking feet.

"Soren. Soren! Can you hear me?"

"Ahh." He likely still hasn't opened his eyes, blocking out the height.

"Soren, let go!"

"What?"

"Trust me. Let go now!"

With a mighty bellow, he releases his grip on the ropes and plummets toward the earth. He crashes into leafy branches, scrapes against a tangling of vines, gets whipped in the face by another branch—

And then I catch him.

We both go sprawling onto the ground.

I can't breathe, and I scramble to get Soren off. He groans and rolls over, but the wind's been knocked out of me.

"I take back what I said," Soren mumbles. "Your idea was terrible."

My breath whooshes back into me, and I find my feet before reaching a hand down to Soren and helping him up.

The trees above us crack, branches ripping from their trunks. Instinctively, I go for my ax.

Not fast enough.

I'm on the ground again. A sharp, tearing pain flares up in my arm, and I look up to see a smear of blood against one of the otti's talons. Leaves and twigs stick out of her feathers. A patch of sap clings to the side of her head. She must have let herself fall through the trees, talons first, getting lucky by nicking me on the way down.

The bird tries going for Soren with her sharp beak, but Soren has his ax out. He blocks and slashes, cutting through feathers and drawing blood.

The bird shrieks and rises into the air a few feet, this time darting out with her talons. Soren rolls, the talons glancing off the armor on his back as he does so.

I move.

Stepping up next to Soren, I brandish my ax, making huge sweeping motions with it from side to side. The twirling makes me seem larger, makes it harder for the bird to focus on one point as her eyes try to follow the ax's movements when she turns for her next attack.

With my distraction, Soren launches forward and prods the otti in the chest. Not deeply, but enough to puncture her. He doesn't want to kill her, I suspect.

With brown-black blood coating her beautiful azure feathers, the otti finally retreats. She leaps into the air, angling her body like a knife to slice through the canopy, and sails for her nest and little ones.

When she leaves, Soren and I look at each other.

I'm struck by the thought that we make a great team. We don't even need to communicate when fighting. Moving in tandem is instinctual, somehow. Together, the two of us are unstoppable with our axes.

Soren leans a shoulder against the nearest tree. "You're hurt."

"I'll be fine. We have to circle back around for the packs."

"The feather?"

"It's safe."

He lets out a breathy laugh.

I hide my glare by looking at the ground. "Tell me, what did you think you would accomplish by getting hoisted into the air? Were you in the mood for a stroll over the *treetops*?"

"If I hadn't, the bird would have attacked you. I didn't know what else to do, so I held on."

"Attacked me?" I ask incredulously. "Soren, I am a warrior! We could have fought her on the ground together. Like we just did!"

"I wasn't thinking!"

"I've been telling you to start thinking about yourself. Your safety is just as important as everyone else's!"

He steps up to me, forces my chin up with a finger. "Not to me it isn't. I want to keep you safe. I will always protect you. Please don't be angry for that."

I swallow. What was it Iric once said? Something about how hard it is to stay angry at Soren because of his loyalty.

"Don't scare me like that again," I say.

Soren leans in and presses a kiss to my lips. "I'll try not to. Thank you for your help."

My legs leave the ground as Soren sweeps me off my feet, holding me in his arms before I can protest.

"What are you doing?" I exclaim.

"You're injured. I'm carrying you."

"My legs are fine," I say as I swat his arm.

"I want to hold you. Now stop wiggling, and let's get you over to the medical supplies in the packs."

"I'm bleeding all over you."

"I don't care."

He silences my next protest with another kiss.

CHAPTER

20

Soren carries me the long way around to reach our packs, because he doesn't want to risk another run-in with the enormous bird. I protest the entire way, but secretly, I'm pleased. Maybe once I would have had an issue with it. I did ask Soren to treat me as he would any other warrior. But I've given myself permission to behave as I wish in the wild. I love how strong Soren is, and I love the feeling of being in his arms.

He sets me down once we reach the packs and retrieves strips of cloth from one of them to wrap my arm. Later we'll find clean water to rinse the injury. It might even need sewing. But neither of us can do that. That is more Iric's territory. He has experience from all the leather work that goes along with weapon-making.

Not that I care.

What's one more scar?

The god has scarred me. The hyggja has scarred me. A mountain cat. Now the otti. Each scar marks me as a survivor.

A warrior of the wild.

WE FIND OUR SHELTER from the previous night and decide to reuse it rather than make more progress down the mountain. We're both exhausted from the day's events anyway.

It's not even close to sunset, so Soren builds a fire, just so he has something to do. We don't have anything to cook over it. It's not even that cold yet. There's no practical reason for it.

I'm glad for it, though. The crackling of a fire is familiar and comforting. It reminds me of the hearth in my room. I remember nights when Irrenia would sneak out of bed and join me in mine. We'd talk for hours—about how our days went, about our struggles in our chosen professions, about the future and what we hoped for most.

I don't know what my future holds. Or even if my life will be long or short. But the present is full of more hope than ever before.

Soren holds the sky-blue feather in his left hand, while his right fingers brush the smooth strands. His eyes are on the fire.

I sit opposite him on a flat rock, the fire between us. Soren has grown quiet. I'm desperate to know his thoughts, but I won't ask unless he wants to offer them up.

"Iric was right," he says at last. "It doesn't feel any different. I've got the feather, but what does it prove? And the goddess—if her Paradise is now open to me again, shouldn't I *feel* it?"

I watch the flames twist around each other. "I've suspected for a while now that the mattugrs are no punishment devised by the goddess. I think they are something born of the traditions of men."

"I know I should be glad that I can finally return home, but I can't help but think of all the people who lost their lives to their mattugrs. How many died because they were left out here alone by their own kind?"

I rise from my seat and walk around the fire to kneel in front of Soren. "We can't change what happened, but I will make changes for the future. When I rule Seravin, I will try my best to make things right for my village. We can only hope to inspire change in the others as well."

Soren returns the feather to his pack before tugging on my hands. My head comes to rest against his shoulder.

"Is there a place for me by your side?" he asks quietly, tentatively. "While you inspire change and rule a village, will there be any room for me in your life?"

I smile, knowing he can't see it. "You're free to go home now. You can have your pick of all the girls back in Restin. I'm not your only option anymore. You wouldn't want to restrict your attention to just one woman, now, would you?"

His hands go to my shoulders; they tug me back gently so he can look at me. I can tell he's about to sputter off a series of protests, but then he sees my face. "You're messing with me."

I nod.

He brings his lips to my ear. "You might not be my only option anymore, but you're the one I choose. My fierce warrior woman."

"My helpless warrior man."

"You're never going to let me live down that ziken horde, are you?"

"Never."

I'm startled by the sudden pressure of his lips against my forehead. It's not like when I felt his lips against mine. The way I felt his heat and desire for me. This is different. It's loving. Makes me feel precious. As though gifting him with myself is the best thing I could ever do for him.

After his lips linger against my brow, he lowers, kissing each of my closed eyelids, my cheeks, the corners of my mouth.

I get my hands on either side of his face and move him to just where I want. His lips sweep across mine. So slow and smooth and perfect.

Our lips don't part until sometime much later.

We're both gasping for breath.

"We need to douse the fire."

It takes me a moment to realize he's talking about the literal fire behind me. No, in front of us.

When did I end up in his lap? How did we get turned around? And how is night already starting to creep up on us?

"Go douse it and come back, then," I manage.

He shoots me a grin, and it takes away what little breath I'd been gaining back.

While he does that, I prepare the lean-to, arranging the blankets and packs just where we need them.

My heart is pounding when Soren joins me inside. I wonder desperately if he will kiss me again.

He does. One lingering kiss before settling himself beside me. His arms go around me, holding me close.

"It's a good thing you've agreed to let me stay with you," he says. "I don't know if I could ever sleep without you in my arms."

"Not used to sleeping on your own, are you?"

"I went a whole year on my own."

"So there was a girl back in Restin," I say.

Soren presses his lips to my forehead, just as he did before. "There weren't any like you."

MY NOSE WRINKLES BEFORE I even open my eyes the next morning. "What is that smell?" I groan and stretch my limbs. They're sore from sleeping on the rock floor, from climbing this blasted mountain.

"I think that's us." Soren's voice comes from just behind me. "We've been sweating our way up a mountain. I also think I might have gotten otti blood on my clothes."

"Then we'd best find that stream today. Otherwise I don't think I can share another lean-to with you."

"You don't exactly smell like flowers."

I smack him playfully. "You're not supposed to say that."

"I've never lied to you," he says. "And I'm not about to start. Even if it means I have to tell you, you smell." His lips brush the back of my neck.

Oddly, it's one of the most romantic things he's ever said to me.

TRAVELING DOWN THE MOUNTAIN is so much quicker than the trip up. Unfortunately, it's also much easier to stumble. We'll be covered in bruises by the time we reach the bottom.

The otti feather is so long that it won't fit in Soren's pack all the way. The tip pokes out of the leather drawstring by at least five inches, following Soren down the mountain. His salvation.

Rocks skitter out of our way as we travel, some without us even kicking them. Curious, but I don't think much of it as I put most of my focus into not falling down.

It doesn't take long to find the stream (once we manage to navigate back around the invisible walls of the god's power), and we start to follow it downhill, looking for a broader opening where we might fully bathe.

"Yesterday," I say, "with the otti bird. I noticed you weren't trying to kill it. You only injured it enough to make it flee."

"That's right."

"I'm glad, even if it did take a swipe at me." My hand ghosts over the bandaged wound.

"My mattugr was to steal a feather, not kill the bird. The otti wouldn't have bothered us if we hadn't come into her territory. She minds her own business. Only hunts when she needs to. Much less evil than the hyggja."

I shudder. "That thing would eat anything that came close to its resting place, hungry or not. It was enough to make *me* wary of deep water."

"And Peruxolo—he is evil incarnate," Soren says. "He deserves to die for what he's done to our people. You shouldn't even hesitate to take his life when the time comes."

"He may bear the face of a man," I say, "but he is no man. He is something else, and I won't hesitate to end him."

"Good." Soren's gaze flicks past me. "We're in luck. The stream's opening up."

The stream widens and deepens into a slow-moving pool. The water is clear—I can see down to the bottom where the rocks gather. They shimmer at the bottom as the sun filters through the water. They must be filled with metal fragments. This mountain has never been mined. It must be rich with ore and other deposits.

"Ladies first," Soren says. "Let me know how cold it is."

"It's runoff from the mountain. It's going to be freezing."

"Would you rather be clean or warm?"

I take another sniff at my clothing. "Clean."

"I'll keep watch. I promise not to look."

"So noble."

He gives me a wicked grin before walking away, his back to me. I pull the armor sheets from out of my clothes and discard them by a tree. Then I shuck my boots and ax. I grab a bar of soap and clean set of clothes from my pack and walk to the pool's edge. Once there, I take off my clothes and place them within reach of the water.

I dip a single toe into the stream. *Freezing* is too gentle of a term for what it is. I can't fathom why there isn't ice floating along the surface. There's no easy way to do this. I take a deep breath and jump.

The cold is so intense it feels like needles are scraping my skin. I just stand there for a moment, waiting for my body to adjust.

"All good?" Soren shouts, his body facing firmly away.

"Th-the w-water is g-great. Just wait until i-it's your turn."

He laughs lightly. I pretend not to notice.

I soap down every inch of skin on my body twice. I lather the soap in my hair until bubbles stream down my arms. I take a deep breath and go down. A headache starts to form from the cold.

Once done, I heft myself out of the water and don my fresh set of clothing. I pull my hair out of my face, wrapping it into a braid. Then I let Soren know it's safe to look, but he stays where he is, keeping guard while I'm still vulnerable without my armor.

I grab my dirty clothes and plunge them into the water. I only have the one extra set with me for this climb, so I'd better clean these now.

As I scrub and scrub with the bar of soap, one spot won't come out. Blood from the cut on my arm, I think. I need something rougher to take to it.

About an arm's length away, I find a good-sized rock with a rough surface. I reach for it. The top shimmers in the sunlight, a bright metal vein glinting along it. I take the rock to my garment and scrub roughly. It does the trick, the spot coming right out. With the water running downhill, the soap doesn't build up; it washes downstream with everything else, so my clothes are free of soap in no time.

I climb from the pool, wring out my clothes, and find a nearby tree branch to drape them across to dry.

When that's done, I take the rock I found with me. Soren will want it for his clothes, I'm sure.

I start for the tree where I deposited my pack and armor, the rock in hand, when a force bats it from my palm.

I look up, but Soren still has his back to me a ways off. My head spins in a circle, looking for some intruder. I find nothing.

"Did you see anything?" I shout.

"Rasmira, I promise I kept my back to you while you were bathing. I didn't see anything."

My cheeks blush. "No, I mean, did you see someone or something?"

"No, why?" He turns toward me.

I look down at the ground, thinking perhaps someone threw something at my hand, but there's nothing but more rocks.

"I'm not sure yet," I say. I have to take a step backward to retrieve the rock. Gripping it more firmly, I head for my pack once more.

But I can't.

At first, I think it's the god's power that Soren and I keep running into along the mountain, but how could it be? I just walked this way fully clad in my armor. I would have felt it before.

Is there something different about this rock in my hand? Why can't I take it with me? Is it important to Peruxolo? Does he want it to stay near the stream? And if so, why?

Maybe all I need is a running start.

I take a few steps back, dig in my heels, and bound toward the tree. There's pressure against my hands—I almost lose the rock, but then something gives. I hear a crash in front of me, my head snapping up to see my armor no longer propped against the tree but on the ground.

"How did you do that?" Soren asks.

I take another step forward. Though there's extra pressure, the rock moves with me. And my armor—

The sheets skid away from me, never letting me grow closer to them.

All I can do for some time is look back and forth between the rock in my hands and my armor. I step all the way up to my pack, my armor now ten feet away to the side.

"Do you recognize this metal?" I ask, holding up the rock for Soren to see.

"It's brighter than iron," he says.

"And it clearly has a negative reaction with iron."

"Like a lodestone?" Soren asks.

"Yes, exactly like a lodestone, but different than the ones found in my village. This one is so much stronger."

"It's an interesting discovery, but why do you—" He cuts himself off, as he clearly comes to the same realization I've already had.

"This is why we haven't been able to take certain paths up the mountain," I say. "It's coated in whatever makes up this new lodestone, and it won't let our armor come anywhere near it. And Peruxolo's lair? I'll bet this metal rims the whole thing. It's why I wasn't able to enter. I could throw a rock inside because it must have not contained any iron within it. And Peruxolo's armor? It must be made out of this lodestone, too. That's why he was able to fling me around and why my ax couldn't touch him. He's bigger than me and must be wearing even more of the metal than the amount of iron I wear.

"He doesn't have power over metal," I say. "He's only using a lodestone against our iron."

CHAPTER
21

When Soren and I are less than a hundred feet from the mountain's base, we have to duck behind the nearest tree.

Peruxolo is outside of his lair.

"Where is he headed?" Soren whispers.

"I don't know. I've never seen him walk around the mountain's base. Maybe hunting?"

We are as still as the tree trunk at our backs, waiting for the god to move on.

Soren is the first to move once Peruxolo is out of sight, gauging the distance to the ground. "We'd better take a different route home."

"Wait."

"What?"

"Peruxolo is away from his lair."

"So?"

"I'm going in." I practically race the last several paces to the ground, before heading for the seam in the mountain.

Soren hits the ground a few seconds after me. "Rasmira! You can't! What happened to waiting for Iric's armor?"

"It's different now. I know it's not a godly power that's keeping me out, but a natural one! And we *know* Peruxolo isn't home. We're already here. This is too good of an opportunity to pass up."

Soren fidgets with one of the straps on his pack. "What can I do to help?"

"Keep watch. Give me a warning if Peruxolo comes back?"

"You got it. I'll hide over in the tree line. But, Rasmira—" He grabs the arm I'd been using to remove my armor. "Be careful. No risks. You're there to look. Don't touch anything. Just because the god is using a natural substance as a barrier, it doesn't mean there aren't magical defenses also in place."

I hand Soren my ax and armor for safekeeping. "I'll be careful. Now stop worrying."

I turn away from Soren and head for that dark gap in the mountain. My pace is a quick walk. The sensation of being flung around by an unknown power is not one I can easily forget. It makes me cautious, even if I now know the source of that power. I try to remember exactly where the barrier would halt me outside the seam in the mountain. Was it here? Or maybe a few steps forward?

But when my feet stop right outside the entrance, a proximity I *know* I never managed before, I know the truth for certain.

Peruxolo has been taking advantage of our isolated villages. No one else has access to this new lodestone, and he has been using it against us for centuries.

I stare down that dark crevice, wondering what I will find in the god's home.

And I enter.

I cannot see a thing for the first few steps. I stop and blink, willing my eyes to adjust. Eventually, I can make out the walls, made entirely from the new metal that reacts negatively with my armor and ax.

I put one hand to the wall and traverse deeper. The farther I go, the less I can see. Just when I worry the darkness will envelop me completely, my foot bumps against something on the ground.

Bending down, I reach for the item.

A torch, and next to it—

Flint and pyrite.

So the god cannot see in the dark.

I light one of the torches, holding it high in my left hand. If anything or anyone else is in here, I'm doomed, for the torch will give me away immediately.

There's nothing to be done for it now. I'm committed. Whatever secrets this opening holds, I will learn them.

After perhaps twenty more steps, I come to a gate. It's a metal contraption pounded into the rock on either side. It can't be to keep mortals out, for that is the lodestone's job. Perhaps it is to keep the dangerous ziken away?

I find where the gate connects in the center. A length of rope ties the two halves together. I take careful note of the knot, so I can replicate it before I leave, before undoing it and forcing the gate outward.

It opens to a cavern full of comforts.

A massive mattress heaped with blankets and furs. Chairs topped with lavish cushions. Rugs made from animal skins cover the floor. Off to one side are the water barrels from the Payment. A cabinet is full to the brim with the pickled vegetables and preserved fruits from the Estavor village. On a table are leather pouches holding dried meat. Enough food and water to last a single person for several years.

The only things out of place are the shackles dangling from one of the walls, blood crusted to the metal. They rest atop an empty bed. I realize it must be where he keeps the woman sacrificed to him each year. How long was the one I watched dragged away from the clearing kept here before she died? And what did Peruxolo do to her?

Perhaps it's cowardly, but I don't want to know. The important thing is that I can stop another girl from ever being sacrificed if I can kill him.

At the far end of the cavern is another path, and I follow it even deeper into the mountain, wondering what I'll find next. But as I travel, I realize the path doesn't curve deeper, it moves back around toward the mountain's edge. Light filters in up ahead, growing more and more bright as I approach. Another entrance.

Whereas the opening I took was a mere slit in the mountain, this entrance is gaping.

And for good reason.

It's a forge.

Branches hang down over the entrance, providing it with some camouflage while still allowing in plenty of airflow. A larger gate blocks the opening, so nothing can get in. In the ceiling are several openings that appear to have been crafted for ventilation.

The oven is similar in shape to Iric's. But the castings lining the walls are different, and I can't make sense of what they're used to make.

Resting against an anvil are a hammer and a metal sheet about the length of a man's foot. Little metal triangles are scattered across a table, but they are made from a different metal than the new lodestone, something darker. The edges are sharp—I nearly cut my finger when running it against one of the triangles. Also atop the table is one of Iric's traps. Did Peruxolo stumble across one? He's started taking it apart. Was he examining it? Trying to learn how to replicate it?

I hold my hand over a barrel that appears to be full of ash. When I don't feel any heat emanating off it, I dip in my hand and let the substance slip through my fingers.

Metal fragments. Iron, I think. What is that for?

There is much more to see in the god's forge, but I've tarried long enough. It's time to leave.

My head swims with images of all the things I discovered in the god's lair as I trek back through the cavern. I have even more questions than before. What are all the things he builds in his forge used for? Why does an immortal god rely on natural elements to keep us afraid?

At least I can say I've confirmed my theory.

Peruxolo uses lodestones to keep mortals out of his home. He wears them as armor so no one can approach him.

But now I know how I can approach him. I know one of his secrets, and I think it's time someone challenged Peruxolo to a fair fight.

I retie the knot on the gate just as it was so he will be none the wiser and take the spent torch with me. I leave the mountain and head for the tree line where Soren hides.

As we take a long route home, Soren asks what I found, and I tell him everything.

"Iron fragments in a barrel? Sharp metal triangles? What does it all mean?"

"I don't know," I answer. "But I don't care. I think I'm ready to face Peruxolo."

Soren nearly trips. "Ready! How can you be ready? It would take years to study Peruxolo and learn all his secrets. Learning one doesn't mean you'll survive against him in a fight!"

"The important thing is that he doesn't know what I've learned! He'll think I can't get anywhere near him because of the iron. Iric's ziken-hide armor will change that. It will make the battle a fair fight!"

"What about your ax? You still don't have a weapon that can defeat him."

"I have the silver dagger he tried to kill me with."

"It won't do you any good against a battle-ax."

It's true. I need a new weapon, but—"The mountain is full of this new metal! I could ask Iric to make me an ax from the new lodestone. Peruxolo's weapon must be made from the same metal. Then the battle would be fair."

Soren scoffs. "Rasmira, you're forgetting one important thing."

"What's that?"

"Peruxolo is centuries old. He's had *centuries* to practice the ax. You've only had ten years! Just because you can finally reach him with your weapon, it doesn't mean you can defeat him in battle. The battle will in no way be fair."

The words hit home, making me feel like a speck of dirt, an insignificant being when compared to a mighty god.

"Just whose side are you on?" I ask.

Soren reaches out a hand and takes one of mine, never missing a step. "I'm on your side. I just want to make sure that when you go into battle, you will come out the victor." He gives my hand a squeeze.

"There is no guarantee. There never will be. Even if I spent the next fifty years of my life training, I wouldn't catch up to Peruxolo's skill. The only advantage I have is knowing his secret. If I wait for the right time to strike, perhaps he won't see it coming."

"Perhaps." But Soren doesn't sound convinced.

We fall into silence as we walk, but my mind is turning. Soren and Iric have completed their quests. Now it's my turn. I finally have an advantage over Peruxolo.

All I need is a plan.

IT'S NEAR DARK WHEN we finally reach the tree house. Smoke billows out of the chimney, and the smell of meat wafts down to us. I miss hot food.

Soren climbs ahead of me, and when he gets through the trapdoor, I see Iric launch himself at his friend, gripping him in a hug.

"You made it back! The feather?"

Soren turns to the side so Iric can see the hint of blue peeking out of his pack. "Right here."

"Take it out! Let me get a proper look at it!"

I cough loudly. "I don't suppose you two could scoot over so I can come in?"

Iric looks through the hole in the floor. "Raz, you made it, too!" He holds down a hand to me and hoists me the rest of the way up.

"Did you ever doubt I would?"

"Of course not. Now tell me everything."

Iric sews up the gash in my arm while Soren talks. The needle bites into my skin again and again, a pain worse than the initial slash from the bird.

"How is it that you're always the one who gets injured?" Iric asks.

"Probably because I'm always sticking my neck out for you two."

Iric grins while Soren has the good sense to look guilty.

As Iric finishes off the last stitch, he asks, "And did you have a nice time together?" The tone of his voice makes it very clear what exactly he means by that.

My cheeks heat up, and I find myself looking anywhere but at Soren.

Iric laughs. "You two are so utterly predictable."

I hear a smack, probably Soren taking a swing at Iric. "Leave her alone."

"So long as there is no touching in front of me, I won't say another word."

"Why, Iric? Would that make you *uncomfortable*?" I ask. Feeling brave all of a sudden, I stand up, move over to where Soren is seated in his chair, and place myself in his lap.

Iric's eyes narrow. "Stop that."

My arms go around Soren's neck.

"Rasmira, don't you—"

And I lean in for a kiss. Soren is more than happy to play

along. His hands press into my back, and before I know it, he's tilting me backward.

A gagging noise comes from behind us. "Okay, stop! You've made your point. Please! Dear goddess, stop!"

It's awfully difficult to focus on Soren when Iric is yapping in the background. Soren's lips turn up into a smile against mine.

"Do we take pity on him?" I ask.

"I'd rather not."

"Rasmira, I swear I will dump the new armor I made you into the gunda-guts-infested lake if you don't stop this instant!"

That gets my attention. "You finished it?"

"I will not say another word until you sit in your own chair!"

I sigh, but rather than do as he says, I simply turn, pressing my back against Soren's front, so our mouths aren't anywhere near each other.

"That's as good as you're going to get," I say. "Now talk."

Iric narrows his eyes, but he gives in. "It's done. Should fit you like a glove. I'll take you to see it tomorrow."

"Good, I'm going to need it. I think it's time I challenged the god."

Soren freezes underneath me as Iric's eyes widen. Soren hadn't gotten to the part in our story where we learned about the lodestone and I explored Peruxolo's lair, so I tell Iric the rest now.

"So you need a new ax," Iric says after I finish.

"Yes."

"I'll build you a new one. No problem."

"Iric, don't encourage her!" Soren says.

"What are you talking about? This is what we set out to do! We both can go home now, and you want to deny that privilege to Raz?"

"It's not that," Soren says. "I just don't think we're ready for Peruxolo yet. We need a plan on how we'll face him. Where we'll do it."

"I already have most of that figured out," I say.

"You do?" Soren asks.

"Yes, I spent our walk back to the tree house thinking about it. If you spent less time trying to talk me out of it and more time being supportive, we could have discussed it together."

Soren lowers his head to my shoulder. "Sorry. I'm listening now."

"Here's what I think we should do. First, you two need to go home to Restin."

"What?" Both boys snap at the same time.

"Iric's hyggja head isn't going to last out here, and that feather could blow away with a breeze. You two should take your proof home while you can, and I'll come with you in order to see how you're received. I want to know if the village will really welcome you back. That'll change how I decide what to do next."

"How so?" Soren asks.

"If you are not welcomed back, then I'll face Peruxolo alone. Because if your villages still treat you as outcasts, then there's no way my father would show up to witness my battle against the god. But if your village takes you in with open arms? I will formally challenge Peruxolo. I will face him publicly, in the clearing where the villages make the Payment each year. Soren will do his part and invite all seven villages to watch the battle."

"Are you sure?" Soren asks.

"I'm sure. Let's head for Restin tomorrow. Then we'll set our plan into motion."

PART 4

THE
GOD

CHAPTER

22

Before heading out, Iric takes me to his forge.

He comes to a stop at a wooden chest tucked underneath a table full of tools. He bends down, fiddles with a latch, and then hoists up the lid.

Shiny black armor winks from within.

Iric pulls out a gleaming breastplate and holds it out to me. I take it, rubbing my fingers along the bottom edge.

"How?" is all I can manage as I stare at the beautiful craftsmanship.

"Wasn't easy. I made this piece from a single sheet torn from the back of the largest ziken we caught. Had to hammer at it for hours to get it into the right shape. Trimming the edges down was even more difficult. Had to take my ax to it. You should know, now that the armor isn't connected to a living creature, the regenerative properties don't work anymore."

"That hardly matters. It's wonderful."

"Would you like to try it on?"

I replace my iron armor with ziken hides. The new armor is lighter, but just as strong. I walk through a set of warm-up strikes, amazed by how much more quickly I'm able to move.

"It's fantastic! I'll never wear iron again," I say, rubbing my arm over where the guards are tucked into my sleeves.

"Shall we start our journey now? Or are you too busy admiring yourself?"

I smack him.

IRIC LEADS US back to Restin. He is most familiar with the way, having traversed the path once a month for the last year to exchange letters with Aros.

"We're going to see Mother and Father," Iric says feebly, as though he doesn't dare to let himself get too hopeful. He carries his own sack on his back. With all the salt inside slowing the decomposition of the hyggja head, I can't imagine how heavy it must be.

Soren carries his feather on his back, with all our bedding squishing it tight so it doesn't budge. That leaves me to carry all our food and supplies for the three-day journey.

"You are," I say. "You'll see everyone you left behind."

I just hope it will be a happy reunion. At my own banishment, I seem to remember Father mentioning something about what would happen if I actually completed my mattugr, but I hadn't been listening by that point. At the time, I never thought I'd get to go home.

But now, with Iric and Soren heading for their own home, my hope is brighter than ever.

SOREN GIVES ME A quick kiss just outside the borders of Restin. "We won't be long. Wish us luck?"

"You don't need luck," I answer. "You've already done the hard part. Go see your family."

"Thank you again, Raz," Iric says. "For everything. We'll be back out before nightfall."

And then they weave around the inna trees, until they come to the stone archway leading into Restin.

I turn around and climb the tree at my back. The boys helped me select the perfect vantage point to see their homecoming. I wish I could go with them, but it's not possible. When we're banished, we're banished from all villages. Newcomers stand out, and I'd be recognized as an intruder instantly.

I climb the tree higher and higher, feeling lighter as I go. *I helped them go home. They would never have done it without me.*

I may not have been the perfect leader my village deserves. But I did something right out here.

When I've climbed high enough, I find a thick branch to sit on and rest my back against the bark of the trunk. My eyes seek out Soren and Iric.

It's midday, and the village is busy. It's not very different from how Seravin looks. Cut-rock houses. Display tables showcasing foods and hides and gems available for trade. A dog loops around people in the road, trying to catch up to its owner. Children run through the street, making a game of dodging all the people. A scolding mother grabs one of the children before he can run across the path of a nocerotis.

Iric and Soren hover at the edge, watching it all. Perhaps waiting for someone to notice them.

I'm too far away to hear anything, but I watch as one head turns and points. Then another and another, until all the activity in the market stills, as everyone sees the banished boys returned home.

Eventually, a man cuts through the crowd and approaches Iric and Soren. Both boys remove their packs from their backs. Iric sets his on the ground, grips the end of the sack, and pulls it up. A mound of white slips through the opening. When the salt falls away, the head becomes visible for all to see.

I can hear the gasps, and then the cheers.

Soren offers his feather to the man who must be the new village leader of Restin, after the last one was killed by Peruxolo.

He takes it, and the shouts and screams are deafening, as the villagers surround Iric and Soren.

What are they doing? Mauling them?

I'm about to rush out of the tree, when I see Iric and Soren hoisted up in the air on the shoulders of some of the hunters and warriors.

They're welcomed as heroes.

Iric and Soren aren't set back on the ground until two new figures enter the square. I can't see much of their features save their gray heads. They must be Iric's parents, for they're rushing at the boys, smothering them with their bodies in fierce hugs. The woman kisses each of their cheeks before ushering them down the street.

But then one more person makes an appearance.

Iric pulls himself away from his mother.

The newcomer, who I'm sure must be Aros, launches himself at Iric. The two nearly fall over from the force of the hug. Aros doesn't even come up to Iric's chin, so the latter has to bend down so their lips can meet.

A smile comes to my own lips, and I recline my head against the trunk of the tree. They made it. They're home. And all is well for Soren and Iric.

But then a girl breaks out of the crowd, someone with golden locks far brighter than mine. She's dainty, elegant, and I'm sure her face is beautiful. She goes right up next to Soren and wraps her arms around his neck.

My eyes narrow.

Who the hell is that?

Soren detangles himself from the girl, but she doesn't go far, hovering around his shoulder. The proud parents, Pamadel and Newin, hurry their boys down the street, likely to their home, with Aros and the girl following.

I'm leaning forward so far that I nearly lose my balance on the branch. I right myself, scowling at that blond head of hair. Just what does she think she's doing? I stare until the group disappears from sight and the market resumes to its previous state.

And I wait.

One hour. Two hours. Three.

I wait for my boys to come back to me. To help me kill the god and make my own way home.

But they don't come, even after night falls.

For a moment, I wonder if they ever intended to come back

at all. They've got what they wanted. They're reunited with their parents. Iric has Aros, and Soren—

Soren has the blonde.

They have their old lives back.

Maybe they've decided they're done with me.

I shake my head. This is Iric and Soren. If they're late, it's because they've gotten caught up in the excitement of being with their loved ones again.

Nothing more.

I wait one more hour, praying to see their faces come back through the stone archway, but they don't.

I force my stiff limbs to make the climb back down the tree. Though my stomach grumbles, I don't touch the food in my pack as I make the trek back to the tree house.

I'm not hungry at all, despite feeling so hollow.

DAYS LATER, WHEN I make it back, I can't bear to stay in the tree house. I return to my little fort. I haven't been here in weeks.

Before I arrive, it starts to rain, a few drops dampening my hair before I leave the road and cut back into the foliage. My shelter has held, though the place looks a little run-down. Leaves and needles cover the floor, having fallen through the cracks in the logs making up the ceiling. Twigs and moss have scattered onto my things. Smaller plants have broken through the earth in the places I once used as walkways.

The rock I used to carve the clues about the god in my tree seems to have disappeared.

Doesn't matter. I've learned as much as I possibly can about the god. It's all up in my head.

I go to my shelter, pull the bark door aside, and collapse onto the ground.

I sleep, now that I feel utterly defeated.

The next morning, I return to the tree house. There is still no sign of Soren or Iric.

If they're back, maybe they went straight to the forge? Iric still needs to build me a new ax.

I race down the trail to the forge, leaping over the traps Iric placed to keep out critters. The whole place smells like ash, the rain from last night likely churning up the scent.

Iric's tools are neatly in a line, his castings cleaned and stacked. One of his buckets has filled with rain water. Another holds wet coal.

But neither boy is here.

My eyes sting.

But that small pressure only makes me angry.

Fine.

I will defeat Peruxolo on my own. I can try to leave notices outside the villages and hope the hunters from each village find them and take them seriously. Will they travel to the Payment site because a letter from an ostracized girl asks them to?

My throat grows dry. Would my father at least show up? He'd recognize my writing. He'd come, wouldn't he?

But he's let me down before.

Everyone has let me down.

Raz...

The sound is so faint, like a whisper on the wind. I'm certain I've imagined it.

"Rasmira." Louder this time and Soren's deeper tone.

"Raz! Quit playing games. Where are you?"

I pick my head up from where it's fallen against my chest. Not *everyone*.

"I'm over here!" I call out.

There's a smattering of wet footsteps on the rocks, and then both boys come into view. First Soren, with his hair mussed, and his eyes tired. Then Iric, his taller frame hunched slightly and his cheeks red.

I launch myself at Soren. I'm not alone. I never was. Not since the first time I met Soren in the wild.

These boys are everything to me, and they came through when it mattered most.

"Did you run all the way here?" I ask.

"Yes," Soren says irritably, looking at Iric. "We had to make up for lost time. I tried to make him hurry, Rasmira."

"Hurry?" I ask.

Iric's smile stuns me. It's the first I've seen that isn't mocking. It's honest and so *happy*.

"Someone insisted he join us," Iric says.

I was only looking for the faces of my two boys, so I failed to spot a third hiding behind them.

He's at least a couple of inches shorter than I am, with hair so dark it's almost black. He wears a short beard, and his eyes are a striking green. Strapped to his waist are throwing hatchets. A large pack bulges on his back.

"Aros?" I ask.

He throws himself at me, squeezing me against his chest. For one so short, I hadn't expected such strength.

"Thank you," he says, "for bringing this one back to me. I heard what you did, and I can't ever repay you for it."

I think to shrug off the words. To tell him it was nothing. Instead, I say, "You're welcome. It's nice to meet you."

He steps back. "I apologize for delaying them, but I wasn't about to let Iric out of my sight again."

I look at Soren. "I can understand that. I'm glad you decided to join us, Aros. I've been wanting to meet the man who willingly puts up with Iric."

"Hey, now," Iric says.

Aros grins and slides an arm around Iric's waist. "He can be an ass, but I love him anyway."

Iric glares down at him, but he can't hold it. Soon it morphs into a goofy grin.

"Why don't we give you two a moment to get yourselves situated," Soren says. "Rasmira and I are going to head to the tree house."

Iric and Aros don't hear a word he's saying. They're already drawing closer.

Soren threads his fingers through mine and leads me down the trail.

"Sorry we kept you waiting," he says. "I couldn't leave the two of them to make the trip here on their own. They're too busy looking at each other to keep an eye out for danger."

"You made the right choice. I should have been more patient. You both just took so long, and you seemed so happy to be with your parents again. Iric had Aros. And you—I saw a girl. Anyway, I thought you'd both have to be mad to want to come back out here anytime soon."

We stop at the base of the tree house, and Soren pulls me close. "My girl is right here in front of me. The girl you saw in Restin?"

"The blonde."

"Yes, the blonde. She was looking to get some attention. Iric and I were declared village heroes, and she was looking for fame by association. I never spoke to her, except to assure her she was unwanted, and her attempts were petty."

I squeeze my eyes shut tight, a wave of embarrassment taking me over. "I've never been jealous before."

"You never need to be again."

The smile feels so good against my lips. I feel as though I could stand here in this spot with him for an eternity and never be bored.

He leans his forehead against mine, and I relish the closeness. "We should probably go get Iric the metal for my ax."

"In a moment. I want to kiss you first."

SOREN AND I MAKE several trips to and from the mountain, always on the lookout for Peruxolo. Either the goddess is watching out for us, or Peruxolo doesn't leave his lair, because we don't run into trouble. We gather buckets and buckets of lodestones for Iric over the next several days. It's tricky, because Soren isn't able to get too close to the metal while wearing his armor. He drags the lodestones behind him in a net and carries both of our axes on his back.

When we've delivered more than enough of the stuff, Soren says, "It's time for me to go."

I know this, and I know I need him to deliver my invitations to the villages, but I hate seeing him go.

"We're all going home," he reminds me, and he places a kiss against my forehead.

"You be safe," I say. It somehow comes out as a threat instead of a plea.

"I promise."

I watch his back until it disappears to the south. He's going to Seravin first to tell my father I'm alive and I'm going to challenge the god. From there he'll head north to all the other villages.

I return to the forge to take my mind off of worrying over him.

It's fascinating watching Iric work. He melts down the lodestone and separates it from all the other minerals. He patterns my new ax after the one my father gave me, spike and all. I help by pounding at leather hides, dyeing them black, and then wrapping them around the newly finished handle. Aros helps by checking the traps and cooking our meals so we can focus on the work.

It takes a good deal of time and sweat, but in the end, I have an ax that can wage battle against Peruxolo.

I THROW MYSELF INTO Soren's arms when he returns. After weeks of going sick with worry, of toiling over the hot fires in the forge, I have him back.

"Are they coming?" I dare to ask. "Is it done?"

He's covered in weeks of travel grit, but I don't let that stop me from holding on to him. "They're coming. All the leaders seemed quite eager to attend."

"And my father?"

"I spoke with him."

I swallow.

"Torlhon was happy to hear you were alive."

"Happy?" I ask skeptically.

"He may not have said as much, but I could see it in the way his face changed. I told him what you did for Iric and me—how it was because of you we found the strength to complete our tasks. I told him you will make a great leader when you return with glory to Seravin. Torlhon will be at the battle. He is looking forward to it."

I don't know if things can ever be the same for me and my family. After the way my father turned his back on me, I don't know that I could ever welcome him in my life, even if he wants to mend things.

But I am glad that he will be there.

"I also spoke with your sister Irrenia. She tried to give me a pack full of medicinal supplies before I left the village."

"That's Irrenia," I say with a sad smile.

"She wants you to know she will be at the battle. She's eager to see you."

A wave of emotion shoots over me. So many people will come, looking for entertainment. It is such a relief to know my sister will be there to offer support.

"Then we should go scope out the battleground and prepare." Peruxolo will receive his invitation last. I want him to have as little time as possible to prepare for the battle.

THIS SPOT ONCE HELD such awe for me. The Payment site is the first place I ever saw Peruxolo and witnessed his powers. It's fitting that it will be the last as well. Whether I win or die.

The space is large and circular in shape. There will be room for those who want to watch the battle to stand along the outskirts. The road that extends all the way to Peruxolo's mountain ends on the west side of the clearing. That single line will be the easiest place for me to fight him. Since I've seen Peruxolo floating in the air, I doubt he will worry over the rough terrain.

"If I can keep to the road, I'll have an easier time fighting him," I say aloud.

Iric and Soren snort at the same time.

Aros stares the two of them down. "Why do you doubt her? She has saved the both of you from banishment. If anyone is equipped to take on the god, surely it is her."

Sufficiently chastised, they both look toward the ground.

"Thank you, Aros." I continue my assessment of the area and list everything I've learned about the god. "He carries hidden blades on him." The healed wound on my abdomen pulses just at the memory. "I'll have to watch for that."

"And what if he chooses to strike you down with his power?" Soren asks.

"That can be dodged. I've done it before. I recognize what that motion looks like."

Iric kicks at a pebble with his boot. "So you'll battle him ax to ax, while trying to keep to the road. You'll watch for hidden weapons, and you'll try to dodge anytime he uses his power." He pauses. "There has to be more we can do to give you an advantage."

"Can we use this new lodestone against Peruxolo in some way?" Soren asks.

We all think for a moment.

"Rasmira's ax is also made from the new lodestone," Iric says. "Anything we might do with iron will also affect her."

"Perhaps," Aros says. He reaches for a coil of rope at his side. "But this won't react with anything."

ONCE WE'RE DONE SETTING up the area, the boys and I head back to the wild. They wait in the tree house, while I make the trek to the god's lair.

Your silver blade wasn't enough to kill me. Let's finish what we started. The day after tomorrow, at first light, all the villages will be gathered to watch us duel. It ends at the place where our suffering begins.

I attach the note to a sturdy branch and then pound it into the ground like a stake. When I leave the mountain this time, I revel in the feeling that I never have to return.

CHAPTER

23

The rising sun dissipates the morning fog, leaving the clearing dry and bright. This is where our villages sacrifice their livelihoods to Peruxolo. This is where I first laid eyes on the god and saw his mighty power.

This is our battleground.

And this is where either he or I will draw our last breath.

Soren, Iric, Aros, and I arrived hours earlier, when the stars were still out and owls filled the air with their hoots. We brought with us the final touches for the battle, a series of rocks we've placed strategically around the area.

"If things go wrong," Soren said as we lowered the rocks to the ground, "if you need a breather, you get him to follow you to this spot. The boulders will be your marker. Look for them, and Iric and I will handle the rest."

I survey the three boulders around us, hoping they're enough if things do go bad.

I hope the battle doesn't last long enough for us to find out.

A crowd has started to gather. Strangers huddle along the tree line, murmuring to one another. The stench of fear mixed with curiosity wafts over me with the breeze. I am the day's entertainment. This is no mere warrior coming-of-age trial. This is a mortal facing off with a god. It could be quick, over in an instant, but it will be exciting nonetheless.

It feels as though a caged animal lives in my stomach, clawing to get out. Nerves almost consume me. I think I might be sick.

A hand tugs on mine, spinning me around.

Soren is there.

He places a hand on either side of my face.

"Don't think about the crowd. Using an ax is as effortless to you as breathing. But you be smart. And don't you dare die on me. We've come too far for it to end now, do you hear me?"

I'm not about to make promises I don't know if I can keep. "I will do my best."

And standing here, finally taking the focus off myself and looking at him, I realize—

He's a mess. He looks ready to crumble. Ready to grab me and run.

"I can't lose you, Rasmira. Can't we spill Peruxolo's secret and call the whole thing off?"

"No. This is my mattugr. I have to kill him if I'm to return home. And it's not enough to say that this immortal has been using lodestones to instill fear in us. They have to *see*. Their fear is too great."

"I understand, but I still don't like it."

I take his hands in mine, and he lets his forehead rest against mine.

"Will you promise me something?" I ask.

"Yes."

"Do not step in at any point and try to kill the god for me. I *have* to be the one to do it. Iric had to deliver the killing blow to the hyggja. You had to be the one to steal the feather and carry it down the mountain. I have to end Peruxolo. Promise me you won't try to kill him, even if he's about to end me."

"Rasmira—"

"I did it for you, Soren. Now I need you to do it for me."

He closes his eyes, as if it will take all his willpower to make this decision. Finally, he says, "I promise. You can trust me in this."

I kiss him, wrap my arms around his neck, and cling to him, try to remember how it feels to have his lips on mine. In case it never happens again.

"Rasmira!"

I know that voice better than any other.

I pull away from Soren, and a happy cry leaves my throat. "Irrenia!"

Her dainty arms go around me, and I lean into her.

"I thought you were dead," she says, following the words with a sniffle.

"I almost died a few times, but I remembered my promise to you."

She squeezes me until I can't breathe, and I wonder how someone so small can manage it.

"It would seem you've done well for yourself in the wild." Her head rises off my shoulder, and I know she must be looking at Soren. "Very well."

Despite everything that may or may not happen in the next hour, I laugh. Just once, but it is enough to lighten the moment.

"Quit hogging her." Another pair of arms comes around me. Tormosa's. They're quickly followed by Salvanya's, Alara's, and Ashari's, until I can't tell where one sister ends and another begins.

A throat clears. My sisters pull back, and my father steps in front of me.

His hand comes down on my shoulder. "What you are doing is very noble, Rasmira. Death at the hands of your mattugr will open the goddess's paradise to you once more. We will see you again when our times come. This public display is an excellent idea. It will show others that my daughter is no failure."

For so long, all I wanted was to make my father proud. But in all the time I tried to earn his respect, I realize now that he never once earned mine.

"I am not doing this for you or your image, Father. For once, I'm doing something for me. And I don't intend to die today. I'm going to expose Peruxolo for what he really is. I neither want nor need anything from either of you." Mother's stepped up next to Father. "You turned your backs on me, and I won't forget it. I won't let your decisions rule my life any longer. I'll see you both when this is over."

I turn away, desperate for some distance. I don't make it ten feet before a hand clamps down on my arm.

I whirl to find my mother standing before me. I think to pull from her grasp, but then I *really look at her.*

I almost don't recognize her. She's a shadow of her former self:

frail, her eyes somehow duller, her cheeks hollow, her skin ashy, her limbs heavy, her hair without its usual shine. She looks helpless, distraught, as if something inside of her is eating her alive.

She looks broken.

"Rasmira," she says, and even her tone has lost the hateful force it usually contains when speaking to me. "I'm so relieved you're safe!" She throws herself at me, resting her head on my shoulder and letting her hands stroke my hair. I don't return the embrace; I'm too shocked.

And then, in my ear, where no one else can hear: "I know it's too much to ask for forgiveness, so I won't dishonor myself by asking. I don't deserve it. Rexasena has already started to punish me for my crimes, and I know she will continue when this mortal frame passes into the next life. But, you must know how devastated I am by what I did. I regretted it the second you disappeared into the wild. I've been so horrible to you, and it wasn't until I let my own flesh and blood meet death that I realized what I've become." She pulls back, rests her hands on my shoulders. "I will try to stop this. I will tell your father everything. You don't need to go into battle. You can't."

And then she's pulling away from me, waiting before interrupting the conversation Soren and my father are having.

I don't know what is happening. Did the moon rise this morning instead of the sun? Have fish grown legs and crawled on land? Where is my mother and who has replaced her?

I was gone . . . over three months. Could my beautiful, horrible mother really change in that time? I don't trust it. Not one bit. She's going to have to do more than cry on my shoulder. But she's offering to make everything right—to tell my father the truth.

"Wait!" I say, forcing her back to me. "Mother, you can't. I need to carry on with this fight."

"No, you never should have been issued a mattugr. I saw that boy sabotage your test. I'm going to fix it, Rasmira. I swear it."

"Don't, please. I'm asking you to wait."

Her already frail body seems to shrink further. "Why?"

"Because I am ready to face the god. He has been a plague upon our people, and I believe I can end it all. Today. No more Payments. No more worrying about the god who lurks in the wild. No more starving children."

"But—"

"If you truly regret what you've done and wish to make things right with me, you will abide by my wishes."

She licks her cracked lips. "I do, and I will."

"Good. Now please, I need some distance from you."

"Whatever you need." She disappears behind my father's shoulder.

By the goddess, *what was that?*

My heart is throbbing within my chest, and my mind is turning over the conversation again and again.

"Are you all right?" Irrenia asks.

"How long has she been like this?" I ask, pointing to Mother.

"It started just after you left. She won't take any of the treatments I try to give her."

I can't deal with this. Not now. Not when so much is riding on today. Not when I keep wondering if I've made the right choice.

Should I have let her tell Father the truth and call the whole thing off?

No.

The word is absolute, leaving no room to question it. I've challenged the god. There is no taking that back. Regardless of whether my mattugr is lifted or not, he knows I'm alive now. He will look for me, might even punish my village for my challenge if he learns where I'm from. I *have* to see this through.

I start toward the center of the clearing. It's dawn. Peruxolo should be here already. But just like he does with the village leaders during the Payment, he is making me wait.

Soren follows after me silently. There is nothing more to be said until this is done. Iric falls into step with us, leaving Aros to stand with his parents.

We stop in the center of the clearing, in the grooves of the road. For something to do, I windmill my arms, letting the muscles loosen. I walk in place, stretch my legs, prepare my body for what is to come. Soren and Iric stand by my sides, waiting with me.

The sun inches higher in the sky, and still Peruxolo doesn't show.

I send a prayer to the goddess, begging her for guidance and strength. What will I do if the low god doesn't show? How am I to return home and make things right if I can't do the task that was set for me? If he comes for me and my family in the night?

After another ten minutes go by, I realize I needn't have worried.

He appears in the trees, just as he did over three months ago. He steps off a branch and hovers in the air, cape swaying behind him, hood raised.

Terrifying, as always.

But as I watch him, watch how he appears to stand in the air, as though an invisible wall holds him up—I remember the piece of metal I saw in his forge. The one I thought appeared to be the length of a man's foot.

It was.

Exactly the length of this god's foot, in fact.

Peruxolo has lodestones in the base of each boot. He must have iron buried in the ground right there. He climbs the tree and appears to float because of the negative reaction between the metals. Oh, so clever.

Soren gives my shoulder a squeeze, and then I hear him and Iric retreat, leaving me to my task.

"I've been challenged," Peruxolo says in that cutting, dangerous tone he uses. The voice that makes us tremble; the voice we feel in our bones.

Except, now that I don't fear him as I once did, I don't really feel his voice in my bones. That was just my imagination, something born of raw fear.

"You have," I snap. "And you're late."

Gasps sound all around me. No one is short with the god. No one dares ever speak to him in such a way.

I dare.

Because if I already made my intent to kill him clear, he can hardly be offended by my tone.

"A god's time is not dictated by mortals," he says. "I was foolish not to watch you die the last time we met. I will not make that mistake today. I will break your body in every way possible before I end you."

He leaps down from his "floating" position and rises to his full height, well over six feet, but he does not pull his ax from off his back.

Instead he flicks his wrist.

I dodge the move and hear a *chink* as his power hits the rocks where I once stood, but as I look at the space, I see something familiar sticking up out of the ground.

It's small, easily missed if I hadn't already seen one before. I reach for it, and pull the metal triangle from the ground carefully, so as not to cut myself against the edges.

And then I remember the night I saw the previous village leader of Restin fall. Peruxolo flicked his wrist, and he fell over dead with blood pooling around him.

And a thought strikes me.

Iric had to build us spears in order for us to kill the hyggja. My village and all the other villages—we have built our weapons to survive in the wild, to kill our most common enemy, the ziken. That is why we use battle-axes, because they are the only things strong enough to pierce their hides.

The villages all keep to themselves—we've not had battles against one another. Our enemies have never been human. But if one's enemy were human? Well, he would need a weapon that cut through human skin. No need for a battle-ax. Anything sharp and projected quickly enough would draw blood. All someone would have to do is aim for the large vein in the neck and tear right through it.

A sharp pain slices into the side of my leg, right in the small gap where my greaves break to meet the armor on my thighs. I let my new realization distract me, and Peruxolo took the opening I gave him.

I reach down for the triangle and pull it from my skin, wincing at the wave of pain it brings.

I will not let him cut away at me piece by piece like this. He knows where the gaps in my armor are, and he's aiming right for them.

A cruel smile waves across the god's face. He's enjoying this, enjoying the crowd poised to watch, enjoying watching me suffer.

No more.

I advance three steps before Peruxolo lashes out with his wrist again, this time aiming for my collarbone, right where my breast-plate doesn't quite reach.

Instead of trying to dodge it, I raise my battle-ax, placing it between the god's weapon and my vulnerable skin.

Tink.

Light gasps sound around us, and Peruxolo and I stare at the spot where the triangle struck. The tip is wedged into one of the blades. With the hand not holding my ax, I grab the triangle— carefully and without cutting myself—and flick it toward the rocks at my feet. Whatever metal this new weapon is made of, it doesn't appear to react with anything, so it must be neutral—made with the intent to pierce skin and nothing more.

And I keep walking toward my village's oppressive deity.

Peruxolo's eyes grow wide for a moment, but he quickly recovers himself and thrusts his whole arm toward me, putting more dramatics into the motion that will release the metal in my direction. I wonder what sort of contraption he has hidden up his sleeves.

I have only a split second to see the metal dive toward my hips, at the gap in my armor that allows me to bend in half there.

I thrust out my arm, catch the triangle on my ax blade once more, and keep going, this time at a jog.

For a moment, I think I might be irritating him, but I realize—

I've bored him.

I can see it under his hood, the way his eyes look down, as though it's sad, really, that I'm trying so hard.

His right leg slides back on the ground, finding a better position to brace himself, preparing for the moment when my armor will react against his and I'll be thrown backward.

Not this time.

I can't help it, I grin at him as I advance, running now, my ax raised.

Bored. He's *so* bored. So ready to be done with me and done with all these people. Ready to go home and continue to live on as our greatest fear.

I know exactly when I've come too close.

There's a moment when I cross an invisible line, and those thick blond brows shoot up in astonishment. He knew exactly how far out I should be before I was thrown back. His body jolted slightly, as though he would put some of his own force into the impact.

But no.

He's so close now, closer than he's ever been before. My heart hammers from the proximity, my breath rushes out for the excitement of it. Every muscle I possess flexes, ready to fight, ready to win, ready to *go home.*

And I take a swing with my new ax made of lodestone.

Peruxolo barely gets his own ax up in time, and despite not making contact with skin, that resistance, the force of metal on metal is glorious.

Because it means I can hurt him. I made him bleed once, and it will happen again today.

I don't know how many years of training Peruxolo has on me

exactly, but I intend to use every piece of training I know against him. Besides, he's been alone in the wild with no one to fight.

I just completed my training three months ago.

I have never been more ready for this fight.

The shafts of our axes are wedged together, each of us trying to force the other back. I use our closeness to hook my foot behind one of his ankles and tug at the same time my arms heave forward with all my weight.

And Peruxolo, the most feared being in all the world, falls to the ground, flat on his back.

He stares up at me, disbelief and incredulity pouring off him, but before I can get my ax head any closer, he somersaults backward and flicks his cape over his head, coming up first on his knees and then his feet.

"You're not the only one who's learned the wild's secrets," I say, and I bring my ax down on his right arm.

He folds the limb into his body, but I still connect. My ax swipes down the front of his arm, one of the blades pointed toward the ground. It rips into his leather shirt, slices through—wood?—and embeds into the soil.

Shards rain down onto the rocks.

Whatever the contraption was that Peruxolo had strapped under his cloak, I've broken it. No more metal triangles being flung toward me now.

But my ax has caught between two rocks on the ground, and before I can right it, Peruxolo clips me in the chin with the pommel of his weapon.

I go crashing onto rocks and sharp twigs, and one of the muscles in my arm pulls as I land on it awkwardly.

"Recover!" A shout goes up from the sidelines, and I roll, roll, roll, as Peruxolo swings his ax down at me with two hands again and again and again.

When I finally get a chance to come up on my feet, Peruxolo is looking at the crowd.

At Master Burkin.

"I'll deal with you after I finish with her."

My weapon is still in the ground several feet away. All I have are my limbs as weapons.

I fly at Peruxolo while he's distracted with Burkin and knee him in the groin. The god uses a latrine, so I'm fairly certain he has *that part.*

He goes down like a bag of rocks, just like any human man would, and I race over to my ax.

Murmurs rise from the crowd.

"She's struck him twice now—the god!"

"He feels pain."

"He's not invincible."

Peruxolo forces himself to his feet as I turn around with my weapon in hand, and as he does so, his hood falls from his face.

More chittering as the crowd goes on about his human face.

Peruxolo quickly rights it, grimacing as he does so. He's still in pain.

I adjust my position slightly, putting Aros's rope trap between me and Peruxolo.

The god advances, and I duck just a couple of feet into the tree line, keeping my eyes on the god instead of the loop of rope hidden on the ground beneath leaves and twigs.

Peruxolo steps right through it, cracking the stick holding the trap in place. The bent tree beside me swings upward, hoisting Peruxolo up with it by a single foot.

Now the crowd dares to laugh as Peruxolo's cape dangles to the ground, and his whole body swings about madly.

I grin and take a moment to look toward Aros. Iric is elbowing him and likely singing his praises for me.

I put my hand against the god's waist and give him a spin. More laughter. It's contagious. I've never been comfortable being the center of attention. But right here, exposing the god, hearing everyone's reactions—it's easy to get lost in the moment.

"Rasmira!" Soren shouts from the sidelines. "Hurry and end it!"

By the time I look back at Peruxolo, he's already finished sawing at the rope with his ax. He falls in a heap on the ground when the rope snaps, and he finds his feet and blade once more.

Cursing my foolishness, I take up position at the road once more, never giving my back to Peruxolo.

"I've had it with you!" He charges, ax held in front, ready to skewer me. I block it, and in the same motion, I curve my ax back around toward his body.

The blade cuts through armor, skin, and bone. Peruxolo cries out and grips his side.

There it is again.

Blood.

He tries to cover it with his fingers, but red seeps through.

The crowd is practically shouting now. They're growing closer, giving Peruxolo and me less room to move.

"My name is Rasmira Bendrauggo," I say. "I want you to know that before I end you."

"This will not be my end!" He flies at me, more calculated and careful this time.

Our axes connect, and Peruxolo sends a fist sailing at me.

I hear Burkin's cry of outrage as my neck cranes to the right, cracking from the force of it.

"There are no rules out here," Peruxolo seethes.

"I shouldn't have expected you to fight fair."

"I'm a god. This was never a fair fight."

He detangles himself from me. He's no longer running at me, but away from me. In great leaps, he starts scaling the air, as though climbing an invisible staircase. Higher and higher.

There must be more iron plates in the ground, growing in purity, letting the metal soles in his shoes carry him higher and higher. It's an act for the crowd. He's trying to redeem his reputation, make them see him as their powerful god.

It's both fascinating and terrifying to watch, even though this trick is no mystery to me. If only I, too, had lodestone soles in my boots, I could climb just as he does. What would the spectators think then? That I'd suddenly gained godly abilities from being out in the wild? Or would they put it together as I have?

Peruxolo switches his ax to his left hand and reaches behind his back with his right. A gleaming silver dagger, like the one he used to pierce me before, appears in his hand, and he flings it.

I'm ready this time, prepared to flick the weapon away with my ax, but it's not turning end over end in my direction.

Did the wound I dealt to his side throw off his aim?

The dagger sails over my head and lands in the branches of a tree only a few feet away. A cracking noise emits above my head, and I look up in time to see something spinning for me.

It connects with my ax faster than I can even follow. No, it sticks to it. More lodestones at work. It's similar in size to the metal triangles Peruxolo projected from his arms, but this one is circular, with little metal teeth. Only this is another new metal. Something that is drawn to the lodestone just as powerfully as iron repels it.

My stomach sinks as I realize—if I'd been wearing armor made out of the lodestone, this sharp little disc would have punctured straight through and wounded me. A small loop of rope hangs off the disc. When Peruxolo threw his dagger, he must have severed the only thing holding the metal back from connecting with the nearest lodestone.

Despite Peruxolo floating in the air, despite most of the crowd waiting to watch me fail, I laugh.

"You prepared for someone figuring out your secret!" I shout up to him. "If anyone else made an ax out of lodestones, you needed to be ready. You positioned me here, closest to the tree, so this"—I point to the metal disc—"would stick to me."

Peruxolo leaps from his height advantage. I flip the switch on my ax to unleash the spike, readying for him.

Our blades tangle at the tips as he hits the ground, rocks rolling away from his landing. He tips his chin to the side so he can better see me from under his hood. His knuckles whiten on his ax as he pushes toward me, forcing me back a step. Then another, and another.

I try to pull away to the side, but he twists our axes, tangling them together further, herding me toward the crowd. He's going to back me up right into them.

My strength starts to waver, my muscles weakening, until I realize it's not me.

Something is pulling on me from behind, aiding the god, and I think for a moment that maybe someone from the crowd has a hold of my ax.

I tighten my grip as the ax is nearly wrenched from my hands, and get pulled along with it. Peruxolo sneers at me as he halts in place, watching me fly backward.

My fingers gripping the ax crunch under the weight of something, and I think my middle finger might actually be broken. A beat later, my back slams against the ground with my ax pinned above my head.

When I finally adjust to the pain, I note that I haven't actually reached the crowd. No, my ax pins my fingers against a tree trunk. The bark is broken in places, held to the tree by thick nails. And underneath, little slivers of that new metal. It's drawn me here, and no matter how hard I pull, I cannot get my ax to part from it.

"You are beaten, Rasmira Bendrauggo," Peruxolo says. "I send you into the next life to meet Rexasena's wrath. Just as you have met mine."

I'm not afraid. He can't take another step forward without sticking to this tree just as my ax is.

Peruxolo drops his ax to the ground and reaches behind his back once more—for another silver dagger. I pull at my fingers, trying to free them from where the ax has them trapped, glancing over my shoulder at the god.

He pulls back his arm, taking careful aim.

I prop one foot against the bark of the tree and pull.

My head cracks against the rocky ground just as the dagger embeds into the bark where my body was just seconds before.

And though the world spins, I rise to my feet, launching myself at Peruxolo and his confused face.

I plow right into him, and the two of us go crashing to the

ground. I land on top and get my thighs on either side of him to steady myself as I send a closed fist flying toward his head.

"My armor isn't made of metal."

I try to hit him a second time, but he catches it and bucks his hips, sending me flying off.

I land right next to his ax.

Peruxolo eyes it and then me. "No!" he shouts.

I fling it toward that tree. It would have landed no farther than five feet away if the natural forces at work hadn't propelled it onward. It clanks into the bark right next to the ax Iric made me.

Confused grumbles now come from the onlookers as they wonder why Peruxolo would allow his own ax to be trapped by his power.

"Behold Peruxolo!" I shout for the whole crowd to hear. "He who uses nothing more than simple natural forces to keep you afraid and helpless. He is nothing without his lodestones."

"You worthless bitch!" he yells.

We charge each other, colliding in a tangle of limbs and armor. I try to force him toward that tree, where he'll be helpless, sucked against that sheet of metal with his lodestone armor, but there's no denying that he's stronger than I am.

I have lost any advantage I had, and now that our weapons are gone, now that the battle is down to fists and feet, Peruxolo has the upper hand.

He steps on my foot in his haste to force me back. The fingers in my right hand throb and swell from where I grip him. At least one of them is definitely broken. My head still spins.

In the next movement, I strike him on his left side where I sliced him deeply and he cries out.

"I am your god!" he says when the surge of pain passes. He back-hands me, cracking my neck in the opposite direction. "You do not challenge me. You do not tell lies regarding me. You obey. You deliver your Payment. And you stay out of my way! I will have the whole Bendrauggo line for this!"

I backtrack, trying to gain some footing so I can strike, but Peruxolo follows. Knuckles dig into my cheek as he hits me again, and for one brief moment, my gaze lands on Soren, standing at the edge of the clearing. His body is rigid, and his teeth are clenched together.

You promised, I hope my look says.

I try to dig my hands around Peruxolo's throat, but he's forcing me backward. A fist into my throat has me choking for air. My eyes water, my throat burns. Every appendage throbs with pain.

I'm going to lose the fight.

But then Soren's voice trails through my mind.

If things go wrong, if you need a breather, you get him to follow you to this spot.

I make sure I land a little more to the left after his next strike.

I want everything to end. I want my people safe. I want to go home. I want Peruxolo's tyranny over.

He steps on my hand, the one with the broken finger, and I scream. He sends a kick into my stomach with his other leg. I can just imagine the satisfaction on Havard's face at that move.

But I can't let him kill me. Not here. I look around. There are the boulders. I need to get him closer.

I pull my hand free of his foot, even though it feels as though I'm pulling my finger off. I roll in the right direction, the move sending more pain shooting through all my injuries. I still can't breathe from the kick that stunned my lungs.

When I stop, I look up, trying to find the boulders.

Just a few more steps.

I right myself, back up some more, my breaths coming faster than ever.

And then I watch the god take his last step.

Peruxolo reaches for me, only his hands stop midair, as though crashing into an invisible wall. He pulls back, examining his own fingers, before trying to grab me again.

He can't advance toward me any farther. Not with the boulder of iron at my back, holding him off. There's another a few paces to his left and a third to his right. Iric, Soren, and I placed them carefully, testing them on lodestones to gauge the appropriate distance.

A large thud sounds behind Peruxolo, and he turns to see Iric and Soren dusting the dirt off their hands from the boulder they dropped behind him. He didn't notice the two of them coming up from behind, hauling the rock from the sidelines of the battle.

And now Peruxolo is boxed in, unable to move, the natural forces of the metals working against him.

"That's your brilliant plan?" he asks with a laugh. "You forget that I know how this works. And *you have no weapon.*"

He reaches between the leathers on his forearm and starts to pull the sheet of armor out from there.

It doesn't give an inch before I rise and reach down into my boot. From it, I pull out a silver dagger. The one Peruxolo used to stab me. His eyes widen in recognition as I plunge the silver tip into the skin at his neck. He goes down.

Blood oozes from the wound, seeps out the side of his mouth, drips onto the pebbles beneath his head. I pull the dagger out, and the stream turns to a pour, as the blood is freed from the large vein there.

He's dead in seconds.

And the crowd is silent.

Not a soul stirs or really even breathes as I stand over Peruxolo's body.

I kneel down beside him and pull the armor sheets from his arms and legs. I tug off his boots, unclasp the cloak from off his shoulders, and unstrap his breastplate.

I want to drop onto the ground and sleep. I want the pain to stop and the crowd to go away, but there is still one last thing I have to do.

I've finally put it together. The last of the mystery. Why a god would rely on natural forces instead of his power. I know what the rest of the things I saw in Peruxolo's lair are for.

I grip Peruxolo by his hands and drag him across the ground. Rocks scrape against his back and blood still trickles from his neck, leaving a bloody trail in our wake. But the progress is too slow. I can't bear it.

I kneel down and manage to heft his weight onto my back.

With an arm and leg on either side of my head, I walk toward my father, who stands at the front of the crowd.

His eyes meet mine. Open wide. Wondering.

I imagine mine like daggers poised to strike. He is why I am here. He sealed my fate.

But now I'm free.

I dump the body at his feet and let everything that has been burdening me fall off with it. No more worries concerning my family. No more thinking little of myself or thinking I'm not good enough for things.

I nudge the body with a foot, look up at my father, and say, "Here is your god."

CHAPTER

24

Only then does the stillness evaporate. Cheering erupts so loudly, I think my ears will burst. People rush at me, trying to clap me on the back, ruffle my hair, or skim my clothes—they try to touch me as though I'm the goddess herself.

But one figure breaks through the crowd.

"She's injured. Everyone back off!" Irrenia nudges bodies away with her shoulders in her haste to get to me.

She opens a bag of supplies and starts prodding at the bones in my right hand. People from all villages rush around us, eager to kick at or spit on the god's body.

"Silence!" A voice breaks through the ruckus, and I recognize the leader of the Mallimer village from the clearing—the one who supplied Peruxolo with a girl once a year for sacrificing.

Those closest to us still, but excitement is tangible in the air, nevertheless.

"I recognize him," the village leader says. "That's Cadmael. He was banished fifteen years ago for failing his warrior trial."

"Yes," I say. Though I didn't know the man's name or where he came from, I did know he was a mortal man. "This is who you've been giving your Payment to each year."

"No," he says. "I've been paying tribute to Peruxolo for over thirty years, and Cadmael has only been banished for fifteen."

"Peruxolo is just a name. My guess is that over the years, the mantle has been passed down from one banished man from the villages to another so he can collect tribute and silently punish the village that sent him to die in the first place. They've been at it for centuries, which is why the tale of Peruxolo goes back so far."

"No!" the leader says more emphatically. "We sacrifice a girl every year for his blessing."

"No," I say, deadpan. "You send a girl to be raped and tortured by a man to satisfy his whims year after year."

Women nearby start wailing. Mothers of those girls who were sacrificed.

"No," he says again.

"Naftali," Father says. "Stop arguing and let her speak."

"He's killed entire villages!" the leader, Naftali, says. "Without even showing his face! How do you explain that?"

Father turns to me. Irrenia wraps my fingers while I talk.

"Poison," I answer. "I've been to the seam in the mountain where this man lived. There were barrels of iron fragments. All he had to do was drop them into a well, and the whole village would die."

"And all his powers?" Father asks.

"All simple uses of lodestones. He's found those that react strongly with one another in the wild. He has metal buried in the ground and strapped to his feet to make it look as though he can fly. There's a sheet of iron nailed to that tree." I point to where my ax still rests in midair.

There's nothing but contemplative looks from the village leaders now.

That resignation, their failure to acknowledge their guilt—it infuriates me. I rip my hand out of Irrenia's and stand.

"This is all your fault. The stupid mattugrs prove nothing. All they did was make those banished hate you enough to starve you, to hurt your women, to place burdens on your backs for revenge. You have no one to blame but yourselves."

"Rasmira," Irrenia says as a warning. These men all hold my fate in their hands, and I don't care one bit. I survived the wild. I survived a god. And whatever else they decide to do to me next, I will survive that, too.

"Perhaps," my father finally says. "But we have *you* to thank for our salvation."

Father reaches down and hoists me onto one of his shoulders. I nearly lose my balance, because I'm unprepared for the movement. "All hail Rasmira Bendrauggo, God Killer!"

Deafening noise engulfs me. I know Father tacked on my surname so he would receive recognition, so all would know it was his daughter that slew the man who terrorized all the villages.

And for once, I don't care.

I feel whole.

EVERYONE GOES HOME TO their villages afterward. And Peruxolo—Cadmael? The leaders decide to leave him right where he is. For the ziken to feed on, just as he'd doomed the previous leader of Restin. An order, I now realize, Cadmael gave to hide the metallic triangle he used to kill him.

It's difficult dragging myself away from the crowd. Shouts of "God Killer" follow me all the way from the Payment site to the village. People swarm me, want to talk to me, want to offer compliments up to the goddess on my behalf, thank me for killing the false god.

It's only by Irrenia insisting she needs to tend to me back at the house, where her supplies are, that Father finally makes the crowds go away.

He's only too happy to turn their attention onto himself.

Now I sit on Irrenia's mattress, with an army of ointments staring at me from the shelves in the room. Soren, Iric, and Aros sit on the pillows and furs on the floor of the room, watching. Despite witnessing me kill the god, they insisted they would see me home.

So here we are.

"Are you almost done, Irrenia?" I ask. "I'm ready to sleep in my own bed."

"Not even close," she says. "I still have to treat the cuts on your face."

"They're barely scratches!"

"You're my patient, and you will sit through any treatments I deem necessary."

As I've long learned, arguing is pointless. It's partly an act, anyway. The familiarity of my sister tending to my injuries is a balm to my homesick heart. I was not lying about my bed, though. I crave it desperately.

"And I thought Rasmira was bossy," Iric whispers to Soren.

"I heard that," Irrenia says.

Iric grins before scooting closer to Aros.

"If she decides to smack you, I won't stop her," Aros says.

"To think I suffered through monsters only to be done in by Raz's little sister."

"I'm *older*," Irrenia says.

"But littler."

Irrenia closes her eyes and draws in a deep breath. "You willingly lived with this person?" she asks.

"I didn't have much of a choice," I assure her.

She throws a look over her shoulder toward Soren, who watches her administrations carefully. "I suppose I would have suffered through it, too, if it meant spending more time with the handsome one."

Soren's cheeks redden, but Iric speaks before he can say anything. "*I'm* the handsome one!"

"No, you're not."

"Yes, he is," Aros says.

I can't help it. The bickering is contagious. "No, he's not."

Soren rewards me with a perfectly handsome smile.

"Two against two," Irrenia says. "That means Soren has the tie-breaking vote."

"He doesn't get the tie-breaking vote regarding his own looks!" Iric says.

"In that case, your vote doesn't count, either. So Soren wins."

Aros eventually calms down Iric's outrage. Iric doesn't know

Irrenia enough to know she's only teasing him, and I'm far too amused by the exchange to make her put a stop to it.

The door opens suddenly, and all talking comes to a halt as my father steps inside.

Inwardly, I groan.

"Are the worst of her injuries tended to?" he asks. "There's a matter Rasmira needs to see to."

"Can it not wait until tomorrow?" I ask. Is he going to make me talk to the elders? If he intends to parade me around to seek more praise from villagers—

"I don't think you'll want to put this off. It's to do with your mother."

That has me on my feet so quickly, Irrenia nearly drops the damp cloth in her hand.

I FOLLOW FATHER THROUGH the streets, Soren behind me. Iric opted to stay and argue with my sister more, but really I don't think he wanted to leave his close proximity to Aros. Fine by me.

"I've had a talk with the elders," Father says. "You should know you have been reinstated as my heir and proclaimed a woman and a warrior for all the village to hear. I would have done that with you present, but I didn't think Irrenia would permit it. This, however, is a matter that needs your immediate attention."

Those in the village have already returned to their work for the day, despite the earlier battle with the god. A blacksmith hammers in his forge. The smell of freshly cooked valder wafts from the open door of an eatery, which will only be available for purchase at an exorbitant price. Peruxolo may have been defeated, but that doesn't mean he didn't already hurt our meat supply—

"Father. In the mountain where the god—Cadmael—lived, there's food. He's dried our meat to preserve it. It's still there. We must send people out to retrieve it. The other villages will want to be notified so they can retrieve their goods as well."

"It will be done," Father says. "Will you lead a group of warriors through the wild?"

If he asked me that question before my banishment, I wouldn't have been able to do it, but now—"Of course."

And that's the end of it.

Father eventually stops in the open air of the village square. The elders of Seravin survey two figures kneeling on the ground, a warrior on each side of them to prevent them from running.

One of the bent figures is my mother. The other is Torrin.

"Kachina Bendrauggo has admitted her guilt before myself and the elders," Father says. "She freely stated that she lied about what happened at your trial and revealed the truth. She says this man, Torrin Grimsson, sabotaged your test.

"This village cannot take back the punishment that was dealt to you. What's done is done. However, these are those who have wronged you. They have told lies before the goddess. And as the person most affected and the future leader of Seravin, I leave it to you, Rasmira, to decide their fate."

I blink. Whatever I thought my father might say, I wasn't expecting this.

"You want *me* to choose their punishment?" I ask.

"It is the least we can do for what you have done for our people."

It is a strange thing to have the two people who caused me the most suffering bowed before me, awaiting my judgment. I could do anything to them. Have them beheaded. Issue them their own mattugrs to see how they like it.

Those are my first thoughts. I can't help it. I suffered greatly because of what they did. But if there is anything I learned out in the wild, it is that a mattugr proves nothing. It does not turn one person from a child to an adult. It does not suddenly turn you into a great warrior or fill your head with wisdom. It is a pointless task meant to restore honor. But honor cannot be given. It is something that you find within yourself.

And I think Mother finally found hers.

Mother cannot bear to maintain eye contact with me, it would seem, for she turns her gaze downward. In a hollow voice, she says, "I begged the goddess for forgiveness every night you were gone. I prayed for your deliverance from the wild. Now that she has answered my pleadings, I will accept any fate you choose for me."

She's probably telling the truth, and there may be hope for our future together—but right now, I don't trust her, and I don't want her in my life.

But I also don't want her dead.

"Mother told a lie," I say, looking into the frail face of the woman who caused me so much pain for so many years. "Her conscience has started to suffer for it, and the goddess will decide what to do with her in the next life. But for this life, I ask that she be removed from me. I don't want to see her. She is not to live in my household. If I enter the eatery, and she is there, she will leave it. If she sees me in the streets, she is to turn around and go in the opposite direction. She will take herself from my path unless I should seek her out directly."

A sigh goes through my father, a small sign of relief. What had he been fearing? Banishment? He does care for her, then. Just not as much as he should. But that is between my parents to work out. It is no fault of mine.

"But Torrin?" I continue, and Torrin's head snaps in my direction at the sound of his name. "Torrin didn't just lie. He intentionally set out to have me banished, hoping that I would die out in the wild. What he did was practically murder."

Out of curiosity, I ask him, "Do you have anything to say to me?"

"It was a joke," Torrin says. "And not my idea. It was Havard's. Besides, surely it was the goddess's will since you rid us all of Peruxolo! I should be thanked, not punished."

But I see through his lies now. It was no joke. He will say anything to save his own skin.

"He is to be banished," I say. "And if he can survive three months in the wild, just like I did, then he is free to return. Havard will share his punishment, for he is just as responsible for what happened to me."

"Wise decisions," Father says. "Kachina, you are free to go, but should you disregard Rasmira's edict, you will be banished yourself. Torrin, you will collect your things and prepare to leave Seravin. Do not seek refuge in another village, for they will be notified of your treachery."

Torrin hurls curses and hateful words my way, but Father hauls him up and shoves him in the direction of his home.

"Hurry, or I will change my mind about allowing you time to grab your things." Then Father stands before Soren and me. "All has been put to rights. You may take as much time as you need to heal before joining the warriors to retrieve our belongings from the mountain. You will now join me in village meetings to further your preparation to rule. I am proud of what I made you. You will do great things, Rasmira."

"I already have, Father. And you may have helped shape me, but I made myself. I've become what *I* wanted."

He seems confused by my response, but he says nothing of it. "As for you," Father says, turning to Soren, "are you courting my daughter?"

"Yes, sir," Soren says.

"You haven't asked my permission."

"You sent your daughter to die out in the wild. Why should I ask you anything where she is concerned?"

It is with great effort that I manage to keep my face still at Soren's audacity.

Father looks down at the ground. "Well answered. I thank you for being there for her when I was not. Will you be returning to Restin? You know Rasmira cannot leave. She is to stay here and rule."

"Father! I am a woman now. What I do is no longer your concern!"

Soren says, "I wouldn't dream of taking her away from here unless she wished it. I'd like to stay in Seravin, if that's all right?"

"It is," Father says after a moment. "You may join the ranks of warriors in the village."

"Thank you."

"Go get some rest. Both of you. There is much to rebuild."

Father walks away, the circle of elders following after him. I take Soren's hand in mine and tug him back toward home.

"Rebuild?" Soren asks. "Nothing was broken."

"Our way of life was," I answer. "No more Peruxolo. The village will need to adjust. And we can improve things! Just wait until we introduce everyone to strong trees, to building with wood!"

Soren doesn't appear to share my enthusiasm. He kicks a loose pebble from the road. "You know, your father is right. You will make a fine leader, but I have to ask, is that even what you want?"

I'm taken aback by the question. "No one has ever bothered to ask me if that's what I want. My father assumed that because I took after him with the ax, I would also become the next ruler and carry on the Bendrauggo legacy. It has been expected of me for as long as I can remember."

"Do you want it?"

Without pause, I answer, "I do. I want to change things. I want to cease punishing failed trials with mattugrs, to save them only as punishment for the gravest of crimes. I can't change things if I'm not ruling, but I will do things differently than my father. I hope that I will better listen to those around me and use the advice of others before making decisions."

Soren grins, but it looks forced somehow, as though his thoughts are somewhere else. I pull him off to the side of the road, away from the busy traffic, down a side street that is much more quiet, before bringing us to a stop.

"What is it?" I ask.

"I'm sorry for presuming with your father back there—I didn't actually get a chance to ask you first. Are you all right if I stay in Seravin with you?" He watches my face carefully, as though he doesn't want to miss any physical reaction to the words.

Is he serious? "Soren, we already talked about this. Yes, of course!"

"But that was back when things were only possibilities. Now this is for real."

"I want you here, for real. For always."

He pulls me to him and brushes his lips against my forehead in just the way I like. I close my eyes against that touch, savoring it.

I know this feeling will not last forever. The ziken are still a constant threat. Father is still a selfish individual. There will always be those who are unfair and cruel. Ruling a village will not be easy.

But I am Rasmira Bendrauggo. God Killer. Survivor of the wild. Future leader of Seravin. I am both a woman and a warrior.

And I will not let anyone cause me to forget.

ACKNOWLEDGMENTS

You WOULD THINK WRITING would get easier with each book, but it doesn't. Each project presents its own challenges, and WotW proved to be the hardest yet. I have so many people to thank for helping make it the book it is.

Rachel Brooks, a huge thank-you for being the best agent a writer could ask for. You helped me pitch and shape this book, and it wouldn't exist if it weren't for you. Thank you for all the phone calls, encouraging emails, and enthusiasm. I'm so glad to have you on my team. #TeamBrooks!

Holly West, as always, thank you for your amazing edits. I'm always blown away by your insights. Thanks for sticking with me through another book! (And I'm so excited about our next one!)

Brittany Pearlman, my tiny general, thank you so much for all the scheduling and planning you do to help me connect with my readers. You're the best publicist!

Lauren Festa, thank you for all the work you did marketing my books! I'm so sad to be losing you, but I hope you have all the fun times at your next job! Caitlin Crocker and Allegra Green, I'm so excited to have you as my new marketing team! I'm looking forward to all the things we're going to do together.

Thank you so much, Nekro, for the breath taking ax illustration! It is better than anything I ever could have imagined. Liz Dresner, thank you for your astonishing design work! I hope you do all my future books, as well!

Starr Baer and Jackie Hornberger, thank you for your copyedits! There's nothing more annoying than getting pulled out of a book because you found a typo. I appreciate the work you do so much!

Dillon James West, thanks for giving the manuscript a read and providing feedback when Holly and I needed fresh eyes! It was so appreciated!

And thank you to everyone else over at Macmillan Children's and BookEnds who worked behind the scenes to make this book possible!

I had so many readers provide feedback on this book. I apologize if I forgot anyone!

Taralyn Johnson, thank you for reading this book so quickly and for going through so many early versions. Your feedback was invaluable, and it gave me the strength to let other people see this book, too.

Shanna, thanks for reading an early version and being so open with your feedback! Guess what? You were right!

Russ, thanks for letting me pepper you with questions about

speargun fishing. I was so sad to have to cut the spearguns, but I still used so many of your insights in my underwater scene.

Thank you so much, Cale Dietrich, for giving this story a read! Publishing twins for life!!!

Charlie N. Holmberg, thank you for reading through my sample chapters and giving feedback. You're awesome. So glad we're friends and CPs.

Thanks, Emily R. King, for reading my initial pitch of this book. You are an amazing person and an inspiration to me. Thank you also to Kyra Nelson and Chersti Nieveen and Bridget Howard, for giving this a read!

Thank you so much, Sarah Talley and Megan Gadd, for reading this manuscript in its rough form. Your friendship means more to me than I can ever express.

Thank you also to all the Bookstagrammers, BookTubers, bloggers, reviewers, Twitter peeps, and internet friends for boosting and supporting my books. There are simply too many of you now for me to name you all, but thank you. I know who you are, and I appreciate all you do.

To my readers, new and old, thank you for supporting me. I wouldn't get to do what I love so much without you. I hope you enjoyed Rasmira's story as much as I enjoyed writing it.

I need to give a quick shout-out to Haley Gibson, who puts up with having a gamer and a writer as a roommate. You are awesome!

And lastly, to my family: Becki, Johnny, and Alisa, thanks for playing *Overwatch* with me in the evenings. I always look forward to it, and you guys give me the breaks I need from writing.

Mom and Dad, thanks for your constant support and love. Parents make such good villains in teen books, but I promise the fictional mothers and fathers are not a reflection of you.

GOFISH

QUESTIONS FOR THE AUTHOR

TRICIA LEVENSELLER

What was the inspiration for *Warrior of the Wild*?
After finishing the Daughter of the Pirate King duology, I knew two things: I wanted to write another action/adventure novel and I was sick of writing sword fights. So I tried to think of ways to make the fight scenes unique for my next book. That's when Gimli from *The Lord of the Rings* popped into my head, holding his battle ax. Right then I decided my next book would have ax battles.

Rasmira's world is very unique. What was the process of building it and coming up with these monster-filled wilds?
Once I decided on battle axes as the main weaponry in the novel, I realized that I had a lot to figure out. Axes are super impractical weapons. They're very heavy, hard to swing, and hard to aim. I had to figure out why a society would choose to use them as their primary weapons. That's when the wild came to me. What if these people lived in a hardened world? What if the predators had thick exoskeletons that could only be penetrated with a heavy swing of an ax? What if the plants were tougher? The vegetables have tough skins and the fruits have thick husks that can only be

broken with axes. I created the entire world around my desire for different fight scenes.

What is your favorite thing that you've ever had to research?

I once researched Ancient Egyptian cosmetics for a book I wanted to do about a girl who is hired to be a makeup artist for a nomarch's son, but that story is shelved for now. The research was so cool, though.

This is your third published novel. Do you feel like you have the process down now, or is it different every time?

Absolutely not. Each novel I write feels like starting over. Because no two novels are written the same way. Each one presents new challenges that I have to overcome. New characters that I have to figure out. Sometimes it feels like each successive book is harder to write than the last. But I love a challenge.

What writing advice do you have to share with the world?

If you've never finished a whole book before, my advice is to finish a book! You learn so much from that first finished novel and the editing process that follows. It will greatly improve your writing and help you decide if this is something you truly wish to do. If you've already finished a book, then my advice is to read deeply in the genre you want to publish in. There are so many people writing these days, and if you want your work to stand out, you need to know what's already been written.

What was your favorite/weirdest fan encounter?
One time these identical twin teenagers were in my signing line. Their mother bought them each their own copy of my book. They were so cute and proceeded to gush about how much they love my work. Most of my readers tend to be adult women (who I also adore!), but it's a special treat for me to have teens come to my events. I love interacting with them and hearing their thoughts.

If you could have dinner with anyone—past, present, or fictional—who would you choose?
Damon Salvatore from *The Vampire Diaries* TV series. Waiting for new episodes on Thursday nights is what got me through college. I feel like dinner with Damon would be downright entertaining.

What book is on your bookstand now?
Wicked Saints by Emily A. Duncan. I've heard nothing but good things about it, and I'm excited to finish!

What question do you get asked the most?
It's definitely, "Will there be a third book in the Daughter of the Pirate King series?" I answer that Alosa's story is finished, but I would love to come back to Maneria someday to write spinoffs about the other kickass female pirates of her crew.

And what question do you wish people would ask you?
Tricia, can I buy you a cheesecake?

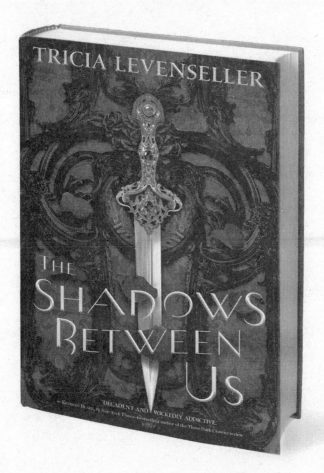

CHAPTER

1

They've never found the body of the first and only boy who broke my heart.

And they never will.

I buried Hektor Galanis in a hole so deep, even the devils of the earth couldn't reach him.

My dream was of him, of the day he told me it had been fun but he was done. Some other girl had caught his fancy. I don't even remember her name. At the time, all I could think of was the fact that I'd given everything to Hektor: my first kiss, my love, my body.

And when I told him I loved him, all he had to say was "Thanks, but I think it's time we moved on."

He had other things to say, too. When I sank my knife into his chest, words came spilling out of him almost as fast as the blood.

He couldn't make sense of it. I couldn't, either. I barely remembered grabbing the knife Father had given to me for my fifteenth birthday, three months previous, with its jeweled handle and silver sheen, but I do remember that Hektor's blood matched the inlaid rubies.

I also remember what finally helped my head catch up with my pounding heart: the last word out of Hektor's lips.

Alessandra.

His last word was my name. His last thought was of me.

I won.

That knowledge settles within me now just as it did three years ago. That sense of rightness, of peace.

I lift my arms into the air, stretching like a cat, before rolling over in bed.

A pair of brown eyes is only inches from my own.

"Devils, Myron, why are you staring at me?" I ask.

He presses a kiss to my bare shoulder. "Because you're beautiful." Myron lies on his side, his head propped up on a closed fist. My bedsheets cover him from the waist down. It's a wonder he fits in my bed, he's so tall. Floppy curls sprawl across his forehead, and he flicks back his head to clear his vision. The scent of sandalwood and sweat wafts over me.

With a hand, I keep the sheets held up over my chest as I rise to a sitting position. "Last night was fun, but you should go. I have much to do today."

Myron stares at my chest, and I roll my eyes.

"Perhaps again later?" I ask.

He looks up at me, before his eyes flit meaningfully to my chest once more.

No, wait. Not my chest. To the hand holding the sheets in place and the extra weight I now feel there.

There's a diamond on my finger. It's beautiful, cut in an egg shape and buried in gold. It winks in the morning light as I tilt my hand from side to side. The ring is by far the most expensive trinket he's ever given me.

"Alessandra Stathos, I love you. Will you marry me?"

Laughter fills the room, and Myron flinches at it. I quickly place my free hand over my lips.

"What are you thinking?" I say a moment later. "Of course not." I stare down at the gorgeous ring once more. With this gift, Myron has outlived his usefulness. For some reason, my lovers cease to give me expensive presents once I turn down their proposals.

Alas.

"But we're so happy together," he says. "I will cherish you every day. Give you everything you deserve. I will treat you like a princess."

If only he knew I have my sights set a bit higher than that. "It's a very kind offer, but I'm not ready to settle down just yet."

"But—I've shared your bed," he splutters.

Yes, he and three other boys this month.

"And now it's time for you to leave it." I move to rise from the bed when the door to my chambers bursts open.

Myron freezes with his hand outstretched toward me, and my father, Sergios Stathos, Lord Masis, looks down at what he can see of our naked bodies.

"Leave," he bites out in a deathly quiet voice. My father is shorter than my five and a half feet, but he's built like a bull with a thick neck, wide shoulders, and keen eyes that pierce to the soul.

Myron tries to take the sheets with him, but I've got them firmly clamped around myself. When he fails to wrest them from me, he reaches down to grab his pants.

"Leave now," Father specifies.

"But—"

"Listen or I will have you whipped!"

Myron stands. Barely. He hunches as though he can hide his tall frame. He makes it halfway to the door before turning. "My ring?"

"Surely you want me to keep it? So I can remember our time together?"

Myron's face twists. He has one foot pointed toward the door and the other toward me.

Father growls.

Myron takes off at a run, nearly tripping over my father's boots as he bolts over the threshold. Once he's gone, Father turns to me.

"You make it difficult for me to find you a suitable match when you're caught with a new bedfellow every night."

"Don't be ridiculous, Father. That was Myron's fifth stay."

"Alessandra! You must stop this. It is time for you to grow up. To settle down."

"Has Chrysantha found a husband, then?" Father knows very well the law forbids me to marry until my older sister does. There is an order to things.

Father treads over to the bed. "The Shadow King has dismissed a number of single women from the palace, Chrysantha among them. I'd hoped your sister would catch his eye, rare beauty that she is."

Oh, yes. Chrysantha is a rare beauty. And she's as dumb as a rock.

"But it was not to be," Father concludes.

"Myron's free," I offer.

Father levels a glare at me. "She will not wed Myron. Chrysantha will be a duchess. I've already made arrangements with the Duke of Pholios. He's an aging man who wants a pretty girl on his arm. It's done. That means it's your turn."

Finally.

"You've suddenly taken an interest in my future, have you?" I ask, just to be difficult.

"I've always had your best interests in mind."

A complete untruth. The only time Father bothers to think of me is when he catches me doing something he thinks I shouldn't. Chrysantha has been his focus my entire life.

Father continues, "I'm going to approach the Earl of Oricos to discuss the match of you and his son, who will inherit one day. Soon, I should think, given Aterxes's ailing health. That should make you happy."

"It doesn't."

"You're certainly not going to remain my problem forever."

"So touching, Father, but I've got my sights set on another man."

"And just whom would that be?"

I stand, pulling the sheet up with me, before tucking it under my arms. "The Shadow King, of course."

Father guffaws. "I think not. With your reputation, it'll be a miracle if I can get any nobleman's son to have you."

"My reputation is known by none, save those whom it directly concerns."

"Men do not keep the exploits of the bedroom to themselves."

I smile. "They do when it's me."

"What is that supposed to mean?"

"I'm not stupid, Father. I have something on every man who has seen the inside of this room. Myron has an unfortunate gambling problem. He lost a family heirloom in a game of cards. Blamed the missing pendant on a servant and got him whipped and fired. His father wouldn't be happy to hear of it. And Damon? I happen to know he's part of a group of smugglers importing illegal weapons into the city. He'd be sent to prison if anyone knew the truth. And let's not forget Nestor, who's quite fond of the opium dens. I could go on naming all my lovers, but I think you get the idea."

Though his face doesn't change, Father's shoulders lose some of their tension. "Such winning gentlemen you keep around, darling."

"The point is, Father, I know what I'm doing. And I'm going to keep doing whatever I wish, because I am the master of myself. And you? You're going to send me to the palace with the next wave of women to see the king, because if there's anything I'm good at, it's getting men to propose to me." I flash the diamond on my finger in his direction.

Father's eyes narrow. "How long have you been planning this?"

"Years."

"You said nothing when I sent Chrysantha to the palace."

"Father, Chrysantha couldn't catch the attention of a rabid dog. Besides, beauty isn't enough to catch the eye of the Shadow King. He has beauties paraded in front of him all year long.

"Send me. I will get us all a palace," I finish.

The room is quiet for a full minute.

"You'll need new dresses," Father says at last, "and I won't get your sister's bride-price for weeks yet. That won't be enough time."

I pull the ring from my finger and stare down at it lovingly. Why does he think I've taken so many lovers? They're fun, to be sure, but most important, they're going to finance my stay at the palace.

I hold up the ring where my father can see it. "There's plenty more where this came from."

>─┼─◇─•─○─•─◇─┼─◁

Sewing has always been a hobby of mine, but it is impossible for me to make all the new clothing required for my upcoming plans in such a short amount of time. Working with my favorite seamstress, I design and commission ten new day outfits, five evening gowns, and three appropriately indecent nightgowns (although those I make myself— Eudora doesn't need to know how I intend to spend my nights).

Father takes no part in the planning, as he is much too busy with his accountant, worrying over the estate. He's bankrupt and desperately trying to hide it. It's not his fault. Father's quite competent, but the land just isn't producing as it once was. Disease swept through a few years ago and killed most of the livestock. Every year, the crops grow thinner. A well has already gone dry, and more and more tenants are leaving.

The Masis estate is dying, and Father needs to acquire decent bride-prices for my sister and me in order to keep his lands running.

Though I'm aware of the situation, I haven't bothered to worry about it. My lovers all feel the need to give me nice things. Very expensive things. It's been a fun game. Learning their secrets. Seducing them. Getting them to shower me with gifts.

But to be honest?

I'm bored with it.

I have a new game in mind.

I'm going to woo the king.

I suspect it won't be longer than a month before he's helplessly in love with me. And when he proposes, I will say yes for the first time.

For once the marriage is official and consummated?

I will kill the Shadow King and take his kingdom for myself.

Only this time, I won't have to bury the body. I'll find a convenient scapegoat and leave the Shadow King for someone to discover. The world will need to know that I'm the last royal left.

Their queen.

CHAPTER

2

Father exits the carriage first and holds out his arm to me. I grasp it with one gloved hand, hold up my heavy overskirt in the other, and descend the steps.

The palace is a grand structure painted entirely in black. It's positively gothic in appearance, with winged creatures resting atop the columns. Round towers sweep up the sides, roofed with shingles, a recent architectural style.

The entire length of the palace is built near the top of a mountain, with most of the city winding its way downward. The Shadow King is a grand conqueror, spreading his influence slowly across all the world, just like his father before him. Since the surrounding kingdoms try to retaliate from time to time, a well-protected city is vital, and the grand palace is said to be impregnable. Guards patrol the grounds with rifles slung over their shoulders, a further deterrent to our enemies.

"I'm not sure black was the best color choice for your attire," Father says as he leads me up the steps to the main entrance. "Everyone knows the king's favorite color is green."

"Every single girl in attendance will be wearing green. The point is to stand out, Father. Not blend in."

"I think you might have erred in excess."

I think not. With the king's conquering of Pegai, some of the ladies at court tried the Pegain style of loose pants with jeweled hems below a fitted top. After a while, the style faded away. It was too different for most ladies to adapt to.

I've designed a combination of the Pegain style and our heavy-skirted Naxosian style. I wear close-fitted pants beneath a floor-length overskirt, which parts in the middle to show off the pants. Heeled boots raise me an extra inch off the floor. The overskirt is short-sleeved, but I wear gloves so long they overlap the sleeves. My top is tied in the back beneath the overskirt, the neckline just short of my collarbone. Modest and yet not matronly.

A black rose pendant rests on a choker around my neck. Matching earrings dangle from my lobes, and my hair is half up in a loose twist.

"I assume you have a plan for once you're introduced to the king?" Father asks. "He will receive each lady one by one up to the dais. He barely even looked at Chrysantha when it was her turn. The Shadow King never descends the steps to interact with the partygoers. He doesn't even ask anyone to dance."

"Of course I have a plan," I respond. One doesn't go into battle unprepared.

"Are you going to tell me this plan?"

"It doesn't involve you. You don't need to know."

The muscles in his arm bunch slightly. "But I could weigh in. Help you. You're not the only one who wants you to succeed."

I pause at the top of the steps. "Have you ever seduced a man before?"

Father's cheeks redden. "Of course not!"

"Then I don't see why I should need you to weigh in on anything. Rest assured, Father, if there's any way in which you could prove useful, I will tell you. For now, I can handle things."

We continue on at a leisurely pace. The doorman nods a greeting at us as we pass him by, and Father leads me toward the ballroom.

But we can't come within a hundred feet of it, because a line of green extends nearly all the way back to the far wall. Nigh a hundred girls chitter with their families and one another, all waiting for an introduction with the king. I'm certain they can't all be eligible for marriage. Many look like younger sisters of the older ladies in line. Still, should the king show any interest in the younger ladies, I'm certain their fathers will *make* them available.

Father tries to take me to the end of that line, and though it appears to be moving at a somewhat quick pace, that simply won't do.

"No, we're not waiting in line," I say.

"That's the only way to get an introduction with the king."

"Let's go into the ballroom first."

"You'll be lost in a sea of people in there. That's not going to catch his attention."

I blow out a breath through my nose before turning to face Father. "If you cannot do as you're told, then you can leave. Remember, Father, all your tutelage with Chrysantha did nothing. Your way doesn't work. I am in charge of this plan, and I will execute it as I see fit. It simply won't do to have us quarreling once we enter the party, so make a decision now."

Father's lips press into a thin line. He doesn't like being told what to do, least of all by me, his youngest child. Perhaps if Mother were still alive, he'd be more gentle and kind, but illness took her when I was eleven.

Finally, Father nods and holds out his free hand in front of us, inviting me to lead the way.

I do.